Trapped

EJ Pay

Copyright © 2019 EJ Pay

All rights reserved. No part of this publication may be reproduced, distributed, or transmitted in any form or by any means, including photocopying, recording, or other electronic or mechanical methods, without the prior written permission of the author, except in the case of brief quotations embodied in critical reviews and certain other noncommercial uses permitted by copyright law. For permission requests, write to the author addressed "Attention: Permissions Coordinator," at the email address below.

ISBN Paperback: 978-1-7331202-4-1
ISBN ebook: 978-1-7331202-3-4

Any references to historical events, real people, or real places are used fictitiously. Names, characters, and places are products of the author's imagination.

Cover design by Mindee Thyrring/PostModernLaundry.com

Printed by Amazon in the United States of America.

First printing edition 2019.

www.ej-pay.com
ejpay01@gmail.com

To my mom
Who is reaching for her future
In her new phase of life

Prologue

We only have one life to live. Well, most of us do, anyway. I have more than one. I am Evelyn Marin. I also trapped in someone else's body, living their life for them. I am trying to find a way to save them. Trying to find a way out and back to my life.

When I left my ocean-fearing mom to attend college in Florida, I thought I would be able to find some satisfaction in being by the water. For years, I felt the pull of the ocean calling to me in my sleep. I wanted to live and breathe and soak in the ocean air. But being so near the ocean wasn't enough. The ocean still called to me and in a moment of frenzy, I went further into the Florida waves than I had ever been before. And I breathed. Not the ocean air, heavy with heat and humidity. I breathed water. For the first time in my life, I learned that I could live and breathe air and water. I was a two-worlder.

But I wasn't the only two-worlder in the Atlantic Ocean. An entire city of two-worlders, including my ex-boyfriend James and my new boyfriend Jack, lived only a few miles from the Florida coastline in the ancient underwater city of Atlantis. They welcomed me as I discovered this new world of possibility. But Atlantis wasn't merely an underwater civilization inhabited by human and sealife alike. No, Atlantis was a city at war and I was asked to be a soldier in their underwater army.

Who could be an enemy to an underwater city? My aunt, Ceto. Ceto had a hatred for land almost as unnerving as the eight tentacle-legs that grew from her waist. She was using her daughter and my best friend, Gwen, to help in her design. Ceto was making plans to use the Atlantean power source to help her cover the entire world with water. No land dwellers would survive her attack. She had to be stopped. Someone had to find the Atlantean power source before she did. That someone was me, and I had an army of revolutionaries formed by the seahorse, Lachlan, ready to follow me wherever I led.

The pull I'd felt my entire life led me to an underwater battle and straight to the power source - the Atlantean pearl. But she was more than a magical embodiment of power. This pearl was a human being from the ancient world. Once filled with power in her human body, she was trapped in the pearl thousands of years ago by an unseen enemy. When I found her and reached out to touch her smooth surface, everything changed. In an instant, I was shown her entire life and in an instant, I entered it. She absorbed me and took me back in time. Now I am living in her body and I have no idea how to get back.

Chapter 1

"Evelyn!" I hear my name fading in the distance, screamed by half a dozen people in a battle undersea. The voices fade, my mind goes black and I struggle for breath.

Fire fills my lungs. Breathing hasn't been painful before. It's sharp and stinging in my chest, and stabbing pains strike my sides. It isn't the feeling I expected when I touched the Atlantis stone. In my dreams, as I'd reached through the water to grasp my destiny, I knew I could no longer breathe. But I thought drowning would feel more like my chest caving in on itself. Like all the air burned out of me while I collapsed from the inside. It wasn't ever *in* my dreams; the actual drowning. But I always imagined how it would be when it finally happened. I feel the burning I envisioned, but not the collapsing.

Everything feels different. The cool, swirling waters from the bottom of the Atlantic Ocean have been replaced by something warmer, dryer. I steady myself and slow down my thoughts so I can see what is around me. I turn to look for my father whose proud and sad eyes were the last thing I registered before reaching out for the pearlescent Atlantean stone. But a large olive tree stands in his place. Its branches are wide and outstretched like they want to wrap me in an embrace. A shudder tingles its way down my spine as I think of those scratchy arms cutting my body and clothing, trying to hold me close.

The water I was floating in is gone. The battle is gone. The people are gone. Nothing is floating groundless around me anymore. I am no longer in an underwater city. Everything is motionless except when an occasional breeze moves across the dry earth. Dry earth.

My feet are standing on the ground. I turn to survey the changed landscape. Rolling hills covered in large orchards of trees are all around me. There is a large home of clay and stone in the valley below. It wraps around a courtyard. An animal pen is near the house. One or two animals move around inside.

I feel something prickly on my feet. I look down to see that dried grass is scraping against the leather sandals which have replaced the underwater shoes I was wearing just moments ago. Instead of battle armor, I am dressed in light linen robes with a leather belt wrapped around my waist. A small charm, a hand with an eye in the palm, hangs from a thin piece of rope around my neck. My body is glistening with sweat like I have been running. My lungs burn.

"Pearl!" I hear a young voice call. I turn to see where it is coming from. A boy about 10 years old with dark, curly hair is staring in my direction. He also wears robes and leather sandals. He is just down the hillside and stands breathless in the long golden grass. He is calling to someone I cannot see.

"Pearl!" He calls again, "You're it. You've got to get me now!" My body remains still while I swivel my head around from side to side to see who he is speaking to. He rolls his eyes and jogs toward me. "Pearl," he grabs my arm and gives it a gentle shake, "are you okay? It's your turn. You are the titan now." He shakes his head at me. When I don't answer, his eyes soften and his voice sounds concerned. "Pearl. Are you okay?" he asks.

I blink several times, trying to understand what is going on. Why is this boy talking to me like he knows me? Why does he keep calling me Pearl? I look around again, trying to recognize anything in my surroundings that might help me understand what is happening. Nothing registers, nothing at all. Until...

I turn to the boy. His skin is golden brown and his eyes are dark like chocolate. His hair is thick and full and his face is familiar. I know I've seen his face before. I know I've seen this moment before. Only a short while ago I was seeing this same moment in time through the memory of the Atlantean stone. The Atlantean pearl.

I stumble backward a few steps, my head swirling with the impossibility of what is happening. I look down at my hands. They are changed. Rather than the rough skin and deep tan I have acquired over the past several months living so much in the ocean, my hands are now soft and small, golden brown tones like boy in front of me. I am small like he is. I reach my hand down to my stomach and run my fingers over my small waist and smaller chest. My hips are smaller, my legs are shorter, everything is different - like it was when I was a preteen. I reach my hands up to my hair. Instead of the long, straight braid I was wearing in battle, I feel thick, soft curls. I pull a section forward in front of my eyes to have a good look at what is growing out of the top of my head. It's black. My brown hair is now black.

I'm not myself anymore. I'm someone else.

I look to the eyes of the boy. This is the boy I saw when I touched the pearl. He, *this* is the first memory she showed me. "Pearl," he says again, his voice gentle and unsure. I think we need to get you home." I nod my head and let go of my hair.

He reaches his hand out to me, and I take it, knowing instinctively that he is a safe place. As soon as our fingers touch, something registers within me. Brother. Twin. Domideus. Dom. This is the pearl's brother. Her twin. Pearl is who she is and what she became. Pearl is who I am now. As I follow dazedly behind him – my brother - focusing on putting one foot in front of the other, her voice enters my soul, filled with a search for freedom.

"You have come."

Chapter 2

A gentle hand brushes across my forehead and I blink my eyes open. When I focus, I see a woman leaning over me. She is completely and utterly beautiful, with dark curls and soft, brown eyes. She looks so much like my mom. But she isn't my mom. She is Pearl's.

She looks deep into my eyes to see if she can decipher what is hiding inside of me. Inside of her daughter.

"Hello, my girl. How are you feeling?" I manage a half smile as an answer. "You've been asleep since yesterday afternoon. No fever though, thank goodness. Would you like a drink of water?" My throat is parched. Water would be wonderful. I give her a small nod and another half-smile. "Just a moment, then," she says and leaves the room.

I stretch my legs and flex my hands, squeezing life back into my tired body and trying to clear my head, remembering the events of yesterday. I touched the pearl of Atlantis, saw her life, embraced it, and stepped into her sandals. I sift carefully through each memory so I don't miss anything. I want to make sense of what is happening. I am Pearl's body, but I have no idea why.

A pang of fear shoots through me. If I am here, what is happening in Atlantis?! Is the battle still raging? Is my family okay? Did Ceto send me here? I try to sit up, but I am too dizzy. I lay my head back on the rough pillows.

I take deep breaths and find things to focus on to calm my racing heart. I turn my head to the side to take in Pearl's home. I feel the coarseness of her blanket when I move on the small bed. It isn't like any bed I've slept on before, not even in Atlantis. It's a straw mattress laying on a wooden platform. The blanket looks handwoven and has an earthy smell. I am still wearing linen robes and the necklace I wore yesterday. I hold the hand and eye charm in my fingers. It is something I've seen before, but I don't know what it means. I stretch my toes beneath the blanket. The sandals are gone, but my feet feel clean and washed free of the dirt that caked them after my day in the orchard.

I turn to my side to face the door and see a soft light coming in through a glass-less, exterior window. The window is covered by a woven cloth that serves as a curtain. The room is clean and comfortable. The walls are plastered in white. Earthen rugs cover the cool, tiled floor. I see a few scrolls on a small wood table in the corner. A short and stubby candle sits there as well. A few clay pots sit against the wall by the door. A wooden wardrobe stands near the foot of the bed and I can see several items folded and hanging inside. A tall basket with used linens is beside it. There is a small chair by the bed. It isn't empty, though.

Dom is sitting in the chair, fast asleep by my side, his head resting on his arm as he leans across the straw mattress. He wears a bracelet of rope around his wrist with a charm like mine strung between the strands. A little bit of drool is dripping down the side of his cheek, and the sight of it makes me smile. I want to wake him up. I want him to tell me about Pearl, about me. Maybe then I can find a way home. I stretch my legs and wiggle my feet until they shove his arm. He raises his head and yawns. Pearl's Mama calls to him to not bother me.

Dom reaches across the bed and pinches my toes. I pull my feet away. I hate having my feet tickled, even in this new body. "Pearl," he says. He sits up and stretches, "how are you feeling?"

That's a question I'm not sure how to answer. "Confused. Hungry. Sad." I have to push each word through the groggy fog in my head. Dom's chocolatey eyes look sad, but then he brightens.

"I can help hungry," he says, and he jumps from the chair and out the bedroom door.

Pearl's Mama comes back in the room just a moment after her son left it. She has a wooden cup and carafe on a woven tray. A single lily lay near the cup. I try to lift myself up so I can sit and drink, but it ends up being more of a shrug. Pearl's Mama sets the tray on the table with the scrolls and comes to help me sit up. Her robes are lighter than mine and she has a red swath of fabric crossing her body over one shoulder. She is so beautiful.

She comes to me and her gentle hand reaches behind the curls cascading down my neck, bracing the back of my shoulders. With her other hand, she takes hold of my arm, and together we get my new body into a proper seated position.

"How are you feeling, my love?" Her voice is creamy and rich and soothing. Her eyes are dark and chocolatey like Dom's and, I assume, like mine. A look of concern crosses her brow, but she covers it with a smile, encouraging me to open up to her.

I remember that she sees her daughter in front of her. If I am unwell, if I tell her what is going on, she will not hide her concern anymore. She will think I am sick. She may send for a doctor. I don't know what time period this is, but it must be hundreds, if not thousands of years ago. There is no buzz of electricity, no sound of airplanes or cars or trains. The home is clean, but looks more like the homes I have seen in paintings of the ancient world. I don't want an ancient doctor looking at me, covering me in leaches, or doing some crazy beating ritual to remove evil spirits from me. So, I decide to be healthy Pearl until I can find my way back home.

"I'm doing better," I manage to croak out. "What happened?"

She holds my head and brings the cup to my lips. I drink the fresh, cool water slowly as she answers. "You came home with Dom yesterday afternoon. You were stumbling about and not making much sense. I brought you to bed and you were quite fitful for a while. I was making ready to have Dom go fetch Doctor Amadeaus when you finally rested your body and your eyes. You were not warm, just restless. When you finally settled down, I decided to watch over you while you slept."

I smile at a mother who loves her little girl enough to go without sleep. My own mom would have done the same. My mom. I ache for her and my smile fades.

Pearl's mother continues, "Dom sat by your feet all night. He fell asleep after several hours. You know how he is."

I smile again and nod. Dom re-enters the room with a torn loaf of bread in one hand and a lump of cheese in the other.

"Pearl was hungry, so I got her some of our morning bread with Acacia's cheese."

"Thank you, Dom. She may not be able to eat much, but it was very thoughtful of you to care for her so."

Smiling with self-satisfaction, Dom returns to my bedside, placing the food on my lap. Slowly, very slowly, I pick up the pita bread. It is flat, brown, and rough in my hands. A dusting of flour covers the outside. I tear off a small piece of the bread and bring it to my mouth. It is chewy with a mildly sweet flavor. I like it. Dom picks up the bread, tearing off a much larger piece and smears its surface with the soft goat cheese he brought. He takes a bite from it first, then puts the remaining portion to my lips. I open my mouth and he puts the bread into it, his clean fingers tapping my chapped lip. The cheese is smooth and creamy with a flavor that is slightly stronger than the cow's cheese I am used to eating. I love it.

Pearl's memory reaches to my mind.

> *She and Dom are hiding behind a tree, eating goat cheese and flatbread as fast as they can. The food was specially prepared for visiting guests, but Pearl and Dom couldn't stand waiting. The smell of the cooking bread and the sun-warmed cheese was too much for them. So, while Cook wasn't looking, they grabbed a small pile of flatbread and scooped a portion of cheese from the platter. They dashed to their favorite tree and ate their prize as quickly as*

they could. Once they finish, they look up with satisfaction and find themselves staring straight into the eyes of Pearl's goat, Acacia. She looks accusingly at them like she knows they took her prize cheese.

The pair can hear the sounds of the farm boy searching for Acacia. It isn't long before they are caught. As he comes upon them, the farm boy, who is 14 or 15-years-old, makes ready to cry out to Cook. But just as he opens his wide mouth with a triumphant face, Dom reaches out and touches the boy's ankle.

"No need to call out, Theodis," Dom says, "You can take the goat to Cook and everything will be fine. Tell her you found the goat wandering in the south field." Without a single utterance, Theodis relaxes his face, closes his mouth, and takes Acacia by her rope back to Cook. Pearl and Dom stifle a laugh as they watch Theodis walk back to the house where Cook boxes his ears and accuses him of taking the food himself. The twins run down the hill, giddy with their feat.

With his touch, Dom made Theodis change his mind.

Mind control. Dom has mind control. When he touches people, he is able to convince them of anything he says. A subtle nudge from Pearl tells me I am right. I look up at her – my – twin, Dom.

Pearl's mother lifts the cup again to my lips to help me swallow the bread and cheese. Does she know what her son can do? Dom has another piece of bread ready for me and pops it into my mouth. I cannot take my eyes off of him, and for over half an hour, I eat slowly while I listen to him prattle on to his Mama about his friends and the games he has been playing. But I cannot stop thinking about what he is capable of. That kind of gift could go so wrong in the hands of a madman. Will Dom become a madman? My mind races through the terrible scenarios that could take place if this power is set loose in Atlantis – or the rest of the world. I shake off my thoughts when I realize Pearl's mother has been speaking to me.

"Pearl. Pearl, darling." Her concern is there again. I offer another smile. I am able to straighten up as well and sit without the help of her support. She rubs my back before pulling her hand away again. "Darling, I don't think you are going to be able to participate in the Celebrations of Zeus today." I'm not sure what she is talking about, but Dom's reaction gives me a clue.

"Mama! No! She can't miss the Celebrations of Zeus!" Dom yells, "It's the opening day of the festival! She'll be fine, Mom. See? She ate almost the entire pita bread, and you know how healing Acacia's cheese is." His eyes are pleading now and his voice goes up an entire octave. But his pleas have fallen on deaf ears. His Mama gives him "the look."

"Dom, you ate most of the bread," she responds. "Your sister is still unwell and needs more time to rest and recover. We don't even know what brought on her spell yet."

It's my turn to act. "But Mama," I whine weakly, "Dom and I have been talking about the festival all week. I just *have* to go." I give my best sad eyes, but I can already see that this mother isn't going to budge. I pull a sad face and slink, dejected, back onto the feather pillows. Dom's entire countenance falls. There will be no winning here.

"You can go next year, Pearl. This is for the best. And, Dom, you can go with your cousins and Theodis." I see frustration and mischief both mingling on Dom's face.

"Okay," he sighs, "but it won't be as much fun."

"Yes, I know," their mother replies. She puts her hand on her son's shoulder. "Now, go get cleaned up and ready for the festival. Your sister needs to rest and regain her strength."

Dom walks out of the room, shoulders bowed, head turned toward me, eyes wishing he wasn't going without me. He pauses and his face lights up as he turns to his mother. "Mama! Can I bring home some festival treats for Pearl?" No doubt, he will be getting treats for his sister, but he will also get an item or two for himself. Their mother sighs as she answers her son.

"Of course you can, Dom. Now off with you. Your sister needs some quiet."

"Don't worry, Pearl! I won't eat all of your sweets!" And with a giggle, he is gone. Their mother puts her hand against my head, checking for a fever that isn't there. She smiles contentedly and kisses the curly locks that brush against my cheek.

"Rest well, my love," she whispers, "I'm glad you are doing better."

"Me too, Mama," I reply, Pearl's favorite name for her mother coming easily from my lips. "Thank you." She gives me a gentle smile and sits in the chair by the bed. She hums a tune that feels familiar to me. I feel a wave of warmth and comfort. My stomach is content, my body is tired. My mind is being lulled to sleep. I close my eyes, knowing that I will be safe, wishing this all to be a dream, hoping that I will awaken in my own bed to the face of my own Mama. Yet, I somehow understand that my time in Pearl's body isn't over.

Chapter 3

After several days, I feel more like myself (or at least like Pearl's self). I have strength back and my mind is clear, giving me the brain power to think about my situation and how to find my way out of it. I yearn for my family, hoping and praying that they are safe in Atlantis, that they were able to defeat Ceto. The sooner I get home to them, the sooner I will feel peace.

Dom enjoyed his time at the festival and spent several hours telling me about the magicians, actors, and street vendors. As promised, he brought back several treats for me: fish, which I couldn't bring myself to eat, Greece's traditional spanakotropita - its fragrant odor of spinach and cheese making my mouth water, and stafidopsomo bread (a few of its sweet, raisin-filled slices missing). We ate the treats together, Dom always out-eating what I could handle in a sitting, and we talked.

Today, I am up and doing some of Pearl's chores. I've just finished cleaning up after our morning meal and am sweeping the kitchen when Dom comes bounding in from outside.

"Pearl!" he says, face flushed from his run in the warm, Grecian air. "Are you finished with your chores yet? I want to play in the olive orchard."

"She hasn't milked Acacia yet," Cook says. Milk Acacia? I didn't know that was one of my chores. Not to mention, I have no idea how on earth to milk a goat. I've seen people milk cows in old movies, but the only milking I've seen first-hand was done by machine.

I'm standing still with my mouth hanging open when Cook gives me a glowering stare. "What's this, girl? You still too sick to milk a goat?" Her tone is patronizing and she is annoyed. "I've had Theodis milking your precious goat for you while you've been cooped up, and he's nowhere near as good or as fast at it as you are. I suggest that you make yourself feel well enough and go milk that goat if you'd like to see any cheese or butter on your table."

I nod and set the broom against the wall. Dom takes me by the hand and we head out the door to the goat pen. I'm hoping that Pearl's brother can milk the goat. But how do I get him to help without letting on what is happening to me?

"So... do you want to milk Acacia for me today?" I use my best begging eyes, but I didn't grow up with a brother. I have made the wrong move. He looks at me like I have gone mad, which maybe I have.

"Um, no way. She's your goat. I don't milk her." Then he gets a huge grin. "I just eat her cheese. Now, hurry up so we can go play. I want to get back to our game."

Pearl's goat, Acacia, trots up to me and nibbles my clothing. I gently push her face away and grab the rope around her neck. I look around the pen until I see a stool and bucket. They are near a wooden framework that looks like it is meant to hold Acacia. I take the goat by the rope and pull her over to the milking stand. Dom watches while I try to force Acacia into the stall. I pull her to the framework and tie her to it.

Dom walks over and says, "Did you forget how to tie her up, Pearl?" He takes the goat's rope, untying what I have done.

"Sorry," I say. "I guess I'm not myself yet." Dom looks at me with a single raised eyebrow and a small frown. He brings Acacia up to the top of the framework, forcing her head between the slats I tied her to. He ties her rope to a small hook, puts the bucket under her swollen belly, and steps aside. It's my turn now.

I bring the stool next to Acacia and sit down. Acacia is bleating and sounds cranky. She is restless and eager to get this over with. I grip her warm teat and pull down. It is fleshy and squishy, warm and weird. And it doesn't work. Acacia stomps her hind leg and bleats at me again. Dom is still looking over my shoulder, watching my milking attempts. I try again so I won't give away that I have no idea what I am doing.

Again and again, I grab Acacia and pull. Again and again, she bleats at me but doesn't give me any milk. My hands are getting wet and Acacia is getting red from my pulling. Once or twice a random squirt of milk escapes into the bucket, but I have no idea why it happens or how to repeat it. Finally, Acacia has had enough. She stomps angrily, kicking the bucket away and bleating louder than before. Her hooves keep stomping and I have to move out of the way to keep from being kicked. I am frustrated and for the first time in my life, I wish I knew how to milk a goat.

I turn to face Dom, his eyes are narrowed and his arms are folded. He is staring me down.

"Pearl, what's going on?" he asks. "What are you doing to your poor goat?" I blink to keep myself from letting a tear fall, but I can't keep the tears out of my voice. So, I do the next best thing and stand there silently, willing this boy to understand what is going on and why I cannot do what he thinks his sister should be able to do. I cannot hold the tears in any longer. I start to cry. Not just cry the quiet tears of a teenager trying to save face, but the heaving sobs of a ten-year-old girl who messed up in front of her brother. A few of the workers in the fields turn their heads my way when they hear me. All they see is a ten-year-old girl crying by her goat. But Dom is with me. I am fine, so they turn back to their pruning.

Dom sighs and sits on the ground, looking up into my face. "What is it, Pearl?" I shake my head, determined to not tell him what is going on. He puts his hand on my arm and I am unable to keep my struggle to myself. I let it all pour out of me, sure that he will tell his Mama and I will be sent to bed for more rest.

"I...I...I'm not really Pearl," I manage to stammer out between runny nose sniffs. "I...I'm stuck in her body." Dom busts out with laughter. He doesn't believe me. I start crying even harder. My shoulders are shaking now with the force of my tears. I cannot stand what is happening to me. I am stuck with the emotional capabilities of a ten-year-old girl and I feel all of it keenly.

After a few moments of laughter, Dom takes a deep breath and lets out a sigh as he puts his hand on my shoulder. I am still shaking and sniffing.

"Oh, Evelyn," he says. The sound of my own name for the first time in days silences me. Hiccups are the only sound I make. "I know you aren't Pearl."

I hiccup and sniff again. "How did you know?" I ask.

Dom lets a smirk creep onto his face. "Well, there's a lot about Pearl that you don't know. Or at least you don't know it yet. I've been reading your mind for days. Pearl would never let me do that. She also wouldn't let me manipulate her into telling me a secret."

My breathing slows and I let a smile creep onto my face. It's my first genuine smile since I arrived here in Pearl's body. Dom used his mind control on me, something his sister would never let him get away with. I shake my head, trying to clear it. "What else do you know about me?" I ask.

Dom lets out a chuckle. "I know you're super old. Not like mom or anything, but way older than me." I almost protest. After all, he was born a llloooooooonnnnnnggggg time before I was. Who's really older? But rather than argue, I listen, wondering what all he has seen. "I know you saved my sister from something terrible. That's why I haven't told mama. That, and she's been sad since Papa died."

"I'm sorry, Dom. I didn't know about your Papa," I say.

"Well, how would you know? You've only been Pearl for a couple of days." His voice grows softer. "My Papa was robbed and killed during a trade expedition over a year ago. I'm okay now, but Mom is sad a lot. She still has to deal with Grandpa, and he can be a little cranky." Dom gives me a rueful smile and wipes at my teary face with the edge of his sleeve. "Let me teach you how to milk Pearl's poor goat before she refuses to give us any more milk. I need some cheese!"

I follow Dom back to the goat whose stomping has slowed. Dom grabs another bucket near the stall and fills it with feed. He places the bucket on the platform in front of Acacia.

"Giving her food helps her stay steady while you milk her. She would rather focus on food than on you."

"Okay," I say.

Dom pulls the stool and milking bucket back into place and sits down. I move nearer and watch what he is doing.

"You were pulling on her like that would make something happen. That's a mistake that only street urchins make." I flush with embarrassment. Dom wets a cloth in Acacia's water and wipes her udder and teat, cleaning away the dust that covers her. He rubs his hands together rapidly, warming them up. Then he wets his hands on the cloth and places his warm, wet hands on Acacia. "It's warm and wet like a baby goat's mouth," he explains. "Then her milk will let down for you." He shows me what he is doing as he continues.

"You gotta start by wrapping your hand around her udder and teat. Grab a little milk from the udder with your top finger. Then all you have to do is squeeze one finger at a time all the way down." I watch closely as Dom works. Acacia's udder is large and full. Dom uses his pointer finger to grab at the fullness and squeezes it down, one finger at a time. A powerful stream of milk hits the side and bottom of the milk bucket and Dom does the same maneuver again, more milk shooting out of the goat.

Dom works for several minutes, giving me little tips as he goes. He wipes Acacia's udder with a damp cloth periodically to keep her clean and comfortable. He is careful with her and she is much happier. But I can't watch him forever. This is Pearl's goat and I am living in Pearl's body. I have to be the one to take care of Acacia.

Dom gets up from the stool and I take his place. Acacia is still chomping on her food and doesn't notice that Dom and I have switched places. She shuffles her hooves from side to side, finding a more comfortable position. Sweat beads on my forehead. For a moment, I imagine myself back in Atlantis, hoping the will and image are enough to transport me home to my own place and time. It doesn't work any better than it has the last dozen times I've tried. I am stuck in this body and I have to learn how to use it as Pearl would.

I warm and wet my hands like Dom. I reach up and grab Acacia's teat again, this time starting much higher and grabbing the swollen udder in my top two fingers. Her udder is warm and soft and squishy. The portion of milk I grabb creates a small pocket in my fingers. I work the pocket of milk down, one finger at a time, making a long and satisfying stream of milk shoot out of Acacia.

I let out a laugh. This is unlike anything I've ever done and the ten-year-old girl I'm living inside of is proud and happy. I'm excited to keep going and rewet and rewarm my hands. Acacia continues to chomp her food, and Dom teaches me more about Pearl while I work. Acacia's udder grows smaller and smaller until there is nothing left for me to milk. Together, Dom and I clean up the area and put Acacia back in her pen with more food and water.

Dom takes me to the kitchen and helps me strain Acacia's milk and prepare it for cheese. Cook is watching us through narrowed eyes, accusing me of pretending illness so my brother will do my work. She huffs and bustles around, constantly complaining. Dom and I do all we can to avoid having to talk to her as we finish the chore. It is a pleasant thing to work with Pearl's brother – my new brother. I feel the warmth and affection Pearl has for her twin. With him as my companion, I know I'll be able to find my way through this new place.

Chapter 4

For several days, Dom and I spend time talking to each other. He tells me about Pearl – I learn about the limited schooling she receives with other daughters of wealthy landowners. I learn who her friends are, which chores are her least favorite, and how to turn Acacia's milk into butter and cheese. We are living in Ancient Greece on an estate outside the city of Argos. Pearl's and Dom's family have lived here for generations. When their father passed away, they went with their mother, Helena, to live with their grandfather. Their grandfather, Vasilios, is one of the most prominent figures in the area. He is a wealthy landowner and aristocrat. His olive orchards provide some of the best oil in the region. Dom will soon begin training to take over the business. Oh, and he can manipulate the minds of people just by touching their skin.

Dom tells me Pearl has powers too, even more powerful than his. But he and Pearl made a pact – Dom protects his sister. Pearl's powers stay hidden. Their own mother doesn't even know about their powers. Their father did and he taught them to keep the powers hidden for their own safety. Dom tries to hide his abilities, but sometimes he can't help himself. He promises to teach me some of the things Pearl can do. He starts by teaching me how to block him from reading my mind.

I tell Dom about my life. It is all fantastical to him. I'm from the future, and as far as he can tell, most of what I tell him isn't possible. Since he has magical powers of his own, when I tell him about the two-worlders who inhabit Atlantis, it doesn't seem strange to him. But the idea of movies and cell phones is completely out of his ability to understand.

"Metal and glass, smooth enough to see into, and you can use it to talk to people anywhere?"

"Yep."

"And you're sure it isn't magic?"

"No magic. No one really believes in magic where I am from."

"They don't believe in magic, but they know Atlantis is underwater. Morons." He shakes his head.

We are eating grapes and bread under an olive tree in their grandfather's fields. I tell Dom almost everything that might be useful in getting me out of Pearl's body. I tell him how, as I reached out for the floating pearl, I first realized that Pearl was – is – a real person. I leave out her life story that I saw, especially the part where Dom dies, and I just say that I saw his face somehow.

Even with all of his help and teaching, there are still some things I don't understand.

"Dom?" I ask, "How did you and Pearl get these powers in the first place? Do they run in your family or something?"

After a moment of contemplation, Dom's mood shifts to something more serious. "Evelyn, there are things I haven't told you. Things you need to know."

I sit up and turn to face him, piqued by this revelation that he has been hiding things from me.

"Mama and Papa were so happy together," Dom begins, "Papa always talked about how Mama saved his life. He was sad and making bad choices. Mama came along, saw the good in Papa and rescued him."

"What choices was he making?" I ask. "What did she rescue him from?"

"Not what," Dom says, "Who."

"Was he a slave or something? Was he being held captive? Who did she rescue him from?"

"He was a slave, but not like the ones from the north," Dom says, "He was under a spell, a love spell, placed on him by Queen Nyobi Kadul."

"Who?" I ask.

Dom rolls his eyes. "Don't they teach you *anything* in your time? Nyobi Kadul was a princess living off the coast of Jaffa a hundred years ago. She was the most beautiful woman on the coast. You can find murals about her life when you travel the coast during the trade season." Dom's eyes are hooded as he adds, "Well, *I* can see them anyway. You...well, Pearl can't go with the caravans."

I feel a pinch of jealousy from Pearl. She is a girl so she doesn't get to follow the caravans when they go out to trade. She wishes she could go. She's dreamed of it and begged for it all her life. Even after her father was killed, she wanted to go on the caravans. I feel and see it all clearly. But it's all new to me, to Evelyn. I am not jealous of Dom. I'd rather know the history he is telling me.

"Nyobi fell in love with a married man and plotted to have his wife killed," Dom continues. "The man's wife was the daughter of a magician. When her father found out about Nyobi, he gave his daughter the gift of absolute beauty. But he cursed Nyobi with a hideous face. Her skin turned green and lumpy. Her eyes drooped down her face and her ears became slits on the sides of her head.

"His curse also made it impossible for Nyobi to live on land. She couldn't breathe the air anymore. She had to live in water."

Is this how two-worlders began, I wonder? Is this Queen Nyobi Kadul the ancestor of all the two-worlders? I drift into thinking of my life in Atlantis but pull myself away from those memories. I need to learn something here in Argos, not lose time mourning for my future and past. "What happened to the princess once she was cast into the water?" I ask.

"Well," Dom continues, "she wasn't heard from for years. Then rumors began. People, all men, were disappearing from the Jaffa coastline. At first, no one knew it was Nyobi. Then they realized there was a link to the disappearances. All of the men who disappeared had green eyes."

"What does that have to do with Nyobi?" I ask.

"You may have noticed, Pear...Evelyn, we all have dark eyes here. Green eyes don't happen very often. The man Nyobi loved had green eyes. She was drawing men to her to replace the man she loved."

"Oh," I say. I feel uneasy as I ask the next question. "Dom, did your papa have green eyes?"

Dom is silent for a moment before answering. "Yes," he says. "His eyes were green."

"So, what happened to him? Did Nyobi get him? How did your mama save him? How was he a slave?" It is a lot of questions for a young boy to answer, I know, but Dom knows the answers and is ready to tell me.

"Nyobi tried to get my Papa to come to her when she saw him one day fishing on the coast. She has some kind of mind control powers and draws men to their deaths. They drown as soon as she wraps them in her arms. It's all a part of the curse the magician put on her."

"Then how did your father survive?" I ask.

Dom sighs and says, "For months Nyobi tried to get him, but he wouldn't come to her. Her mind control powers didn't work on him. Eventually, she started luring young children to the ocean – angry that my Papa would not come. Most of the children died. Some my Papa was able to save.

"Finally, he agreed to come to Nyobi if she would stop killing the children. But Nyobi didn't want him dead. She had fallen in love with him. No other man had been able to escape her. She looked deep in the ocean for ancient magic. Then, one day the princess came for him in a spout of water.

"She had a shell in her hand and told my papa that if he would drink the water from the shell, he would be able to live underwater. She wanted him to marry her and rule the ocean with her.

"He was sad, but he knew the princess would keep killing the children if he did not do what she wanted." Dom's eyes are downcast and his voice is quiet as he continues the story. I take his hand in mine.

"He drank from the shell and entered the water with the princess. She took my father to the depths of the sea and they were married by magic. That magic then lived in him, became a part of him. He was now a king of the ocean and Nyobi was his queen.

"But Papa was miserable. Queen Nyobi was a jealous wife. Anything Papa did made her more and more mad. She started cursing everything that she thought he loved. She cursed the fishing boats that my father looked for. She cursed the colorful fish that he liked. She cursed the happy families onshore.

"Papa grew weak and old under his Queen's control. He knew he had to stop her and free himself, but he didn't have the strength for it. Then, one day, as he was near the shore, floating the body of a dead fisherman toward the beach, he saw my Mama. He had never been caught covering the crimes of his Queen before. He had never been seen mourning as he rid the sea of the dead she killed. He looked at my Mama and his heart filled with sadness and regret. He wanted freedom.

"My Mama called out to him. Her heart ached for to him. She could see that he was broken, sad, and trapped. She just wanted to help him. The strength of her yearning for good broke the spell that bound my father to Queen Nyobi Kadul. As soon as he felt the tether snap that tied him to his evil bride, a weight lifted from his chest and youth returned to his features. My Mama saw the change and her heart grew. Papa came to shore and Mama met him there. They took each other by the hand and walked away from the evil in the ocean."

"When did the Queen find out?" I ask. "What did she do?"

"When the binding spell that united my father to her broke," Dom replied, "the Queen felt it and she raced to the shoreline. But by the time she arrived, my father and Mama were gone. But in the water was the lily my mama had been wearing in her hair. Nyobi found it and knew it belonged to someone who took Papa from her. Using most of her remaining power, she cursed the flower and cursed my Mama."

"What did Queen Nyobi curse your Mama with, Dom?"

Dom raises his eyes to meet mine. "The Queen cursed my Mama's womb, Evelyn. Anything growing from my mama and papa would be cursed. Cursed with power. Cursed with ability. Cursed so that if anyone knew about the child, they would hunt it and destroy it.

"My father was the only other person who knew about our power, Evelyn. He felt the curse the moment it was cast. He was so familiar with Nyobi's methods. He was ashamed. He blamed himself for our powers. He loved Mama too much to tell her. He knew she wanted to have children. He didn't want to make her sad or afraid. That's why he and Pearl and I kept it to ourselves."

I pull away from Dom's gaze, realizing what he is telling me. I take deep breaths in an effort to slow the beating of my heart. The powers he and Pearl have and share were bestowed on them through a jealous curse. He is cursed. Pearl is cursed. I am in Pearl's body.

I am cursed.

Chapter 5

"I'm living in a cursed body." I didn't mean to say it out loud. Dom lowers his gaze and looks down at the dry grass he is playing with beneath his legs. Guilt sweeps through me. I have hurt Dom's feelings, made him feel less than me through my shame and fear.

"I'm sorry," I say. I need to make this better. "I didn't mean that the way it sounded."

Dom looks away from me as he responds. His dark skin is flushing red in his cheeks. "Don't worry about it," he says. "I thought you would understand. It's okay if you don't. But you still need to know if you are going to keep safe." Dom's eyes are fixed on the olive orchard in the distance. "There's more you need to know," he says. He moves so he is sitting tall, facing me. He clears his throat and looks me in the eyes.

"The other week at the festival," he says, "something happened. I didn't tell you because you didn't know our secret yet. I wasn't sure if I could trust you." Dom looks down just for a moment before meeting my gaze again.

"Pearl and I have a code of secrecy. We don't tell other people certain things. This should be *our* secret." His eyes are sad and I feel how much he misses his twin. I feel Pearl's love for her brother. "But, it doesn't look like Pearl will be coming back soon," he says. I look down at the ground, too ashamed to face him. I have taken over his sister's body. Not by choice, but by the cursed magic that lives within her *and* him.

Dom clears his throat and shakes off whatever sad emotions were creeping into his young heart and continues. "Anyway, since you're older, maybe you can help us. Help me and Pearl, I mean. That's probably why you're still here anyway." I lift my head and give him an apologetic look. I want to get out of this body and back into my own as much as he wants his sister back.

"I want to help, Dom," I say. "Maybe we can figure this out. I want to help Pearl. I want to help you." I look down and whisper, "I want to go home." Three tears escape from my eyes and I cannot speak. I let myself think of my mom, my father, the life I was taken from. But only for a moment. When I am calm again, I sit up and ask, "What else do you have to tell me?"

Dom's face is filled with the trust of a ten-year-old boy confiding his secrets to his sister. I know I will never reveal his secret. Too much of Pearl is living inside me. I cannot betray them.

"So, at the festival, a man came up to me," Dom says, "He said my mother was looking for me. I started to go with him, but then I saw a parade of acrobats and got distracted. When I turned my head, he grabbed my arm and pulled me behind him."

"What?!" I yell. "Dom, who was it?!" My heart is beating faster and I can't breathe. Why was someone trying to take Dom?

"I don't know who it was. He looked familiar. He was real big and strong and was wearing a long purple robe. I kept trying to get away, but his grip was so hard, I couldn't get loose."

"Wait. You can read minds, Dom. You can make people feel things. Weren't you able to make him think whatever you wanted? Couldn't you make him want to let you go?"

"He was wearing gloves, Pearl. Ugh! Evelyn! I couldn't touch his skin. He was covered. He got me pulled behind some of the buildings and tried to shove me into the back of a cart. I bit his robes and kicked him and he hit me across my face."

"Dom!" I yell. "Why didn't you tell your mama?"

"Shhh!!" Dom says. "Let me finish. It's like I said. Mama has enough to deal with. I'm fine now, so what? I'm becoming a man. It doesn't really matter anyway."

I roll my eyes at his naiveté. He is so clueless, he'll get himself killed. "Dom, you don't know what people can do to kids."

He gives me an uncomfortable glance. "I know enough of what they can do to kids, Evelyn. Theodis has told me."

I cringe just thinking about what Theodis has told Dom and how he knew. I feel sick inside.

"But he didn't want that from me, Evelyn," Dom says. I look up into his eyes.

"How can you be sure?" I ask.

"Because after he hit me, he said, 'Oh, no you don't, you little brat. There'll be no getting away from me. I have something for you to do.'"

"Dom, what did he mean? What did he have for you to do?"

Dom reaches out, grabbing me by the arms and shaking me. His eyes are large and angry. His voice grows deep as he reenacts his ordeal. "He shook me by both arms and told me he knew what I was capable of. He said he had some friends who needed some persuading."

My hand flies to my mouth as I gasp. How could he know? Whoever he was. I know Dom and Pearl have been careful with their secret.

"I froze and he laughed" Dom continues. "Then he laughed louder and his grip loosened on me a little bit. I yanked as hard as I could and fell backward. He tripped when he tried grabbing me again. It was all I needed to get away. The last I saw him, he was tangled in his robes on the ground."

I am so upset and shocked by what Dom is telling me that I grab his arm, digging my nails into the skin.

"You can let me go now, Evelyn. I got away and I'm fine," he says. Dom looks away from my face and into the field behind me. I turn to see what has caught his attention and I see Theodis walking across the field, a large bruise on his cheek. He has been getting into fights lately. He hasn't been doing a very good job of winning.

Dom and I sit for a few minutes, watching Theodis as he walks. Then it comes to us at the same time. Theodis. Just how often has Dom used his powers against Theodis? Dom and I turn to face each other. I see in an instant a dozen or more memories where Dom has practiced his power on the servant boy. Dom using his mind altering powers to convince Theodis to get a pastry from the kitchen. Getting Theodis to sneak milk for him from Acacia's pail before it is sieved. Making him say he broke something that Dom actually broke.

I look Dom straight in the eye and I know that he knows what I saw and remembered from Pearl. He looks away from me and back to Theodis. We watch silently as Theodis goes into the animal pen with a container of slop for the pigs.

"Dom, do you think he knows what you've been doing to him?" I ask in a whispered tone.

"I don't know," Dom says. "I hadn't thought of that before. I don't know if anyone can tell when I'm reaching into their thoughts."

"I didn't know when you were reading my thoughts, but that doesn't mean no one can feel it," I say.

Theodis comes out from the pen, empty container in hand. He pauses to close the gate then catches a glimpse of us as he turns to leave. He meets our eyes and holds our gaze for several moments. The message is clear: *I know what you've done and now I'm paying for it.* He strokes his bruised cheek, shakes his head, then lets out a small huff of derision. That's all we need to know for sure. Theodis told someone about Dom and he is still in danger.

"Dom, we have to tell your mama what happened," I say. "She needs to know."

"What good would that do?!" Dom asks. "She just wouldn't let me go out anymore. She doesn't know about our powers, remember? We have to keep her safe."

"Dom," I say, "we don't have to tell her about your powers. We can just tell her someone tried to take you. She needs to know."

"Again, Pearl," Dom says, "Why? It's over and I got away. Besides, what would she do? She isn't going to know who it was or why they would try anything. She would start sending someone with me anytime I go anywhere and she'd worry all the time. It wouldn't do any good. It wouldn't help anything."

I shake my head and open my mouth to argue. Dom grabs my arm and starts messing with my head.

"It's going to be okay, Pearl," he says to me. I can feel him trying to manipulate my mind. I'm still new at resisting him and he is determined. I yank my arm away.

"It isn't okay, Dom," I say. "And stop calling me Pearl! I am here to help her and I can't if you don't let me ask for the help you both need!" Dom's nostrils flare and he stands up, putting his fists on his hips and stomping his foot on the ground. He grabs my arm again.

"Evelyn," he says, "you will not tell Mama. She doesn't need to know." As soon as he says my name, my real name, my brain goes foggy. Dom is blurry. Theodis is blurry. Everything is blurry. I am under his control. My mind obeys his power. My will is overcome by his. I will not tell his Mama.

Chapter 6

For the next several weeks, Dom and I keep a low profile. We stick to our chores and our schoolwork. We spend less time talking, always nervous that Theodis will be watching or that someone will jump out and grab Dom. When his mama's sister and her family come to visit, I spend the entire time with my eyes on Dom. There are so many people around, it is easy to lose track of him. I am afraid for him but my mind is bound by him.

We have taken more precautions to stay safe. Dom goes nowhere alone and has stopped visiting with his friends. It's exactly what he was afraid his mama would do to him, and he is doing it to himself. But one day, our efforts are almost ruined. We are alone together for just a few moments in the animal pen, milking Acacia. We have been giving each other quick clues when we have to talk. A tug of our ear lets the other know that we need to meet. The animal pen has been our meeting place for the past week

"I've been trying to stay away from Theodis, but I feel like he is always hiding around some corner," Dom says in hurried whispers. "I feel like we aren't doing anything to get Pearl back. Do you have anything new? Any leads?"

I stare at the ground. "No," I say. "I have nothing. I tried looking through some of your mama's things to see if maybe there was some sort of clue there, but Cook called me into the kitchen to sweep again. I swear that woman is out to get me."

"If it's any help, she actually doesn't like Pearl very much," Dom tells me. "She has been with the family a long time and has always acted like she was mad at us most of the time. I think she wishes she had some of the money we have. She thinks Pearl and I are spoiled – hasn't liked us since we came to live here. So, at least it's not just you."

I shake my head. The family servant feels more like a family enemy.

"I'm sorry I haven't found anything," I say. "What about you? Have you had any luck?"

Dom's face grows serious. He glances from left to right, making sure we are absolutely alone. "I saw him, Evelyn." He says in a hurried whisper. "I saw the man in the purple robe who tried to kidnap me. He was coming to talk to Grandfather."

My heart beats clear into my throat. "Did he see you, Dom? Did he try anything?" I ask.

Dom leans closer, his face almost touching mine. "Evelyn, he looked me straight in the face. He stared at me with an angry look I don't ever want to see again." Dom leans back on his heels and shakes his head.

"What happened next?" I ask, a cold sweat breaking through my brow.

"I froze," Dom says, "I didn't move near him or try to use any of my powers. All I could do was stand there. I knew I was safe in the house. He can't do anything to me while Grandpa's around. But then, he reached into his satchel. I was scared. I didn't know what he would have in there."

"Well, what was it?"

"Gloves."

"Gloves?"

"Gloves, Evelyn. Gloves. Because he knows how my talents work. He knows that I need skin to skin contact to sway anyone. If only Pearl were here. I could do more if Pearl were here."

I feel inadequate when I see the fear in Dom's eyes. Pearl would know how to use her own powers to help her brother. She knows his strengths better than I do in ways she cannot explain to me.

"Dom. We have to figure this out," I say. "Maybe we can ask your grandpa about the man in the purple robe. Maybe we could follow *him* and get you to touch his skin and make him forget and, and…"

Dom's eyes light up. "Grandpa always keeps a record of his business," he says. "Maybe he was pretending to be here on business. If that's right, we can get into the record room and see who he is. Then, then yeah, we can sneak to his place or hide somewhere he wouldn't be able to see us. Then…"

Someone sneezes. Dom and I freeze where we are and turn our heads up. The hayloft. We sit silently, waiting for more sounds from whoever is there. Is it someone we can sway? How much have they heard? The questions lay quietly between us as we hold our breath and wait.

We don't have to wait long for another stifled sneeze and a sniff from above.

"Who's up there?" Dom calls out to our spy. Silence. In a louder voice, Dom yells, "I said, 'who is up there?' Come out now! You'd better come out or I'll get Grandpa. He won't put up with servants spying."

Theodis jumps out of a pile of hay and makes a running start for the edge of the loft. Before we realize what he is doing, he jumps on top of Dom, tackling him to the ground. I fly backward as Theodis slams into Dom. Theodis is at least four years older than Dom and nearly double his size. If it were a simple matter of hand-to-hand combat, there's no way Dom would stand a chance. But Dom can touch Theodis' skin. He can make him see anything, do anything, think anything.

I jump toward the pair, swinging my arms wildly at Theodis' back. I pull at his hair and scratch at his exposed neck. "Dom!" I yell, "Dom! You've got to control him!"

Dom's arms are flailing wildly, trying to reach for Theodis' face.

"Oh no, you don't," Theodis says with a mocking tone. "You don't get to touch me. I know what you'll do."

Dom reaches for Theodis' arm and gets ahold of his wrist. Theodis is momentarily weakened as he becomes susceptible to whatever Dom is making him feel. I have a good grip on Theodis' hair and I'm not about to let go. He releases his grip on Dom and stands. Dom stands with him, holding tightly to his wrist. I let go of his hair, knowing that Dom can control him now.

We are walking to the gate when Dom slips on a puddle in the animal pen. In less than a second, he is flat on the ground, his hand no longer holding Theodis' wrist. I turn to Dom, helping him from the ground. Theodis shakes his head and spins to face us.

"Oh no, you don't, you spoiled freak!" Theodis shouts at Dom as he tries to get up and grab him again. Theodis grabs a hemp sack from the fence. In an instant, he has it wrapped around Dom and is lifting him off the ground.

I jump onto Theodis' back and he drops Dom again. He turns and I slip to the ground. He gives me a swift kick in the side. "Take that, you little brat. Nobody wants you. You aren't worth anything next to your brother here. Or is he even your brother? I heard you talking." He is kicking me with each sentence and I do all I can to move out of the way. He grabs at my hair and tosses me to the side, tearing Pearl's hamsa talisman from around my neck. He tosses it to the ground and picks up the sack, walking to Dom again.

Dom is lying on the ground, trying to get up. As Theodis reaches toward him with the sack, Dom lifts his hand to keep him away. But Theodis uses the sack to grab hold of Dom's outstretched arm, grabbing him by the wrist. He twists and yanks as hard as he can and Dom screams out in pain. As Theodis reaches for Dom again, all I can see is red. This boy will NOT harm Dom!!!!!

I let out a scream unlike anything I have ever heard from the mouth of a ten-year-old girl. It is loud and low and rumbling. It sounds like a lion calling out in the Sahara. I feel complete and total rage coursing through my body. I envision Theodis crumpling to the ground by Dom, holding his own head and screaming in pain. I let out another yell and imagine the scene again – Theodis falling in pain.

As I finish my second yell, I am totally weak. I look to Dom who is near me. His eyes are fearful, his skin pale from the shock of his broken arm. But he looks at me as though I have done something horrible.

I look to where I last saw Theodis standing over Dom. He is a heap on the ground, his hands clasping the sides of his ears. Blood is leaking out from between his fingers and small rivulets of bloody tears are coming from his eyes. Pearl's hamsa talisman lays on the ground by his hands.

Dom is frozen on the ground, in too much pain to move. In the silence, I can hear the yells and footsteps of the adults running from the house. Just as they reach us, I feel so light-headed that I have to lie back down again. I turn my head and see Pearl's Mama reaching my side, kneeling to check on me. As she touches my head and I see her lips move in questions, I close my eyes and sleep.

∞ ∞ ∞

My eyes flash open and I awake from the nightmare. A ferocious, pounding headache pulses behind my eyes and I am in a cold sweat. I hate these kinds of dreams. They always leave me with a sense of something ominous coming toward me. I have so many ominous dreams. I wish they would stop.

I reach my hand out of my blanket and touch my sweaty brow. I wipe at the wetness with the edge of my covers, drying my entire face from the nightmare I have awoken from. I stretch the stiffness from my limbs and sit myself up in the bed. The room is still dark, but the tiniest hint of dawn is making its way through the edges of my window curtains. My stomach growls and I move out of my bed, across my room, and into the dark kitchen.

It is too early yet for Cook to be awake, so I rummage through the wooden bowls on the table, looking for the best fruit to eat. An uneaten piece of flatbread is sitting by the fruit bowl, and I take it along with some dried figs Cook keeps hidden in her secret drawer. I bring the food back into my room. I sit on my, Pearl's, bed and watch the day begin its journey into the tiny space.

As I finish the bread, I hear stirring coming from the corner. Someone is in here. Have they been here all night? I sit silently on my bed, waiting to see who will walk from the dark corner and into the light.

Just as I start worrying that someone bad is in my room, Dom steps into the early light. His eyes are bleary and his hair is disheveled. I didn't see him when I left my room. He must have been sleeping in my chair again. I smile, ready to make a joke about his wild hair, when I see the sling hanging over his shoulder, holding his bandaged arm.

The painful reality hits me with blunt force as I realize that I hadn't been dreaming. Last night, two nights ago, whenever it was – it happened. It really happened. What happened?! What happened in the animal pen?

What did I do?

I feel the color draining from my face and the food I just ate turns flips in my stomach. My vision blurs when sleepy-eyed Dom snaps awake and hurries to the bed. He sits on the blankets next to me and puts his good hand on my shoulder.

"Evelyn," he whispers. Why is he calling me that? Oh, yes. That's me.

"Evelyn," he whispers again, this time giving my shoulder a gentle shake.

I let out a small groan and lay back on my pillows. Things are spinning, but they are also clearing. I wasn't dreaming. I wasn't dreaming. Theodis. Dom.

"Dom!" I sit up, wanting to ask him what happened and if he is alright. Dom's hand pushes gently on my shoulder, making me rest on the pillows again.

"Settle down, Evelyn," Dom whispers, "We can't be too loud or Cook will wake up."

"What happened, Dom?" I ask. "How long have I been asleep?"

Dom pulls his feet up on the bed, facing me.

"Theodis was working for the purple-robed man who tried to take me, Evelyn. He heard us talking in the animal pen. He was going to take me to the purple robed man." Dom's eyes shine with the wetness of strained and fearful tears. "Theodis tried to hurt me, but you and I both fought him off. He threw you down and broke my arm. The rope for Pearl's hamsa charm must have broken off somewhere in the fighting." Dom sits up and pulls something from the small bag around his waist. He lays it on the bed. It is the necklace I have worn since entering Pearl's body. The thin jute that held it around my neck has snapped near the knot that held it all together. The blue-painted, wooden hand lay on top of the pile of jute, the eye in the center staring at me in harsh judgement.

"What happened, Dom?" I sit up and ask the questions that I fear most. "What did I do? What does this necklace have to do with anything?"

Dom looks up at me sadly, a single tear rolling from his cheek. He opens his mouth to speak and we hear Cook shuffle from her bed. She is waking up. Our conversation will have to wait. Dom picks up the necklace and hands it to me. I put it around my neck and head to the kitchen to begin my chores.

Chapter 7

Pearl's mother has fussed over me all morning. She's asked me nearly a dozen times if I am sure I want to be up. She insists that I should still be in my bed, that I've had too much of a shock, that I need to recover. When I ask what I need to recover from, she grows quiet, mumbling something about "unfortunate" and "how glad I am that you and Dom are well." She pats my shoulder and kisses my forehead, a tear or two escaping her eyes. "If I had lost you, my only Pearl," she sighs, holds me close, then allows me out for a walk outside, sure that the fresh air will do me good.

Cook is in a harsh mood as neither Dom nor I are fit to do anything useful in the house. With his broken arm and my recent dizziness and fainting, we have both been sent outside. It doesn't take long before we reach our favorite tree. After half an hour of sitting and staring at the animal pen in the distance, I begin the conversation we started this morning.

"Dom," I break the silence, "what happened? Please tell me."

Dom shakes his head, at war within himself over what to say.

"It was my fault," he says at last. "If I had told you earlier about what Pearl can do, what you can do, you would have been able to control your mind better."

"What do you mean control *my* mind? What can I do, Dom?"

Dom looks at me for a moment, then he takes a deep breath and says, "There's a reason why Pearl never uses her powers, Evelyn."

I am jolted for a moment, forgetting that I am *not* Pearl. I am Evelyn. I am living in Pearl's body, here to help her escape her future.

"Pearl is so much stronger than me," Dom continues. "She can manipulate minds without touching people. She can see inside of minds and make people go completely crazy. The hamsa necklace was the only thing that was keeping you sane. Once Theodis pulled it off of you, your...*Pearl's* power couldn't be contained." I reach up and feel the talisman, again tied around my neck.

Dom pauses then says, "*You* have to learn how to do these things, Evelyn. *You* have to learn how to protect yourself, in case I am not around."

My heart races and I avert my eyes. I recall Pearl's memory of Dom's death. It's a memory he hasn't found yet. She has kept it hidden so far inside of me that he cannot find it. I cannot picture his body in death, I just know it happens. Death. Theodis. What happened to Theodis?

"Dom," I ask, "what happened to Theodis? Is he okay? Dom, what happened to him? What did I do?"

Dom turns his head away and sighs. "Theodis isn't here anymore, Evelyn. He just kept screaming and screaming, holding his head, blood coming from his ears and eyes." I am sick to my stomach as Dom continues, "Grandpa called for the physician, but by the time he arrived, Theodis was quiet."

I am still as a statue. Theodis' silence was the sign of his death. I don't know what could have been done for him with modern medicine, but there is no way that ancient doctors could have helped him in any way.

A moan escapes my lips as I hold back the nausea rising from my stomach. Dom puts his hand on my shoulder and I cry. I am filled with a power I have never felt before. I don't understand it. It is deadly and I have used it.

I have killed someone.

∞ ∞ ∞

Dom stands behind me, holding my hair as I throw up in the grass beneath our tree. I think I am done. I sit up and Dom wipes my face with the bottom of his robes, my tears adding to the moisture on my face. I have killed someone.

"No one else knows about your powers, Pearl...Evelyn...Ugh! Can I just call you Pearl? I can't keep doing this!" Dom's face is red and his eyes are shining. He is holding back the wave of emotion he feels over being afraid and separated from his sister. He needs comfort. He needs to feel that she is with him. I nod, letting him know that calling me Pearl is okay. I know who I am.

Dom closes his eyes, sighing as his shoulders sink an inch. "To everyone there, it looked like Theodis was possessed by Achlys or something. It looked like he was poisoned. Servants screamed and ran, saying Theodis was cursed. They said Grandfather brought the wrath of the gods on him."

I am dumbfounded by what Dom is saying. I forgot that I am living in a time where people believe in pagan gods and worship idols and find fear and suspicion everywhere they turn. A 21st century crowd would suspect terrorism or drugs. But not here. Here they are rooted in myth and legend. They aren't far from the truth. But I'm not a god. I'm a displaced two-worlder.

"What do they think he did to bring the gods' wrath on him?" I ask, still clutching the hamsa medallion in my hand. I run my fingers over the palm of the hand, feeling the raised eye in the center. As I do, a memory flashes across my mind. It isn't my memory. I can see myself, Pearl, screaming. She is facing the person whose mind I am channeling. She screams at such a high pitch, I can see hands raising to cover ears. The memory of pain sears through my brain. The memory won't stop. It's all screaming and pain until red seeps into the corners of my vision. It is wet and warm. The hands move down and they are covered in blood. The memory looks again at Pearl. Then everything goes black. My eyes open to the painful reality that I have just seen Theodis' last memory.

"People will believe anything they want to believe," Dom says. He hasn't seen me waver. "Grandfather has a lot of power here and a lot of money. People are jealous of our family, Pearl. People like Cook." I blink my eyes, trying to shake the vision I saw as I listen to Dom's explanation.

"Cook is probably getting paid by someone to say the things she is saying. As for those who believe it, well, Cook's family has been here nearly as long as Grandfather's. Her opinion means something. She doesn't want to see our family succeed. She wants us to fall and she will take as many followers with her as she can."

I sigh and take Dom's hand. "It will be okay, Dom. You'll see," I tell him. "This will blow over and things will return to how they were before." Dom's eyebrows remain furrowed and the corners of his mouth droop a little lower as he turns his gaze over the countryside, shaking his head. My confidence fades and my heart sinks into my stomach when I look at the fear in this young boy's eyes. I lay my hand again on the ground and let a hot tear roll out of the corner of my eye. Guilt sweeps over me as I think of the part I have played in Dom's fears. He knows Pearl better than I do. He knows the depth of her powers and capabilities. He knows why they are something to be feared. I know next to nothing. Dom clears his throat and brings his eyes to meet mine. His gaze is strong and steady and determined as he speaks.

"I think it's time for you to learn how to use your powers, Pearl. If something happens again and you lose the hamsa, you need to know how to protect yourself. I don't want you to make another mistake and have someone find out what you can do. There is no telling what they would do to you." He stares at me, unblinking, willing my soul to commune with his, convinced that he can persuade me to believe him. But he doesn't need to persuade me. I felt Pearl's power completely out of control within me. The result was disastrous. I have to know how to control this power. I have to delve deeper into Pearl's being to learn how to protect her, save Dom, and return to my own home and body and life.

I nod to my twin, to Pearl's twin. "Yes, Dom," I tell him. "I want to know. I want to learn."

But there isn't much time for learning in the next few months. Cook left, but that was just the beginning of the servants' exodus. We've lost two more housemaids and three field hands since Theodis' death. Dom and I are given more responsibilities to keep things moving as they should until we can get more servants. More servants who haven't heard about Theodis, who don't know Cook, and who will be loyal to Grandfather.

Mama's sister, Oronia, comes to visit for several weeks when she learns about what happened. I eavesdrop on their conversations so I can know how close the rumors are to the truth.

"It was horrible, Nia," Pearl's mama tells her sister when they think they are out of earshot. "The boy was covered in blood. Dom was screaming. Pearl's eyes were rolling back into her head."

"What happened to them, Helena?" Oronia asks. A momentary pause follows before Mama answers.

"I don't know, Nia," she says. "The servants blame father. They say he has cheated in his business and brought the wrath of the gods on our family. Father says Theodis was taking some kind of drug, that he shared it with the children, then went into hysterics."

"But what do you think happened, Helena?" Oronia asks. "Do you think it has anything to do with Pontus?" I hold my breath when I hear his name. Pontus was Pearl's father. What does Oronia know of his past?

"It isn't polite to spy, Pearl." I jump back when I hear the voice of Pearl's cousin, Ananke. She is 18 years old and betrothed to a merchant in the south. She is here visiting with her mother, trying to help the family.

"I'm sorry," I tell her. "I was just..."

Ananke smiles at me. She is tall and light-skinned with sloping shoulders and golden hair. Her eyes are the color of the ocean on a stormy day. She is an anomaly in this family. She puts her hand around my shoulder and leads me away from my hiding place.

"I know it's hard to not listen, Pearl," she says, "but no good will come of it. Let the adults take care of the situation. You and Dom just need to worry about getting well." I know Ananke is well-intentioned, but I can't help but worry about the situation. Our family is in a precarious position and it is my fault.

Aunt Oronia and Ananke stay for a few weeks to help get the family settled into a new routine. Ananke keeps an eye on me and Dom, not giving us a moment to ourselves. Though they are both kind and love us, I am happy when they finally leave and we are left to settle into our new way of life.

I had to quit school. Not that I mind missing the education. It is primitive, but still interesting to hear their theories, knowing myself which are true and which are not. I am sad to have lost the opportunity for Pearl, though. Hopefully, when I can fix everything, Pearl will be able to go to school again.

I lay awake many nights and think of my mom and my life in Atlantis. I think about Jack and wonder if he has met another girl who interests him. I picture the Atlantean army at war with Ceto's army. I worry over them and how they are doing. I dream and have nightmares that plague me, but I am no closer to finding my way back to them - back to my real family and my real life. I am working harder and eating less - a nasty combination in a growing girl. I have frequent headaches. I am growing used to them.

Dom is still attending school and helps Grandfather when he gets home. We only have a few minutes together after the evening meal. But summer is approaching and Dom will soon have a break from school. We both hope to have more time to teach me what I need to know.

I have taken over cooking. Pearl's mama has been teaching me my way around the kitchen, but soon it is all in my hands as she continues to manage the few remaining servants and pick up more chores in Grandfather's home. Most of the meals I make are simple like olive, tomato, cucumber, onion and feta horiatiki salad. Dom teases me because I burn even the simplest dishes. But tonight, I think I have found my niche in the kitchen. I am excited to see Dom's reaction.

"Oh, no. Do we have to eat more of Pearl's burned food tonight?" Dom asks as he comes to the table. Grandfather is traveling tonight, looking ever farther for business partners and customers who have not been tainted by Cook's rumors. So it is just me and Dom and his mama seated at the table.

"Dom," his mama says as she shakes her head at her son. "Pearl has spent the past few months learning and trying just as you have done." She glances at me then back at Dom. "And just as *you* have made mistakes in your accounting with Grandfather and work in the fields, Pearl has made mistakes with the food. But just as *you* have improved in your new responsibilities, Pearl has improved in hers. You are both getting older. You're almost 11 now. Please treat your sister with the respect and maturity you are capable of and she deserves." Dom sighs and looks down at the table sitting quietly to wait for the meal.

First, I bring out the horiatiki. Dom eats it without complaint since it is one dish that no one can mess up. Before his salad is eaten, I bring out the second dish – keftedes. The mild-flavored meatballs aren't dry like they have been the past few months. They are juicy and flavorful and covered in the traditional cream sauce. The pita bread I made to go with the keftedes is perfect. The garlic flavor peeks through the layers of unleavened bread and adds the perfect touch to the meat and sauce. I can see Dom's mouth watering as he reaches for another serving of the keftedes, but his mama puts her hand on his wrist.

"No, Dom. You must leave room in your stomach for the dessert Pearl has prepared."

"She made dessert, too?!" he asks. He looks at me with a big grin on his face. It's enough of an apology for me for the way he was abusing my cooking earlier. I head to the kitchen to grab the loukoumades for dessert.

As I lift the towel from the bowl, the smell of warm cinnamon makes its way to my nose. I stumble backward for a moment. The scent hits me in the face like a stinging memory. Something about the smell is overwhelming and familiar. I see images in my mind. A boy with red hair who always smells like cinnamon. My heart feels like it is going to break and a tear finds its way onto my cheek. I feel like I have been crushed with the weight of lost love, though I cannot place the who or the why.

"Are you ever going to bring the dessert?!" Dom's excited voice brings me back to my senses. I reach for the jug of syrup and pour it sparingly over the fried dough dusted in cinnamon and rolled in walnuts. I wipe my cheek with the back of my hand and bring my masterpiece to the table.

Dom and his mother clap for the dessert when it arrives. Mama doesn't stop Dom from eating seconds and he reaches into the wooden bowl for more loukoumades. We talk and we laugh as the evening sun reaches for the horizon. The days are growing longer and Dom and I will have more time together this evening after dinner.

"Dom," his mother says to him. "Since your sister made such a lovely meal, I say we celebrate."

"Absolutely!" Dom agrees.

"We will celebrate by helping Pearl clean the kitchen together." Dom's eyes grow wide and he opens his mouth in protest, but Mama stops him. "As we work together, the load will be lighter and you and Pearl will have time to play this evening." Dom shoots a quick glance in my direction. This is a chance to teach me how to use my powers.

"Yes, Mama," he agrees. "I will gladly help tonight. Thank you!" Then turning to me, "Thank you, Pearl. Dinner was so good."

I smile and nod my acceptance of his compliment. It is fitting that on the night I will be learning more about my… Pearl's powers, that I am feeling more at home and successful in her body.

Chapter 8

It's a warm evening and Dom and I are sitting under our olive tree – the same tree I saw greeting me when I first entered Pearl's body. It is a lonely outcast of a tree. The rest of the orchard is all gathered together in neat rows on the hillside. But this tree, a renegade seedling making its own home on the hilltop, has no other trees around it. From where we sit, we can see the rolling hills of Grandfather's orchards with the olive press and the house in the valley. It is all Grandfather's land and will all one day belong to Dom. Our tree is like our own little hideaway from the world when we want to be alone. It gives Dom and me all the shade we need on a warm day and all the cover we need on a night of discovery.

Dom sits cross-legged in the dry grass beneath the tree. I am kneeling on my robes. Dom looks me in the eye, assessing if I am really ready to learn about the magic inside of me.

"I'm ready, Dom," I assure him. "This is the only way to get Pearl back home."

Dom's eyes widen and he takes in a quick, sharp breath. He has grown accustomed to calling me Pearl and started to forget that I am really Evelyn. I understand his confusion. I sometimes forget myself.

Dom shakes his head, clearing his thoughts, and says, "Hold out your hand."

I put out my right hand, my left hand still holding the hamsa medallion around my neck. Dom takes my open hand and places his closed fist into it. When he pulls his hand away, there is a small, black pearl in my open palm. Recognition sweeps over me again. I know this stone. Yes, it is smaller than the one I held nearly a year ago, but the shape and color is still the same. This is the pearl I grasped when I was last in Atlantis. This is the pearl that brought me here.

"Pearl," Dom gets my attention. "You are going to start your lessons by moving *this* pearl with your mind." He doesn't know. Dom has no idea that this pearl is a link to everything. For him, it is just an object – something to use as a learning tool.

Of course, maybe it's a sign to me from Pearl. Or from Fate. Or from Destiny. All I am sure of is that I MUST pay very close attention to whatever comes next. Dom mistakes my quiet fascination for confusion or fear.

"You don't need to worry, Pearl," he assures me. "This is the easy stuff. I've done it lots of times. You'll remember."

As he says the words, an image flashes through my mind. I see Theodis working at his regular chores in the animal pen. He is pouring slop into troughs and refreshing the hay. He stops his work near the wall of the house and looks around to make sure no one can see him. He digs through the hay pile and pulls out an amphora. The ceramic pottery piece is one from a set that I recognize from Grandfather's rooms. They are all filled with some of Grandfather's prize liquors. Fine paintings like I've seen on museum field trips cover their sides. Images of harvest, of moon and sky, of royalty all cover the valuable set. Dark wines and light champagnes and a dozen more liquids I cannot name fill those amphorae. Theodis helped himself to Grandfather's store.

Just as Theodis gets ready to take a drink, I see a small bucket rising over the railing behind him. I look for the hand holding the bucket, but I see none. Then the bucket floats above Theodis and dumps upside down over his head, filthy water from the trough soaking his clothing before falling to the ground. Theodis jumps to his feet, shoving the amphora of wine into the hay. He looks left and right, trying to find the person who embarrassed him. Trying to find Dom.

In this memory, I turn to see a younger Dom at my side, under the same olive tree we are sitting under now. He is laughing and I am laughing with him. He is the one who poured the water on Theodis. But he could not be caught because he was nowhere near Theodis when it happened.

The memory vanishes and the hand holding the hamsa is burning hot. I drop my hand to my leg, wiping the heat on my robes.

"I just want you to focus on the pearl," Dom says, oblivious to the memory I've just seen. "Are you focusing?"

"Yes!" I answer. I return my attention to the small, black object in my hand.

"Good," Dom continues. "Now, I want you to focus all your thoughts on the very center of the pearl." Atlantis is the first place I learned to focus my attention on inanimate objects to discover the life within. I found the life in water, in temperature, in sea life, in air. Now I am looking for it in the stone that I think will take me home. I use my mind to reach out to the heart of the pearl in my hand. I feel it instantly, reaching out to me, using silky tendrils of thought to tickle my brain. I laugh as I meet the heart of this stone.

"Okay, Pearl," Dom says. "I want you to ask the pearl to do something."

"What should I ask?" I wonder aloud.

"Ask it to roll around in the palm of your hand," Dom replies.

With my eyes focused on the pearl, I reach out and speak to it with my thoughts.

Hello, I say. *I am Evelyn.*

ARE YOU?! The pearl yells into my mind. I am taken aback by the force of her speaking. She is not at all gentle. I feel the tendrils of her thoughts turn to distrust as she searches my mind for what I want from her.

Yes, I respond quietly. *I am Evelyn.*

The pearl laughs at my words. *YOU ARE NO EVELYN. YOU ARE ME AND I AM YOU! YOU CANNOT FOOL ME!*

Please, I respond. *I am not trying to fool you. I just have a favor to ask.*

OH REALLY, the pearl responds, *AND JUST WHAT KIND OF FAVOR IS IT THAT YOU WANT TO ASK OF ME?*

Well, I begin, *I wonder if you might roll around in my palm a bit. I'm learning levitation from Pearl's brother, Dom, and he says this is the way it is done.*

The tone of the pearl softens and she whispers to my mind, *Dom? Dom is a sweet boy. He has carried me with him since you gave me to him those many years ago. I am always in his satchel.* I feel the warmth and tenderness the pearl has for Dom. It is enough to catch in my heart. A tear falls to my hand, landing near the pearl I hold.

Ah, she whispers to me again, *you have grown fond of the boy. It is fitting since he is your brother.* I don't have the heart to correct her. She was so angry with me when I said my real name. I let her believe I am Pearl. I hope that will encourage her to help me.

The pearl makes tiny circles in my hand. They are very small at first, but the circles grow wider until she reaches the small drop that fell from my eye. She rolls through the tear then stops. She rolls back into the remaining water, rolling in it until it is all off of my hand and onto her body.

Is there anything else? She whispers. I look up at Dom, willing him to not make me do anything more with the pearl. She is aching inside. I don't know why, but it breaks my heart to ask more of her. But Dom's face is jubilant. His eyes are lit by a smile that stretches from ear to ear.

"Pearl! You did it!" He shouts, "I knew you weren't lost! I knew you were in there!" The pearl in my hand is growing hot. Dom hugs me and just before I can close my fist around the pearl, it leaps up from my hand. I pull away from Dom to catch it before it falls, but it isn't falling. The pearl is simply floating in the air in front of me and Dom.

Dom's smile softens and he reaches his hand toward the pearl. When his palm opens beneath the black stone, it lowers into his grasp. He folds his fingers around the pearl and holds it to his chest.

"Do you remember when you gave me this, Pearl?" He asks with tenderness in his voice. "It was a perfect day. Before we lived here. Father brought home a sack of oysters from his trip to the coast. You and I sat on our bench under the pomegranate tree, opening each oyster with rocks we found. We were eating ourselves silly. You had the last oyster. When you opened it, the pearl was inside. We were both so excited. It was yours. It was in your oyster. But you gave it to me. Do you remember what you said?"

I sit quietly, waiting for Dom to answer his own question.

"'Here,' you said. 'I am already a pearl. You need a pearl to always keep with you too. That way we will always be together.'"

My heart is about to burst with feeling for this sweet boy. I want to tell him I am not Pearl, but I cannot do that to him. He needs me to be Pearl. He needs me to be his sister. So, instead, I ask him a question.

"How old were we when that happened?"

Dom calculates the few years of our lives on his fingers. "It was before we moved here," he says to himself. "That's at least three-and-a-half years. And we've been 10 forever, so...six or seven, I guess."

I smile and nod and put my hand on Dom's shoulder. I love Dom like a brother, even if he isn't really mine. It's nice to have a brother for a while.

We both look up as we hear our Mama calling us from the porch. The sun is behind the hills now and the first stars of evening have been twinkling at us for quite a while. We stand up under our tree, stretching and breathing in the cooling air. Dom places the black pearl back inside his satchel and we race down the hill to our home.

The evenings will only grow longer. We will have even more time together. I will be able to learn all I need to know to go back to my own home. I ache to go home. But I also ache over leaving.

Chapter 9

It seems like an eternity that I have lived here in Argos. Dom and I are 11 now and things for the family are worse than ever. Most of the servants have left the place altogether and the estate is falling apart with just our care. Dom still continues to go to school, but his added responsibilities at home mean that he misses several mornings each week. I cook all the meals now and Mama does what she can to keep the house running. But the orchards are showing signs of neglect. Many of the tree tops are outgrowing the roots and we can't get to all of the pruning. Some of the trees are starving for nutrients, but we can't turn the soil as often as it needs. Some of the orchards are infested with disease and the trees are dying. Grandfather spends all of his time in his various rooms, meeting with visitors out of our sight and hearing. The man with the purple robe has started visiting Grandfather often. Dom and I wonder if he is trying to seek to marry Mama. It makes sense. That would be a sure ticket to Dom and his powers. If we become desperate, I will use my powers.

I have become better and better with my powers. The black pearl only comes out on occasion. I convinced Dom to let me use other objects for my practice. I told him I was afraid to lose his pearl. We used sticks and rocks for a while until I fine-tuned the proper voice and method of address for objects I want to levitate. The elements are a little more moody on land than they are in the sea. At least when compared to the sea life in 2,400 years. I am often rebuffed or turned away with comments like, *Someone thinks she can control me. Well, I have news for her. I will not be controlled any more by these ridiculous humans.*

The plants give the most trouble. Sticks, trees, even fruit can be temperamental. Give me a rock any day. The rocks and soil are so happy to have attention paid to them. Most of their life is spent being moved out of the way for trees and other plants to grow. They give all the nutrients they have so the flora can flourish. All they need is a little gratitude.

Hello, generous soil, I will say.

Well, hello there. The soil responds. *Aren't you just a polite person? What can I do for you today?* I then continue to ask the soil (or rocks) to do something for me. At first it was simple stuff like creating a small mound. But now I can get items to move through the air, floating here and there above the ground. The trick is the air itself.

When I lived in Atlantis (how I miss it), I had communication skills with the air above the ocean water. That skill has translated beautifully to all air here in Argos. It doesn't know me or my father like the air above Atlantis did, but my ability to communicate with it is just as strong.

Welcome again, Pearl Evelyn, the air whispers to me.

Hello, friends, I say. Then we have a lovely conversation about the weather and how hard the air has been working to keep things in their proper season. I have become good friends with the air around me and they have helped me learn proper levitation.

My friends, I say. *This is my rock friend Hortius* (or whatever the rock is named). *He is generously willing to help me learn today* (manners go a VERY long way with all communications). *Would you please be so kind as to work with us?*

The air and other elements and I then work together to do some pretty amazing things. Last week, Dom and I worked to repair a low rock wall. Because of our powers, the work didn't take as long as Mama expected it to. We had several extra hours to ourselves. Dom is a genius when it comes to talking to the plants. They respect him and will very often work to impress him. Sometimes I think they do it just to show me up.

After we finished the wall, Dom pulled out several corn kernels from his satchel. Together we coaxed the kernels into the ground and asked the ground to share its water and nutrients with the little seeds. We worked for twenty minutes or more, both of us talking to the elements around us, encouraging, thanking, and asking. When we finished, we had a tall, grown corn stalk with four or five ears of corn, full and ripe and ready to be picked.

Once we pulled the ears from the stock and shucked several of them clean, the stock withered into a dried heap. Then I reached out to the air to work with the dried stalk to create a fire. Once we had a small blaze going, we roasted our corn near the flames in their husks and let the cleaned ears rest in the heat. As we ate the roasted corn, the ears in the fire began to pop. We laughed and talked and ate before we finally headed back home.

I have started learning the mind control Dom says Pearl is so natural with. But I don't have many opportunities to practice it. I won't practice on Dom's Mama. She is too kind and I cannot bring myself to disturb her in any way. A few times I have made Dom think his pants are wet, but that is only when he is tired and his defenses are down. He is the only one who can keep me from influencing him.

Once at the market, I persuaded a vendor to give bread and cheese to some homeless children near his stall. That felt good. If I can use mind manipulation to help others, I will feel successful.

I cannot help but wonder if some of these skills will stay with me when I am able to return to Atlantis. I feel like I am on the edge of discovering something that will take me home and free me from Pearl's body. I have to work hard to remember things from my life, my real life. Dom hasn't called me Evelyn in so long. I wonder if he has completely forgotten who I really am. I wonder if I will forget.

I ponder these things as I stand at the kitchen counter, preparing some of Acacia's cheese to be fried. I hear her bleating coming from the animal pen. The sound is so loud and frightening, I drop what I am doing and run out to see what the matter is. When I arrive at her pen, I start screaming for help and run to my little goat.

Acacia is standing near her trough, bleating like mad, blood pouring from her mouth. I kneel by her side to see how she has hurt herself, but with all of the blood, I cannot see where a cut might be. I dip the end of my robe into her water so I can clean her mouth, but when my fingers touch the water, they burn. Acacia's water is rancid. No wonder she is bleeding.

I jump up and scream for Dom and Mama. Soon, they are by my side with Grandfather storming from the house to see what the problem is.

"Dom! Her water is bad!" I shout as Dom hurries through the gate. But Mama is right behind him and pulls his arm toward her.

"Dom!" she yells, "Run as fast as you can to the house. Get the last container of the kitchen water and bring it here with rags. QUICKLY!"

Dom runs into the house faster than I've ever seen him run before. Grandfather arrives at the animal pen, his expression softening when he sees me cradling Acacia in my arms. Her bleating is still loud and she will hardly let me hold her. She tries to kick and butt her head into me, but I hold on tight.

Pearl's mama is with me, on the ground, kneeling by Acacia and wiping at the goat's face with her beautiful scarf. The fine, creamy linen is easily stained by the bright blood from Acacia. Dom arrives in an instant with the clean water and rags.

"That's a good boy, Dom," Mama says. "Now go stand by Grandfather and let Pearl and me work." Dom obeys and walks to the outside of the pen with Grandfather.

Tears stream down my face as Mama dips the rags into the clean water from the house. This time there is no burning. Our water is safe. She squeezes the fresh water into Acacia's open mouth and the goat's bleating pauses for a moment. More and more water from our pot makes its way into the mouth of my precious goat. Her bleating quiets as the poison is rinsed away.

"We need to get her to eat, Pearl," Mama whispers. "The bad water is still in her stomach."

"Don't we want to make her throw it up?" I ask. "She needs to get it out."

"No, Pearl," she whispers again. "If it comes up again, it will burn her throat again." She turns her face to Dom whose eyes are pouring tears almost as much as my own. "Dom, please go and fetch some of the cornmeal from the house. Bring the small honey pot as well."

"Yes, Mama," Dom says and he runs into the house. Grandfather is still standing by the pen. His expression is hard and he sighs heavily.

"Helena, we cannot waste our good food on the goat." Grandfather's gruff voice is harsh against my heart. Mama remains silent as she continues to wipe Acacia's face.

Acacia is laying in the dirt beside me now, her head resting in my lap. Her breathing is labored and rough. I stroke her neck and cry quietly over her. Dom is by our side in a moment.

"Dom," Mama says, "please make a little cake of the cornmeal and honey." Grandfather huffs angrily and storms away from us, back to the fortress of his rooms and his failing estate. The air is calmer and quieter with him gone. I can focus on my animal. My mind is too harried to speak to Acacia's mind directly, so I do the next best thing and hum songs to her as she quiets.

Dom makes a little ball of the cornmeal and honey then hands it to Mama.

"Thank you my son," she says quietly as she accepts the ball. She flattens it in her fingers then puts a tiny piece on Acacia's tongue. Acacia isn't aware that the food is in her mouth. Mama pours in a little more water to get Acacia to swallow. Acacia moves her tongue around in her mouth like she wants to get the food in, but she is weak and tired. Mama sets the remainder of the cake on the ground and joins me in stroking Acacia's neck. Soon Dom is petting her belly.

We sit like that, the three of us with my little goat, singing to her and petting her as her breathing becomes more labored. She finally makes a choking sound, kicks her hooves twice, and lies still.

We sit with her and give her our love until the sun is gone and the air grows cold. There is no one else to take care of my little goat. The three of us will have to bury her ourselves. Mama lifts the goat in her arms as Dom helps her to her feet. I follow numbly behind as Dom leads us through the gate, up the hill, and to our olive tree. He grabs a small shovel along the way and digs near the base of the tree. Mama rests Acacia's lifeless body on the ground and makes a small wreath from the tall grass around us. I lie down next to my Acacia and cry into her rough fur.

When the grave is ready, I help Mama ease my goat into it. Mama lays her beautiful scarf across the body of my goat. Dom commences covering the tiny opening with the shovel. Dom's hands have grown strong and calloused from his work in the orchards, but he is working so feverishly on Acacia's grave that cracks are opening up in his hands. A few drops of his blood and tears drip into the soil, a small offering that the earth takes quietly down to my Acacia.

We place Mama's wreath on top of the little grave and walk quietly back to our dark house, our hearts too broken to speak.

Chapter 10

Mama has made dinner for the past several nights. I try to help, but until Acacia's milk and cheese are gone, I don't think I can make anything decent. I have taken over some of Mama's duties instead. The days are long and difficult and they are beginning to blend into each other. I am afraid I will never make it out of this place. Acacia's loss has made me more homesick than ever. I want to cry to my own mother, not Pearl's. I want to hold my friends and sleep in my bed and go to school and forget the craziness that is my life.

I have some time this evening to sit alone under our olive tree. The mound of Acacia's grave has little blades of grass sprouting all over the top of it. She would have liked to eat the grass and lay in the dirt beside me. I wrap my arms around my knees and cry hot and angry tears onto my robes. I hit the ground with my fists and let out a scream into the evening air.

Dom comes running up the tiny hill, yelling something I cannot hear. Nothing is wrong with me. I am fine. I just want time to be alone. But it doesn't take long for me to see that Dom is waving his arms frantically in the air while he runs toward me. I stand and race to him straining to hear.

"Pearl! Pearl!" he shouts to me. I feel anger flaring up at Pearl's twin for not calling me Evelyn. I just want to be Evelyn! But I can't be. Not anymore. "Pearl! He's after me again! The man in the purple robe!"

I freeze where I stand. The man in the purple robe has been here many times to see Grandfather and occasionally takes a moment to speak to Mama, but he hasn't come anywhere near Dom or me. We knew he would make a move eventually, but I am still on edge as Dom tells me the time is finally here.

"What happened?!" I ask him. He reaches me, out of breath and grabs my shoulders to steady himself while he speaks.

"I was coming home from school today and passing by the field where we fixed the wall. Cook was there and jumped out in front of me!"

"Cook?!" I yell. "What was *she* doing there?" I haven't seen Cook since she convinced the staff we were cursed and left the estate. I'd like to curse her.

"She is working for the man in the purple robe," he replies, "She was wearing a servant's ring on her pinky. There was a purple stone set in its center. That's *HIS* ring, Pearl!"

I feel a chill run up my heated neck and I shiver. Cook is now working for the man in the purple robe. This is bad. This is very, very bad.

"What did she say to you, Dom?" I ask as we head back to the safety of our tree.

"She said she knew all about us, Pearl. She said she watched us that day we fixed the wall."

My heart stops beating for a moment. Cook was *there*? I feel the color draining from my face as I remember what we did that day. We fixed the wall without our hands and we grew corn and roasted it with fire and ate it. Cook saw all of it. Despite my speechlessness, Dom continues to tell me the horrid details of his encounter with Cook.

"She stood with her fists on her hips," he says, "and she said, 'I wet myself I had to stay so long watching you two. I got a backhand to my cheek when I finally made it home to my new kitchen estate because I was so late. But that just added to the pleasure I'm a gonna get from watching you and your sister get what you deserve.'"

"What did she mean, Dom? What did she mean?!" I ask him.

Dom looks me in the eyes, his brows furrowed above his nose. He whispers to me, "She said she went straight to her new master and told him everything she saw. He sent her to watch over us ever since. She saw Acacia die and she said she knows who did it."

"What do you mean, 'who did it?' Do you mean that someone poisoned her water?" I ask. "I thought it just went bad. I thought we did something wrong that spoiled it."

Dom shakes his head. "No, Pearl. Mama and I knew from the start that someone put something in her water. It wasn't you or me or Mama or Grandfather. Someone was trying to send us a message."

Bile rises in my throat. I think of my goat, poisoned by someone who wanted to get at Pearl. At *ME*. Why would they harm a defenseless animal? Why would they hurt Acacia? She didn't deserve to die.

"Pearl," Dom continues, "Cook slapped me after she told me about Acacia. She slapped me and said, 'Boy, you better be watchful of yourself. I thought it was just your sister. But now I know *you* are just as bad a seed as she is.' She slapped me again and laughed then turned and went back down the road where she came from."

Tears sting my eyes and it is all I can do to keep from throwing up. I am so sick inside. Dom and I are being watched. We are being hunted.

"What do we do?" I ask him.

"We leave," Dom tells me.

"Leave? What do you mean? Where would we go?" I ask him. "We are just kids. How will we survive on our own? What about Mama and Grandfather?"

"I think I can follow the trade routes and get us to the coast. We can change our names. We will have to find work, Pearl. I can be a field hand anywhere and you can cook."

"But why Dom?" I ask. "What are we working for? What is our plan? Where do we end up?"

"We just have to survive for a while," he answers, "and keep Mama safe. In a few years, we can act normal again. I mean we won't be able to come back here, but we can find our lives and our futures somewhere else."

I feel hot blood rising into my face. "Somewhere else?" I ask. "How could we leave Mama? She will be devastated if we run away. Besides, the man in the purple robe will ask questions. Once he knows we have run away, he will start looking for us again."

Dom sighs, frustrated that I am not embracing his plan.

"I agree," he says. "But the less Mama and Grandfather know the safer it will be for them and for us. We have to either make them forget us or make them think we have died. They don't know about our powers, Pearl. It's like the pact we made before we were born. They can't know and we need to look out for them and for each other."

"But you FORCED me to not tell Mama anything!" I scream at Dom. I am scared and I want to go home, but I know I have to save Pearl and her brother to make that happen. "I am NOT PEARL!!!!!" I grab him by the shoulders and shake him while I yell. He has to know who I am! He has to remember!

Dom flings my arms from him and takes a step back. He stares at me with his nostrils flared for a moment before turning and running down the hill back to his home.

What have I done?

I run after him, shouting his name, but he is faster than I am and he makes it to the house before I do. Mama is in the kitchen, ready to feed us dinner. She sees me chasing after Dom and intervenes.

"Let him go, Pearl," she says as she holds me back. "Whatever you two have argued about, it will not get better if you push him to talk to you." I push against her hands, but she is bigger and stronger than I am in this eleven-year-old body. Finally, she wraps her arms around me and holds me as more angry tears burn through my eyes.

"Do you want to tell me what you two are fighting about?" she asks. But the remnants of Dom's power keep me silent. It is killing me inside, but I know I cannot tell her what is going on. I have to let go of any ideas I have of leaving Pearl's life. I have to let go of Evelyn if I am going to help Pearl and Dom. If I cannot get help from the adults in this place, then I'll do all I can to help Dom. I am convinced that it is the only way to keep us both safe and for me to find my way back to my real home.

"No," I answer as I heave great sobs into her chest. "No, no, no, no, no." I let myself cry, once again letting go of the old Evelyn, and becoming the new Pearl.

Chapter 11

My travel bag is packed and hidden beneath the bed in my room. Dom and I haven't spoken or spent much time talking in the past few weeks, but I left him a note under his door, apologizing and reassuring him that I am Pearl. He left me a note last night, detailing the plan.

Our cousin, Ananke, is traveling to her fiancé in the south. Dom and I will travel with her, putting as much distance between ourselves and the man in the purple robe as we can. The estate is in danger of total ruin and collapse. Any extra money we earn will be used by Grandfather. It is hard for Mama to let us go, but even she understands that the estate is failing and will not support our small family forever. Once we are away from the estate, Mama and Grandfather will be safer and Dom and I can find a safe place to live and work. Dom has traveled enough with the trade expeditions that he thinks he can get us all the way to the coast. He talks about Atlantis being the biggest, brightest city. If we can get there one day, we can be safe. The idea of being in Atlantis again is enough to make my head spin. I am convinced that the answers are there for Dom and me.

I am working in the kitchen again, mincing the meat for tonight's meal. Moussaka. The meat and tomato sauce are layered with eggplant. It's the latest dish I have learned to make and I want to leave this new family on the good memory of a full stomach. I gather the stone and wood cookware and head outside to wash it.

I have finished washing the rest of the blood from the meat off my hands when I feel a small rock hit the side of my head. I whip around to see where it came from and I scratch the temple where it hit when I feel another small rock striking my neck. I whip back around in time to see a small, black rock flying through the air toward my face. My hand flies up to catch it before it can hit its mark. I grasp it in my fingers and open them to look at the missive that was about to hit me. I stop and my breath catches. It isn't a rock. It is Dom's black pearl.

I look all around for Dom, wondering if he is ready to make up and that is why he is making his pearl whap my face. But my hand burns.

I look down and see the pearl rolling in circles, my hand heating beneath her movements. She is reaching out to me with her mind.

Pearl Evelyn, you must listen to me, she says.

I am not Evelyn anymore, I tell her, *just Pearl.*

I sense irritation from her over my interruption. She is fully aware of who I am and she doesn't want to talk about it.

Dom is in trouble! She shouts to my mind. I shake my head wildly.

What happened?! I shout back.

This morning as he was walking to school, he was grabbed by two large men, she tells me. *They gagged his mouth and put a bag over his head so he could not see and tied his arms to his sides. They tossed him into the back of a wagon and covered him with sacks of flour. We traveled for over an hour that way. Dom spoke to me the entire time. He told me all of your plans and how to help you escape.*

Escape?! Me?! Why do *I* need to escape? Dom is the one who is trapped!

I am not going anywhere without Dom! I yell at the pearl. A cold slap hits my mind and it freezes my thoughts. This is no ordinary pearl. She is powerful.

I am not here to argue with you, she says. *I am here to do as Dom has asked me to do and to help you. He has a plan in place and you are to follow it.*

I hold my forehead to bring it out of the freeze. If only Ananke could have taken us a day earlier. *What is the plan?* I ask of the pearl. *Will it allow us to save Dom?*

Of course it will, she responds. Her words bristle with offense. *I would not have left him if I was not fully certain that he would be saved.*

I calm myself. Dom will be okay. He has a plan. I have to listen to the pearl so I can help him and save him.

Where is he? I ask of the pearl.

He is in one of the lower rooms of the man in the purple robe, she replies. *Dom is safe there for now. The man in the purple robe has been asking him for parlor tricks, simple things that any child could do.* She says this with a pointed nod my direction. I know I don't understand how to use all of the powers this body possesses, but I resent being referred to as a simple child. But I have to put aside my resentment so I can help Dom.

What is Dom doing for him and what is the man in the purple robe saying to Dom? I ask, eager for all the information the pearl can give to me.

At this point, all Dom has done for the man is levitate small objects like vases and platters, she responds. *All of the objects in the house are prepared to help Dom in any way they can. They know too much of what their owner is capable of doing. They have all been encouraging Dom. I left Dom in good hands when I came to you.*

I shudder as I think of what the objects in that house have seen, but I am equally as grateful that they are willing to help Dom. I know how powerful that kind of communication and support is.

What am I to do? I ask. *What is the plan and my part in it?*

I feel satisfaction from the pearl as she senses my devotion to Dom. I am glad to be gaining her trust. I need to be able to work with her if Dom and I are ever going to be free.

You are to stick with the plan currently in place, she says to my mind. *Dom is going to use his mind manipulation to free himself from his captors tonight. You will need to bring his bag with you to the meeting place.*

I don't know how I will be able to keep myself occupied until then. It is close to dinner time and Dom should be heading home at any moment.

What happens when he doesn't come home tonight? I ask.

The pearl is silent for a moment before she responds. *You will use your mind manipulation skills, Pearl. You must make them feel that everything is alright.*

My stomach drops a few inches. Using mind manipulation to help our escape tonight was always part of the plan. We were going to reassure Mama that this is the best way to care for the family, letting Dom and me travel with another adult, finding a good and steady source of income, bringing her comfort. But that was going to rely heavily on Dom's skills. I am still new in trying to understand what I am supposed to do.

The pearl senses my hesitance. *You must control your fears, Pearl,* she warns. *Dom's entire plan rests on you doing your part.* She is angry with me, frustrated that I do not see the path clearly before me.

You must do your part, she admonishes again. The pearl is staring me down mentally from the palm of my hand. The force of her will is overpowering. She is firm in her belief in Dom and in his plan. She is not as firm in her belief in me, but she expects me to rise to the occasion.

Please tell Dom I will not let him down, I say to her with all the confidence of an eleven-year-old girl. I am being forced to lie to our family when Dom is in danger. My confidence is not strong. The pearl sighs from the depths of her soul. She still knows I am lacking, but I am all she's got.

I will tell him, she replies. She is willing to buoy him up with my words at least. Anything to give him the confidence to see this thing through. Even if I mess this up with the family tonight, Dom will be able to clean it up before we leave together.

The little pearl rolls from my hands and falls until she is only an inch or two from the ground. I can hear the air molecules talking to one another as they keep her aloft. They are eager to help Dom, but they are more eager to help *me*.

Just as the pearl is rolling away, a gut wrenching pain sears through my abdomen. I scream in pain, wrapping my arms around myself and falling to the ground. The little pearl is by my head in an instant.

What is it?! She questions. *What is going on?* Images flash through my mind of a stone room with no windows. I see armed men standing around me as I lay on the floor. A large foot swings toward me and strikes at my stomach. But it is not my stomach I am seeing. It is Dom's. And just before my mind goes dark, I see the edges of a purple robe.

Chapter 12

When I come to, the pearl is gone. A light breeze brushes against my cheek and I hear the air speaking to me.

Pearl. Pearl, it says. *You must get up. Pearl.*

I sit up and feel that only a few moments have passed since I saw the vision of Dom being beaten. I jump to my feet and run to find Mama. A strong wind hits me in the face.

You must not run to your Mama like this, it says. *The pearl was clear. In order to save Dom, you must take over your part of the plan.*

Every fiber in my body wants to run to Mama and Grandfather and beg them to help Dom - to save him. But the elements refuse to let me deviate from the plan. I have to do as they say. They will help me.

We have been in communion with our sisters where he is being kept, the air tells me. *He is already working on his plan to escape. He will be successful, Pearl. You must trust us. This is not the first time we have helped a human in need.*

I feel the collective age of the air around me. How old is it and how much has it seen and done? Will it be the same air that comes to me in over two thousand years?

I inhale deeply and let the breeze calm my racing heart. The air is with me, around me, in me. It is with Dom. I will wait as long as I can, trusting that this older, wiser element is able to see my twin.

I walk into the kitchen and see Mama setting the table with Ananke. As Dom's place is set, I send an image to Mama's mind: *Dom is working in a neighboring field tonight. He will meet up with Pearl and Ananke. You hugged him and bid him farewell this morning.* As soon as the thought finishes in my mind, Mama picks up Dom's plate, silently chiding herself for forgetting he would not be joining us this evening. She wipes a stress-filled tear from her cheek. Money is tight and her boy has to find work away from home. How can she stand the strain? My heart breaks for her.

I make my way to the moussaka I was working on earlier and mix in the tomato sauce. Mama and Ananke have been helping in the kitchen but I need to finish preparing the meal. In the stone pan, I layer the eggplant and beef, topping it off with white sauce and placing it on the fire. I watch it warm through in the embers while I inhale the scent of meat and smoke.

I sit without eating at the table. Everyone is quiet, but Mama can see that I am shaken.

"Pearl, darling," she says. "Please eat more of your meal." She places her hand on my arm and sighs. "We have all been working so hard lately. You need your strength, Love. Please eat a little more and I'll clean up the kitchen tonight." Grandfather, who is rarely with us for any meal, grunts to himself. I know he thinks I have been babied too much and maybe he is right. I'm ready to take my place and do my part.

I give Mama a small smile. "That's alright," I tell her. "I was just daydreaming. I will handle the kitchen." I eat more to build my energy for the travel ahead of me. I go over the list of food and clothing I have in my small traveling bag. I plan to pack a few more pasteli into the bag just in case Dom didn't pack enough food. The small honey and sesame seed bars will provide much needed energy in a pinch.

When the dishes are cleaned up and I am ready for bed, I hold Mama a little while longer. I send waves of the love her daughter has for her. She squeezes me tightly and kisses my head. I feel her love and try to hide it safely within me for my own memory later. It will be a long time before I am embraced by her again.

I wait in my room, eyes wide open in the darkness as the last of the household sounds settle down for the night. The plan is to leave before dawn with Ananke. We want to cover as much ground as we can for our journey. When I know the time is near, I reach for the bag under my bed. Everything I will be taking with me is inside. It will all help keep me alive until Dom and I can find work in a safe place. I shoulder Dom's bag as well and head out of the room, taking one last look at the space I have lived in for almost two years.

With Dom's and my bag in hand, I tiptoe to Ananke's room. She is dressed and ready to go as well.

"Are you ready, my Pearl?" she asks with a tired smile. My heart is racing. I cannot get out of here fast enough.

"I am," I reply. "Are you eager to go?" It has been a long engagement for Ananke. She has met her fiancé only once or twice and has corresponded with him solely by letter. I do not know if she even loves him.

"I am eager for my new life, Pearl," she answers, "but I am nervous as well. I am leaving so much behind. You are too." Ananke has no idea how much I am leaving or how much I am running to. She takes my hand in hers and together we leave the estate of our grandfather.

We make our way to the edge of Grandfather's land. The breeze assures me that Dom is on his way to our meeting place. I whisper a goodbye to my olive tree and to my little Acacia buried beneath it. I whisper goodbye to all the other versions of myself that I have had in this home. If we are going to be safe, if we are going to protect Mama and Grandfather, we are both going to have to forget. I let out the last sigh of my old life and take the first deep breath of the new as Ananke and I leave the estate, heading to the wild trees that line the road leading to town.

When we arrive at our designated spot, I pace from side to side. I try to not imagine what could be happening to Dom. Was he really able to escape his captors? How much was he hurt before he got away? How far away is he now? Does he need me to come to him?

"Patience, Pearl," Ananke says, "Dom will be here soon enough." But I can see Ananke tapping her own fingers against her leg.

After almost an hour of waiting, I feel the little pearl coming to me again. But this time she is not alone, she is in Dom's satchel. As soon as I see Dom, we run to each other and embrace. His clothing is torn and he is filthy. Bruises are beginning to show through the welts on his arms. I am sick inside to know that he has been hurt in this way. I cry as I hand him his bag. Ananke reaches us just a moment later.

"Dom!" she says. "What in the name of Zeus happened to you?!"

"Oh, it's nothing," Dom assures her. "I got in a fight with some kids in the fields. They were saying stuff about Grandpapa and I wouldn't let them. I won!" His eyes are bright and his voice is triumphant, but Ananke isn't buying it.

"Dom," she says, "we should take you to the house to get you cleaned up and get your wounds tended to. You are in no condition to travel." Dom reaches out and takes Ananke by the hand. He speaks to her with his mind and his mouth as he leads her back to the road to Argos.

"It will be fine, Ananke. You'll see," he says. "I'm not in bad shape. We can keep traveling now. You want to get going as much as we do."

I see the change come over Ananke's countenance. It's an eerie sight to see someone forget what they were doing, knowing that it's your fault their memory has changed.

"You're right," she tells Dom. She walks steadily forward, never letting go of his hand. "You look fine. We can get you cleaned up when we get to where we are going." She pauses. "Where are we going?" she asks as she looks at Dom.

"Don't you remember?" Dom asks. "We are heading to Thyrea so you can get married. You're going to live with your fiancé's family for a few months before the wedding." Ananke nods as she continues again on the road.

"That's right," she says. "I'm starting a new life."

"And you don't want to listen to me and Pearl while we walk," Dom says. "You have other things on your mind." Ananke is quiet. She nods and walks.

Dom and I watch Ananke for a few more minutes before he starts talking to me again. He continues to hold her hand, assuring that she won't come out of her trance.

"Dom, tell me what happened to you," I say after several minutes.

He is silent for a moment before he begins his story.

"Men grabbed me while I was walking toward the school," he says. "I tried to scream, but they were too quick with their hands and they gagged me before I could make any real sound." He rubs his jaw. "I couldn't reach any of their skin, they were covered well, so I had to wait for my time to come. They tossed me into a wagon, covered me with heavy material, and took me to an estate to the north.

"Once we got to the place, they carried me into the house and tied me to a chair. I sat in a great room for a long time before the man in the purple robe came to see me. I was still working on how to get out of there, so I decided to be safe and do whatever he asked."

"What did he ask you to do?" I question. The man already had contact with Dom. He knew he could manipulate minds. But the pearl said Dom was doing simple levitation tricks.

"He started by telling me that he heard an interesting story about a boy and a girl who could command nature," Dom tells me. "I knew he was talking about the rocks and the corn, but I knew I had to keep you out of it. I told him that I didn't know that kind of story, I only knew of a boy who could do those things."

"What did he say?" I ask.

"He laughed. He said, 'Boy, there is no need to fear for your sister. As long as you cooperate, she will be fine.'" Dom lowers his voice as he mimics the man in the purple robe. Some part of him thinks this is funny.

"I asked him what he wanted me to do," Dom continues. "I knew I had to keep you safe. He said he wanted me to do what I did in the field. He brought me to a small garden off of the house kitchen and put some corn on the ground. My hands were still tied and I asked to have them let go so I could work. He laughed again and said I could do it with my hands tied or they would get you to do it for them."

My heart beats faster. I love him for protecting me, but I wish I could have helped him sooner.

"So, I did what he asked," Dom continues. "I spoke to the earth and grew the corn. He pulled off the top ear of corn and inspected it. He mumbled something to his servant and that guy ran off. Then the robed man said, 'Into the house,' all low. He led the way and his guards grabbed my arms and yanked me along."

I wince. I know the guards did more, so I wait for Dom to reach that part of the story.

"He didn't lead us back into the grand room we were in before," Dom says. "He took me to another room with no windows. Before they shut the door, I told the pearl to find you. I had a plan." Dom puffs out his chest and smiles. He gives me a wink and I roll my eyes. Even when kidnapped, he boasts.

"Once the pearl was gone and I was sure you would know what to do, I focused on touching skin. All I needed was to touch anyone's skin and I could manipulate my way out of there. But the purple robed man knew that. He was wearing gloves and was covered everywhere but his face. He took one of his gloves off and walked toward me. He was smiling while he walked but once he reached me he snarled and yelled, 'demon child!' and hit my face with the glove." I wince again.

"He put the glove back on and smiled," Dom continues. "'Now,' he said, 'you will help me with what I am asking you or you will receive more of that.' I knew what I had to do, Pearl. I had to let myself be hit and kicked so I could have skin on skin contact.

"I told the robed man I wouldn't do anything else for him. He let out just one laugh. One 'ha' then looked at his guards. 'Make sure he submits by sundown,' he said. 'I want him in good working order when my guests arrive tomorrow.'"

"What guests did he mean?" I ask Dom.

"Judges and political leaders," he says. "He wants my mind manipulation to help him gain power."

"What does he want them to do?" I ask.

"I don't know for sure," Dom says. "But when he left the room, he turned to me and said, 'If you aren't ready to help me by tomorrow, young Domideus, I will have to visit your Grandfather and bring your sister home with me.'" Dom looks at me and says, "No way *that's* gonna happen." I shake my head. He thinks he is my protector.

"I can take care of myself, Dom," I tell him. Then I look at his face, swollen and bloody in the moonlight. "But I love you. Thank you."

Dom gives me a swollen smile and puffs his chest out again. "*You* are welcome. Now, back to my story. Just as the robed man was leaving the room, the first guard punched me in the gut."

"I felt that!" I interrupt.

"I told you that you are better at this stuff than I am," he says. "I can't read anyone's mind across that kind of distance, not even yours."

I blush with pride. I accomplished something big with my powers today, even if I didn't intend to.

"Anyway," Dom says, "the guards had their gloves on at first, but once the robed man was gone, their gloves came off. They grabbed me by my hair and sat me on a stool in a corner of the room. They started slapping me. Once I had the rhythm of their hits down, I turned the tables on them."

Dom laughs to himself and continues. "I made them think I wasn't on the stool anymore. I made them see my face on each other and their faces on me. Pretty soon, they untied me and started slapping each other around. Once they were fully fighting on the ground, I got out of there."

"You got out without anyone noticing you?" I ask.

"Well, I found things to hide behind. The doors all opened for me when I asked. There were some dogs, but all they did was sniff me and lick my hands. I got a few cuts on my legs from climbing over the outer walls and through weeds and stuff, but once I was outside, the pearl helped me figure out which way to go to find you."

Dom pulls the little black pearl from his satchel and hands her to me. She is glistening and quiet in the moonlight, happy to be praised by Dom. She is warm in my hand and I wonder why we create this heat whenever we touch. I am about to ask Dom about it when he stops and jerks his head to the side, grabbing my arm. Ananke stops with us, her eyes staring forward into the darkness of the early morning hours.

Soon I hear something, too. Far away, but getting closer, we hear the barking of dogs.

"Run!" is all there is time to say and we take off down the road, Ananke trailing behind Dom as he yanks her along. We are still several miles from the closest homes. No one can help us. Dom lets go of Ananke and pushes me off the road. I fall into scratchy bushes, getting cut by the branches as I land on the ground.

"This is it, Pearl," Dom says through ragged breaths. "We have to split up. They still don't know we are together, but it won't take long for them to figure it out. I can draw them away, but you and Ananke have to get moving on your own."

I freeze where I am. I don't want to separate from Dom. I've seen too much of his future to be able to leave him alone. If I let him go now, everything I have seen will happen. Dom will be captured and he will be killed.

I open my mouth to protest and try to get up, but Dom pushes me further into the bushes, his hands on my neck and shoulders. "No, Pearl. You are strong enough to do this. You and Ananke need to get to safety. She will know where to go."

"Dom, I won't let you leave me," I say through gritted teeth as I push at his arms. But it is no use. Dom is stronger than I am. "We *have to* stay together. It's the only way we can bring Pearl back!"

Dom looks at me with angry eyes and shoves me again. "This is the only way to bring her back to me," he says and he grabs the hamsa medallion from around my neck. Before I can understand what he is doing, the necklace is off of me and in Dom's hands.

Dom is immune to the powers I have to control and manipulate minds and kill, but anyone else would be in danger if they came near me without that medallion on. Any shepherd in a field or weary traveler to cross my path while I am angry will die the same painful death that Theodis did. I might even kill Ananke if she tries to hold me back.

Dom runs like mad toward the dogs and away with my medallion. I watch helplessly as he tosses it into the field. I have to find it and find it fast. It takes at least ten minutes to get out of the tangle of branches and thorns Dom shoved me into. Once I am free, I can no longer see him in the distance. Ananke is sitting on the ground, a blank stare still covering her face.

I head the same direction Dom was running and look for the medallion in the tall grass by the side of the road. I am on my hands and knees, running my fingers through the grass. The sound of dogs echoes in the distance, but I hear something else. Something is hissing in the grass beside me.

I freeze where I am and look around slowly. Not three feet away from me, coiled and head raised defensively, is a shiny silver snake. A small, scaled horn lifts up at the tip of its nose and laying on its coiled body is my hamsa medallion.

I don't take time to think. I need that medallion and I need to get to Dom. I reach forward as quickly as I can, yanking the necklace from the body of the horned viper and roll away as quickly as I can. But the necklace was caught in the coils of the snake. When I yanked it to me, the snake yanked with it and now I am laying on my back with a snake on my arm.

Before I can stand or run, the hissing snake strikes at my arm, making contact with my bicep. The pain is searing and dizziness fills my head. I drop my medallion and the result is immediate. My arm burns with unbearable heat and I scream at the snake. It makes a sizzling, screeching, hissing sound and is blown off my arm with the force of my power and lands, lifeless, several feet away.

I stagger to my feet, grabbing the hamsa medallion and putting it safely around my neck. The burning I created with the snake was enough to minimize the most dangerous effects of the venom, but I am still dizzy and my limp arm tingles by my side.

I stumble back toward the road, determined to find and help Dom when I hear a familiar voice in my mind.

Pearl! Pearl! Come to me! I am here!

The pearl is calling to me. I had her in my hand when the dogs began to bark. Dom had just given her to me. I forgot her when I started chasing after Dom. I cannot leave her here and I know it.

I make my way as quickly as I can to where I dropped her in the bushes. She is buried tightly under the thick bramble and I scrape my arm trying to get her free from her prison. When there is enough room for her to move, I urge her out from the bush and into my hand. She is sleek and shiny as ever - totally unaffected by the thorns that have cut my flesh.

We have to get to Dom, I say to her, but as soon as I try to stand again, all the blood rushes from my head and I fall to the ground in a quiet, black sleep.

Chapter 13

When I wake up from my venom-induced sleep, the sun is burning bright in the sky overhead. I am shaded by the bushes I fell into. My arm is throbbing and so is my head. I open my eyes slowly and blink the light into my eyes. As I do, I see a small black dot in front of my face. I reach out for it. It is the little pearl. As soon as my fingers brush her surface, I am flooded with sadness. She doesn't say a word, she just conveys images to my mind.

I see Dom, running from guards again, leading them away from the place where he left me. The dogs who sniffed his clothes and licked his hand earlier in the day are chasing him and barking like mad. He cannot outrun them. It doesn't take long for the dogs to be on top of him, pinning him down and biting at their master's command. The guards beat Dom at first then remain at a distance from his body, letting the dogs maul him. After a while, the guards tell their dogs to halt. Dom has lost too much blood and he lies moaning on the ground.

"You shouldn't have played your little mind tricks on us," one of the guards says. He has a swollen eye, doubtless inflicted by the man in the purple robe when he discovered his prisoner had escaped. "Now we know not to touch you," the guard continues. "We have to let the dogs take care of you for us."

I know Dom could have manipulated the dogs. He was trying to keep them away from me. So he let them maul him as he lay submissive on the ground.

"But guess what, little master," the guard says to Dom, "*our* master wasn't kidding when he said he would have your sister help. In fact, he's on his way to your house right now to find her and bring her home with him. If she's a good girl, she won't need the dogs to protect her."

I hear a gurgling sound coming from Dom. He is laughing while his lungs fill with deadly fluid. He knows that I am not home. He knows I manipulated Mama's mind into believing I traveled north with Ananke, not south. The man in the purple robe will be led on a goose chase looking for me. By the time he discovers the trap, I will be long gone and Dom will be too.

The image of my twin fades as the little pearl's vision is blurred by salty tears. Dom's pain is over now. His secret is safe. I couldn't save him, but he saved me.

Chapter 14

For days, Ananke and I travel by night with the little pearl in my satchel. Ananke is still in a daze. Dom held her hand for too long without paying attention. His power is lasting with her longer than intended. The pearl and I say nothing. Our hearts are heavy and I stumble about as we make our way into the heart of Argos. We move past bustling vendors and dirty alleyways. I run into people because I am not watching where I am going. My feet move ahead in blind obedience to the instructions Dom gave me. We only stop to sleep when the air is absent of all human sound. We only stop to eat when we don't have the energy to go further. Why do we keep moving? Why are we running? Where are we going?

"Thyrea," Ananke says when I have these thoughts. Dom said she would know the way. Maybe that is all that is left in her mind.

We continue forward, following Dom's plan. He wanted us to run. He wanted us to be safe. I run for him. I run for me. Dom said we could find safety, that we could lead a normal life again. I don't believe that anymore. But I cannot bring myself to ignore what he told me. So, I keep walking, Ananke just a few steps ahead.

We travel by some of the most extravagant city homes, multiple stories high with tile roofs, ornate garden courtyards, and fine cloth covering the windows. But we also travel through some of the most desperate and destitute neighborhoods where the only shelter is from dead branches woven together like a tent. In the brief moments when my mind is clear, I think of how unfeeling humanity can be. That opulence and poverty can live so close together. Both sides hating the other, perpetuating the disease of class. In a body filled with power, I am still powerless to change human nature. In these moments, I am glad my Dom is not here to see what I see. Then I cry and I miss him again. He would help me understand that I am not powerless to change things.

The little pearl and I communicate only minimally with our minds as we travel through cities, towns, and countryside. We are both in pain, trying to survive Dom's death. Ananke says little or nothing. She just keeps walking, leading us where we are supposed to go. Weeks go by before I use my voice. When I finally do, it is hoarse and raspy from disuse. My mouth and throat are dry and sticky. I am out of food now. Dom's bag went with him and was probably used as a trophy for the guards who captured him. And though I've been careful with my supplies, I knew they couldn't last forever. Ananke's bag is empty.

Trapped

We have finally reached Thyrea. Ananke and I stop by a fountain, washing our bodies in the flowing water and changing into the clean robes we have kept in our bags. We must be close to her fiancé's family home. She will be safe there. I hope she will be anyway. I have decided that I won't be staying with her. I have to break all family ties. I have to find a way back home. Nothing else matters to me anymore.

"Ananke! Ananke!" I hear an older woman's voice calling from a market. Ananke and I both slow our steps, turning our heads toward the sound of the voice. Out from the bustling wood and fabric market stalls, a large woman, plump and happy with graying hair and dancing eyes bounds toward us. When she reaches Ananke, she takes her in her arms and holds her close. Ananke blinks several times and shakes her head. I see recognition filling her face as she is squeezed by the woman.

"Lia," Ananke says. Her voice is a ragged whisper. It is the first I have heard her speak in many days. "My Lia," she says again, hugging the woman back.

"I must take you to Themis," Lia says. "He will be overjoyed to see you." Lia lets go of Ananke and turns to me. "And is this your young cousin?" she asks Ananke. "I thought you were bringing both of them." Ananke's face is a blank expression again when she looks at me. She has forgotten who I am.

"No," I answer Lia, "I am not Ananke's cousin but a servant from her home. I was sent to assist her on her journey. Now that she is safely in your custody, I will be looking for employment in town."

"Two women were sent alone on such a long journey?" Lia asks.

"No, our custodian is looking for an inn where he can rest before returning to Argos," I say. The lie is weak, but it's enough to convince Lia. She returns her attention to Ananke.

"Well, I am so glad you were cared for," she says. "Now, let me get you to the house so you can rest and eat." My stomach growls as Lia takes Ananke by the hand toward the bustling market. Ananke turns back to look at me and smiles. She is grateful. She is pretending to know who I am. I wish her well and hope she will be happy in her new home and life.

As for me, I need food and I need work. My body is numb to any feeling except the pain in my heart. I have to keep going for Dom. I do what I can to make myself presentable and travel through the city to find employment. It is growing dark when I finally find an inn across the city from where I left Ananke.

"Ah, and how can I help you today, my dear?" the rotund wife of the innkeeper asks. She has mistaken me for a guest. But better a guest than a vagrant.

"Please, ma'am," I respond to her, "I am looking for employment. I am a very good cook, and I am eager to find a job where I can earn my keep."

The eyes of the woman lose their merriment in an instant. She pinches them together like it will help her see me more clearly.

"And why would a young lady dressed in such fine robes be needing a job, may I ask?" She looks at me with eyes full of suspicion. "Or are those even your clothes?" She grabs my robes and pulls me close to her face. "I'm willing to bet that you stole those clothes from the line of a proper lady." The woman's breath is foul at this distance and she is strong. "I've a mind to call the authorities on you." That is something I cannot let her do.

With all the skill I can muster in my weakened state, I pour my thoughts into her mind. "No, ma'am," I say to her. "You are mistaken. These clothes are mine and I am only in search of a job. I am reliable and teachable. I will be a good investment for you."

My words and emotion-bending work on the woman's mind and she lets go of my robes. "An investment, did you say?" she asks me with a raised eyebrow. "I've had a mind to make a good investment myself. You look too skinny to be a decent cook, though," I send the promise of improvement into her mind. She harrumphs. "If you get to being too much of a burden, I daresay I could bargain you off."

Her mind is rough and I am weak. If the promise of bargaining me away or selling me is enough to get into the household, I'll take it. At least it will be a safe place to eat and sleep.

"Alright, I'll take you on," she finally says.

I breathe a sigh of relief.

Alright, little pearl, I whisper to my companion, *let's make Dom proud.*

"I haven't any need of a cook at present, though," the woman continues. "My sister-in-law does all our cooking, but I'm willing to bet she could use another kitchen maid."

"That would do very nicely," I reply, "thank you."

"Humph," the woman says. She slows her pace and looks confused as to why we are having this conversation. I don't want her to come to her senses, so I impose on her moment of reflection.

"If you will show me where to go, I can start working now," I say, pouring the words into her mind and ears.

"Yes, well, this way then," she replies and leads me through the crowded rooms to the back of the inn. We enter a room much larger than the household kitchen I'm used to working in. It is bustling with people moving about, chopping, battering, frying, and baking. Herbs hang from the ceiling. A vertical rotisserie spins in the corner with a large leg of lamb attached. Servants run over to it occasionally to slice meat for the gyros or shawarma they are making for the inn guests. The smells and sounds fill my nose and ears with hunger. It's the first time I've noticed that pain in weeks. I try to focus on what the large woman is saying to me.

"And this is Aphrodite, my sister-in-law," she says, leading me to the woman in the middle of the bustling room. "Aphrodite, I have a new kitchen maid for you. This is...well, what *is* your name child?"

"Athena," I answer. The little pearl and I knew I would need to change my name to create another layer of secrecy from the man in the purple robes. He has never seen me up close, so having a different name may be enough to save me if we should cross paths again. I have always loved the name Athena.

"The goddess of wisdom and war, eh?" the large woman asks. "Well, let's just hope you live up to your name in the wisdom part. We can do without the war."

"Des," Aphrodite interjects, "if there is one thing I don't need it's another kitchen hand."

Another servant enters the room and runs to the large woman. "Pardon me Mistress Desdemona, but master Nadir requires your help with a guest."

Desdemona lets out a short sigh, rolls her eyes, and turns to her sister-in-law. "The child is an investment. If that brother of yours keeps running up debts, she will pay for the trouble of keeping her fed. Now, show her the way around the kitchen while I go clean up another mess for your brother." She huffs and stomps after the servant and leaves the kitchen the way we entered it. I turn to Aphrodite for further instruction.

Aphrodite. The goddess of beauty. It is an unfortunate name for someone so unbeautiful. Her dark skin is covered in warts and her kinky hair is riddled with grey. I wonder if perhaps she was a beautiful baby or child and simply lost the worldly beauty as she grew older. I am holding out hopes that perhaps her personality is as beautiful as her name.

"Well, it looks like I'm stuck with you for now," Aphrodite says. "Just mind that you keep your pretty little self workin around here and nothin else. I don't need no runaway pregnant servant girls coming to ask me for help." I am surprised at first by the implication. I am not quite twelve-years-old and I look it. But life here is so short. I suppose I'm really not very young when girls marry at fifteen or younger. I may end up dying by 13 from some disease. It's a miracle I have lived this long.

I nod my promise to not flirt with the servant boys or inn guests and follow Aphrodite out of the inn and across the back courtyard to the servant housing.

"I ain't got a lot a place for you to sleep in," she says as she leads me to a small shed. "All the higher servants is already bunked up doubles and triples. You'll ha' ta stay here 'til someone else leaves or dies."

I swallow hard, "This will do just fine," I say as I enter the small room. "Thank you."

Aphrodite looks me up and down, taking in my good robes and clean face. "Hmmm," she says. "I don't know what brought such a nice young girl ta be a servant, but I don't want ta know. It's easier for us both that aways if we can keep a few secrets t'ourselves." I give her a small smile of appreciation. "But you don't want ta go awearin them nice things in my kitchen." She disappears for half a moment then returns with her hands full of servants' robes. They are darker and coarser than what I have been wearing, but they are clean. "Here," she says as she tosses them to me. "Go ahead and put these on. You can leave them good clothes in here. You can use the washtub every week for your body and your clothes. If you want more cleanin than that, you'll ha' ta take yourself down ta the creek on your off time. Mind you, now, you don't get much off time. But there it is.

"And don't go sneaking around at night. These parts aren't safe for a young girl. One or two goes a missin' every year. Now get yourself changed and we'll see if you live up ta my standards. I'll see you in the kitchen."

I thank Aphrodite again when she leaves and I close the door to my shed. There is a single, high window in the wooden structure. A small cot with a tiny table beside it fill up most of the space. It can't be more than six feet square, but I am small and my needs are few. I set my bag on the table and lay my clothing on the bed. I decide to leave the little pearl in my satchel on the table. The servant clothes have their own satchel and I don't want to risk mixing them up and losing the pearl.

"Well, Dom," I say to the empty space beside me, "I've got work. I won't let you down. If only you stayed." A tiny tear drops to my robes. I wipe it from my face and turn for the door.

Good luck to you, Pearl Athena, she says to me as I head out the door. I give her a small smile. I'm going to need all the luck I can get.

I step into the courtyard. I am bathed in sunlight and a gentle breeze. I feel the wind taking my sorrow for just a moment, granting me peace in its place. I am overwhelmed with a sense of being reborn. And I am being reborn in a way. Letting go of Pearl so I can live as Athena. The sun is burning high in the Karneios sky. This is the month Dom and I celebrate our twelfth birthday. I shield my eyes and welcome the day.

Today, Athena is born.

Chapter 15

Happy birthday to Athena.

Today marks a full year of living and working for this inn. I lay on the cot in my shed and listen to the sounds of early morning outside my door. I am ready to rise and go about my duties, but I want to take a moment to breathe in the past year.

I spent the first several months crying myself to sleep on my cot. The little pearl always lay quietly on the table. After a few months, we started sharing our favorite memories of Dom. I share our childish conversations under our olive tree. The little pearl shares the memories of watching him treat someone kindly. Those times when he thought no one else was around. The memories are good. They help us both remember Dom as the little boy who gave everything. We remember him that way because he was that way. And now we live for his memory.

I barely made it through those first months as a servant here. Whenever I was rested and fed, I had time to think of Dom. The sadness was almost enough to overwhelm me. But a remark from Desdemona about selling me or a threat from Aphrodite to send me out at night to be kidnapped were enough to bring me out of the gloom. At least enough to earn my keep.

Eventually, I began practicing my mind manipulation again. On more than one occasion, I convinced Aphrodite that the servants should have dessert or a night off. The other servants would hear me speaking to her and they loved me for it. They started calling me Athena, the girl with the golden tongue.

I use my communication skills constantly in the kitchen. I make everything sweeter, softer, crunchier, and more savory than the other kitchen maids. I get my work done faster, too, and that has raised me in Aphrodite's esteem. She has started teaching me other Greek dishes and I love it. Last night we made spanakopita and souvlaki for dinner for important inn guests. They raved about the meal and Aphrodite gave me the credit. Desdemona smiled and whispered, "Investment," as Aphrodite and I went back to the kitchen. But the real treat of the evening was the dessert. Revani. My mouth waters at the memory. The dense cake with its nutty, grainy texture and lemony flavor was the most heavenly thing I have had in all my life. Aphrodite saved a special piece just for me. A little celebration for the thirteenth birthday of Athena.

Trapped

There have been no inquiries at the inn for a girl named Pearl. No stories of cursed children bringing death to their families or servants. No politicians looking for a magician to help them destroy their enemies. But as promised, rumors of kidnapped or murdered people reach our ears frequently. Servants and the poor are at the greatest risk. We are near Sparta and have to be watchful over each other.

One girl was dismissed from the inn for being unmarried and with child. I was surprised. The girl was one whom Aphrodite had taught for many years. I thought Aphrodite's feelings for her would have provided leniency or assistance of some kind. But the girl was sent out of the inn without her remaining pay and promised that if she tried to use Aphrodite as a reference, she would regret it.

When I expressed my surprise and concern to a fellow servant, she told me that Aphrodite has a bitter past that leaves her so unkind to girls in need. Aphrodite's sister was blessed with the beauty that Aphrodite lacks. Aphrodite was older, and was therefore the first in line to marry. But her younger, more attractive sister, became pregnant by Aphrodite's fiancé. A marriage was quickly arranged, leaving Aphrodite miserable and alone. When giving birth, her sister lost too much blood and died. The infant died shortly thereafter. But the husband did not return to marry Aphrodite in her sister's place. Instead, he moved to town with his inheritance and his wife's possessions and never looked back. Aphrodite has despised unmarried, pregnant girls ever since.

So, I keep my head down, working hard to keep my place. The longer I can remain invisible here at this inn, the safer I will be. I may be able to live a normal life someday. I stretch and wish my little pearl a lovely day and head into the fresh morning air.

I go about my duties as usual. It is a special day for me. I am grateful for the safety and the growth I've had. I sing as I work, humming here and there where I don't remember the lyrics to the Greek songs.

"That is lovely singing," I hear as I enter the dining room with arms full of clean plates. I didn't expect anyone to be in the room yet. The hour is still early and inn guests sleep later than the servants. This room is usually empty at this time of the morning. The voice speaking to me is low with a booming quality to it. I turn quickly and see one of the important guests from last night's meal sitting at an empty table, an empty glass and amphora for alcohol in front of him.

"Pardon me sir," I say, bowing my way out of the room. "I didn't mean to interrupt you."

"Nonsense, girl. I said the singing was lovely," he is looking at me with half-opened eyes, a line of drool shining on his cheek.

I bow again and set the plates on the closest table to me. I head back toward the kitchen, eager to not be alone with this man.

"I say, girl," he calls out to me, "have you any more of this fine wine in your kitchen?"

I nod and answer, "We do in the cellar sir, I will have one of the servant boys fetch it for you."

"Nonsense, girl," he dribbles out again. "No need to upset the house on my account. When you go back to the cellars, take a look around for me and save me a container of my own. I'll gladly pay you for it."

"I thank you, sir." I say and bow again. "I will look for the wine, but there is no need to pay me for it. The master and mistress of the house are the only ones who need to be compensated." He is making me uncomfortable. I don't want any of his money. I want him to stop talking to me.

The man raises his head and lifts his eyebrows. "Morals, eh? It's not very often that you find a servant with morals, now is it?"

I know the question is rhetorical, but I cannot help but answer. "On the contrary, sir. I believe you will find that all of our servants here are honest and upright. The master and mistress treat us well. We have no need to steal from them."

"Humph," he lets out as he drains the dregs of his already empty glass. "Perhaps I should add to my own household from some of the servants here. Tell me, girl. Would you like to come work in my home?" He raises a corner of his mouth in a crooked, drunken smile.

I keep my face smooth and expressionless as I answer, "Thank you, sir, but I am quite happy here." I bow again and quickly leave the room. My stomach is a knot of anxiety. I am determined to stay away from this man and his household. Something about him makes me feel unsafe.

As I go about my day, I receive many congratulations from my fellow servants for my time spent with them here. As Aphrodite promised, several have died or moved on to other places of employment. But rather than move into their quarters, I decide to stay in my tiny shed. I like the privacy it gives me. I can practice my powers while I am there.

Aphrodite has taken me under her wing after all. I haven't tried to manipulate her mind to make her have friendly feelings toward me. I want to be valued for who I really am and not what I make others think I am. So, her kindness toward me is born out of real feeling. I work with her this morning to plan and prepare for the evening meal. There is a large group of visiting dignitaries here at the inn. Tonight is their sendoff dinner.

"You're a quiet one today, aren't you Athena?" Aphrodite likes to talk while we work. "What's on your mind, young thing?"

"Oh, nothing in particular," I reply. "I've just been thinking about my time here and how I have enjoyed it."

Aphrodite gets a twinkle in her eye along with a raised eyebrow. "You sure it's not feelings of love that has you a thinking so?"

I furrow my brows as I answer. "Love? No. What would make you think that?"

"Oh, I heard some of the other servants talking last night. Many of our young men find you a beautiful thing. An' I heard the gentlemen talking ta you in the dining room this marnin'. He noticed yer beauty too or he wouldn't ha' said anythin' ta you."

I blush at her words, embarrassed to be the object of anyone's attention.

Aphrodite sees my blushing and mistakes it for the feelings of a flirtatious girl, pleased to be the center of attention. "Just a member what I told you," she says. "Any harlotry and you're out. We have a fine and decen' establishment here and my brother an' his wife don't want none of them intrigues amongst their servants. You understand me, Athena?"

I nod and return to my work, determined to let the subject go. It doesn't take long for Aphrodite to find something else to talk about, mainly the guests at the inn. The dignitaries have been staying here for several weeks. Our inn is a resting place for them on a longer journey they are making. They have been visiting other towns and cities in Greece, meeting the people they lead and enforcing laws.

However, several of them are using this as an opportunity to take bribes from the people and have secret dalliances with each other or with servants they meet along the way. The memory of the drunken man in the dining room is enough to keep me away. I want no part of their escapades. I want to keep a low profile. I have to keep safe.

The dinner Aphrodite and I make this evening is one of the best I've been a part of. The meal begins with the horiatiki salad and is followed by tiropita. I mix together the butter and cheese and olive oil and roll them into their triangle pastry shells. We also make tzatziki and serve the thick garlic and dill yogurt with fresh pita bread. Aphrodite shaves lamb from the tall rotisserie to serve with the meal and enough retsina wine to go around. Once dessert makes it to the table, the guests are quiet with full stomachs. The baklava and ellinikos coffee are taken only in small amounts as the guests fight fatigue.

The man from the dining room this morning is here again tonight. I hope he has forgotten all about me since this morning. The amount of wine he must have in him should help him forget. There are so many people in this city and at this inn. But just to be safe, I have one of our younger servant boys bring the man the same wine he was drinking through last night. I think I have played it safe enough, but as I help clear the dessert from the tables, I am forced to walk past the man who is again (or still) drunk.

He reaches out and grabs my elbow and turns me to face him.

"Oh, girl," he stammers. "How would you like to come work for me?" I pull away as much as I can without getting into trouble with the innkeeper.

"I thank you, sir, but I am very happy with my situation here at the inn." I nod again, and try to leave, but he still has ahold of my arm.

"Nadir," he addresses the innkeeper who is overseeing the evening, "how much can I give you for this young girl here? I believe she would be an asset to my home."

Before I even need to try out my mind manipulation on the man, Desdemona steps in. "I'm afraid she isn't for sale, Spiro. She is an investment, you know, and I am not ready to part with her."

"An investment, you say?" the drunken man eyes me for a moment before letting go of my arm. "Perhaps she will be available in a year or two then. I will come and ask after her another time."

I make my way to the kitchen as quickly as I can, listening to the group conversation turn to the subject of investments. I am sick inside from the danger I have just left. How much longer can I remain safe here at the inn? Anywhere?

I sigh as I head to the work piled up in the kitchen. From the corner of my eye, I see Aphrodite watching me quietly.

Chapter 16

Happy birthday to Athena.

I'm fourteen now. This past year has been more turbulent than the first year I lived and worked here. I've grown taller and have started to fill out the curves and shape of a woman. I'm not very happy about it. Besides the frustrations that meet me every month, I have started noticing the attention Aphrodite has been warning me about for the last two years.

Two of the boys who work in the stables have been taking the time to talk to me every night when I finish my work and return to my shed. And at least one of the house boys has been sending me messages. I keep finding little gifts laid at my doorstep. Candies and ribbon, even a small bracelet. I never keep the gifts or use them. I don't want to encourage anyone, but my neglect doesn't faze my admirers. The gifts keep coming. The conversation keeps coming. The attention keeps coming. And Aphrodite notices all of it.

"Ah, you can ignore her," one of the stage hands tells me after dinner. "Aphrodite doesn't let us mess around because she had some bad history with a guy. But we can keep to ourselves and she'll never know."

"I highly doubt that," I respond as I move away from his touch. "Aphrodite always knows what happens here." The boy tries to take my hand, but I pull away. "Look," I tell him, "You are very nice and I appreciate your compliments and offers, but I'm really not interested in a romantic relationship. I like my job here and I don't want to lose it."

The boy lets his arm fall to his side and he looks at me for a moment, thinking about what I could mean.

"You know, Athena, you won't be able to be free forever," he says. I get a chill down my spine as I feel the double meaning in his words. Why does he even think I'm free now? "You are too beautiful to not be taken by someone." My temper rises. I don't want to be in a relationship. My looks have nothing to do with it. I'm just not interested.

"Well," I say, "I would like to be free as long as I can." I walk faster to get distance between me and this boy and I head to my shed. If Dom were still here, he could protect me and I would let him. The boys are less eager to mess with girls whose brothers are here as well.

Where have you been? The little pearl asks when I sit on my cot.

I had to help clean later tonight and one of the stable boys tried holding my hand again. I pull out my bundle of wages. It isn't much, but it is something. I don't know where it can take me, but I want it to take me somewhere.

Which one? She asks about the stable boy. *The one with the longer hair or the shorter hair.*

The one with the longer hair, I reply. *He is a little more bold than the others. He said I couldn't be free forever. I know he's talking about marriage, but I'm hearing more than that.*

I know this must be hard for you, Pearl Athena, the little pearl says, *but you are destined to find the freedom you seek. Don't let a young man from a different land convince you otherwise.*

I smile at the pearl. I pick her up and feel the heat created in my fingers.

Little pearl, I say, *Why are you always so hot when I touch you?*

She is quiet for a moment before she answers.

Pearl Athena, do you remember your past? A breath catches in my throat. My past. It was so long ago.

Sometimes I remember, I tell her. *But other times, I forget who I am, what I am doing, where I am going.*

The little pearl listens and pauses before speaking again.

Pearl Athena, she says, *you and I are connected in more ways than you realize. You sometimes forget who you are, but I never forget. We are a part of one another.*

How? I ask.

I'm not sure of the family line, Pearl Athena, but you and I share so much. The blood in my body is from the same family line as the blood in your future body.

We are related? I ask. I have lived so long with the little pearl, I forgot I'm actually living in her body. I have a body of my own. One from a future time and place that I am forgetting with each passing day.

Yes, the pearl continues, *we share a bloodline. That is why we burn. My power recognizes you and your power recognizes me.*

Family. The little pearl is family. That means Dom is really my family, too. We are related. I start to cry.

Why do you cry, Pearl Athena? the little pearl asks.

You are my family, I say. *Dom is really my family too.*

Yes, she says. *Your love for him is the family love it should be. This is why you can save me, Pearl Athena. You and I are connected. You are saving your ancestors.*

I smile at my companion.

Pearl Athena, she says, *What do you know about my pearl form?* I think for a moment.

You came from an oyster Father brought back from the coast, I say. *You were the only pearl in the bag of oysters and when I found you, I gave you to Dom.*

Yes, she says, *that is how I came to be with Dom and you, but that isn't where this form was created.*

I pause for a moment to consider the options. I am too afraid to mention the one that stands out most. But I know it can't wait forever.

Where was this form created, little pearl? I ask, reluctant to break the band of security that exists between us. The little pearl is silent for a moment, also wanting to maintain our union. Unwilling to let go of the bond we have formed since Dom died. But even she cannot hold it inside.

It is from Jaffa, she whispers.

Jaffa.

Jaffa, the city and port where no one wears green. The sea where Mama's womb was cursed, where Dom and I were given powers that would make us hunted. The sea home where Queen Nyobi Kadul resides.

This is where the little pearl was created.

Why didn't you tell this to me before? I ask. I'm nervous. I'm afraid that the little pearl and I are being used by our enemy. But if that were true, why haven't we been found? Why are we still alive?

I didn't tell you because I wanted to remain with you, the little pearl says. *I know I am from a dangerous and magic place, but Dom was always so tender to me. I was devoted to him. Since his death, I have become devoted to you. I don't have any allegiance to the Queen. My allegiance is with you.*

I feel sadness and fear sweeping from the little pearl. She is afraid I will abandon her, afraid I will run away from her. But how could I do that to her? Dom loved her and she has been good to me since his death. And we are family.

Thank you for telling me now, little pearl, I say to her as I lay her on the table.

I sense her feelings of rejection as I set her down. I want to put her at ease.

I am not putting you away from me, little pearl, I say. *I am just setting you down so I can ready myself for bed.*

Her relief is tangible and fragile. She doesn't know if I am sincere in my statement. I am. I will not send her away. I know she is true to me and to Dom's memory. But if she were to feel rejected, would she become prey to Queen Nyobi Kadul? Would she be able to withstand the power of the evil sea witch?

Yes, she says, *I believe you.* But her words are hesitant and full of uncertainty. It will take time for us to take apart this barrier to our trust.

There is a knock at my door. It is Aphrodite.

"You'll have to put your work clothes back on," she says through the door. "A late party of guests has arrived and you'll be needed in the kitchen." She shuffles away from the door and back to the kitchen. I am called from bed more often than the other servants because I am trusted. Aphrodite knows she can trust me to take care of the new arrivals and their food needs. It is a place of honor even if it means I miss some sleep now and then.

It will be okay, I say to the little pearl. *We can work this out together. Let's just rest tonight. You'll see. Everything will be alright.*

Alright, Pearl Athena, she says to me. *I trust you.*

And I close the door behind me, leaving my little pearl alone and cold in the dark.

Chapter 17

Happy birthday to Athena. 15 years old. The excitement of finally feeling safe has worn off and I am dreaming more and more strange things. Sometimes I recognize the people in my dreams. Sometimes I do not. But there is always a longing to be with all of those people. I cry when I dream of my Dom. Other dreams are of men and women, some of them have legs that have become fins and they swim in water. I swim in the water with them. I sometimes see a girl a little older than me in the water. Her hair and skin are dark like they are here in Greece. Ominous clouds of silt come between us and I lose her from my view. Sometimes I am sitting in a meeting with army generals. The lead general is a woman with a fin. It is fascinating and I wake up feeling like these dreams are memories. Whatever they are and whatever they mean, they leave me with a yearning to travel to Atlantis. I don't know why. Maybe Dom and I were destined to be there together.

I am reliving one of those dreams this morning as I lie in bed. The little pearl is not far from me on the little table with my bag. We have eased into trust again, relying on our family relationship to guide us. It is unnerving still that she is from Jaffa, where Queen Nyobi Kadul reigns and dominates the sea. Knowing she is connected to the curse that binds me nearly drove me crazy. But I could not deny her devotion to Dom and to me.

A loud banging on my shed door pulls me from my thoughts.

"Aphrodite wants you now, Athena!" I hear through the door. "We have a feast to prepare for tonight!" Another feast? This is the third feast this week. Nadir and Desdemona must be trying to gain favor with some of the local politicians. Maybe they are trying to get more money from their pockets. I sometimes hear Desdemona yelling at her husband late at night. He manages to lose money very quickly. As soon as a little money fills his purse, he disappears for a day or two. Then the money is gone. Gone to gambling. Gone to drink. Gone to other women.

"I'll be there," I call out and I hear footsteps running back to the kitchen. I dress quickly and touch the little pearl where she lies. I feel the heat in our touch for a moment, but she is quiet this morning. Probably enjoying the warm morning rest.

I head to the kitchen and meet with Aphrodite in the doorway.

"What are you wearing, Athena?" she asks me. I look down and realize I have on my good robes.

"I'm sorry, Aphrodite," I say. "I grabbed the wrong robes in my hurry to get here." Aphrodite's suspicion about my romantic motives has been increasing over the past several months. She is always reminding me to not get romantically involved with anyone or I will lose my place no matter what Desdemona has to say about it. Everything I do or wear or say has Aphrodite asking me questions about my heart. I assure her constantly that I have no intention of giving my heart away.

"Well," she says, "I guess you are stuck in those today. We have too much to do to take the time to change. Just be sure to leave them in your room tomorrow."

"Yes, Ma'am," I answer.

We head into the kitchen and everything is in disarray. This feast meal is going to be larger than the last two thrown by the inn and everyone is running about trying to fulfill their many tasks. The dining room is busy with the servant boys trying to get everything swept up and in order from the last feast. Women are bustling around the boys, arranging fresh flowers and herbs and finding the right plates for serving.

I work in the kitchen alongside Aphrodite making meats and appetizers, breads and desserts. I am trying to be careful in my good robes, but every time I get anything on them, Aphrodite is after me for wearing them at all. Her reproofs are tiresome and constant. Curse these robes.

The day is especially warm. The sun is melting the butter faster than Aphrodite and I can get it mixed with the cheeses and pastries. This puts her in an even more foul mood. By the time evening rolls around and the guests are arriving for the meal, all of the servants are a hot and tired mess. One or two have to retire for the day, they are so overcome by the heat. I work in the dining room with Aphrodite to make up for the missing servers.

A moment after I set down the main course, I hear a familiar voice.

"Well, girl," he says. I know it is the drunken man, Spiro, who was here two years ago. He hasn't forgotten me. "Desdemona said you were an investment and she was right. You have grown into quite the beauty."

My face is red and the sweat beads roll down my back and face. I look up at Aphrodite who is glaring at me in my cursed good robes. She will be angry with me tomorrow for sure. But there is nothing I can do. Unless...

I reach into the man's mind and change what he sees in me. I make my face pockmarked and I tickle his nose with the foul odor of rotten meat. His nose crinkles as the smell hits his face. I use a new maneuver of thought I have been working on. It is meant to make the impression last, even if I can no longer see the person. This is the first time I have tried it on a human. I move into the kitchen to retrieve more food. When I return, the man looks at me through squinting eyes.

"I could have sworn..." he says. He puts his focus back on his food and eats quietly for the rest of the meal. I continue to work alongside Aphrodite, but she doesn't say a word to me. She is watching my every move, looking for a reason to blame my behavior for his actions. I am determined to not give her anything to find fault with. I keep my eyes on my work and say as little as possible to our guests. I will not be moved from my place.

By the time dessert is set out, Spiro is more drunk than I've seen him. His words slur and he talks constantly about servants and investments. I try to sway his thoughts, but his mind is so fuzzy that he cannot even grasp his own thoughts, let alone the ones I am trying to give him. As I finish clearing the food from the tables, he reaches for my arm. But he is slow and uncoordinated. Instead of grabbing my arm, his grip lands firmly on my thigh.

I can see the anger in Aphrodite before she even realizes it is there. Spiro hiccups and lets go of my leg, "Ever so sorry, my girl," He says through drool and food. "Lost my aim." He then yawns loudly and calls for Nadir.

"Nadir, my fine man. I'd like a word with you if I may." Nadir's face is flushed and he breaks into a sweat. His hands tremble as he follows Spiro from the room. Desdemona glares at her husband. Nadir definitely owes Spiro money.

Aphrodite orders me to the kitchen and tells me I am to continue there for the rest of the night. She will take care of the remainder of the guests in the dining room with the younger serving boys. My face is burning with embarrassment and frustration in addition to the hot weather. I am angry with Aphrodite for blaming me for a drunken man's actions. I will use my mind to put things to rights.

But it isn't long before one of the servant boys comes to the kitchen with a message for me.

"You'd better get to your room quick," he says. "Spiro is talking to Nadir about taking you from the inn. Aphrodite is redder than I've ever seen her. She is doing nothing to help you. You need to be out of sight."

But out of sight for me is out of control. I cannot control them if I cannot see them. I am not strong enough for that. I push my way around the servant boy and head for the dining room. I run into another serving boy entering the kitchen with arms full of dirty dishes. He spills his load and I can't make it past the mess all over the floor.

By the time the dishes are picked up and I enter the dining room, Nadir and Spiro are gone. Aphrodite sees me and points with her stout arm to the kitchen. I send her waves of affection for me, determined to get her help. Her arm wavers and she lowers her finger. She shakes her head in a gesture of pity for her lost Athena.

"We will talk tomorrow," she says to me. "For now, you must go to your room to rest."

The inn guests glance up at us as we openly talk in their presence. I don't want to be in any more trouble than I am already in and I don't want Aphrodite in trouble either. There is no telling what she would say to defend herself if I was not there to feed answers to her.

I turn from the room and go back to my little shed. I am too tired and upset to talk to the little pearl. I try to send her an image or feelings, but my head hurts. I cannot reach her tonight. There will be time to explain in the morning.

As I drift off to sleep, I hold my small bag of money close to my heart. If I am sold and sent to live with Spiro, I will run away. I can figure out something.

Chapter 18

I am dreaming of a city underwater. It looks like the major cities of Greece, but it is in ruins. I see a man's face speaking to me in the water. I can't hear him so I move closer to his face. He is yelling something. His face is distraught and worried. I want to comfort him. Then I hear him.

"They are coming for you! Run!"

A hand grabs my arm and yanks me from my cot. My blankets fall to the ground. I am confused and disoriented on this hot night. I am still trying to wake up and understand what is going on. I open my mouth to scream, but a rag is shoved into my mouth as I do. I kick and thrash but that only lasts for a moment. Soon, I am being held tight and ropes are tied around my arms and legs. Multiple people are holding me. A bag is placed over my head and we step out of my shed into the stifling night air.

I am bound, gagged, and blindfolded for days. I ride in the back of a cart, bouncing along the road to wherever we are going. Twice each day I am lowered to the ground and escorted by a woman to go to the bathroom. My gag is only removed long enough for me to eat a bit of pita bread and drink water. I don't know where I am going. I don't know who has me. I never hear the sounds of civilization so we must be traveling through the countryside. Whether east or west, north or south, I do not know.

On the third day, we make a sharp turn. I roll sideways in the cart as we move onto this new road. Two days later, we finally stop.

Again, I am guided by the hand of a woman. We move through tall grass for a few moments before my feet feel soft and smooth dirt. Soon, we walk on stone. We climb stairs and enter a cool room. I am led to a chair where I sit and wait. My gag is removed again and I am given water. The gag is left out of my mouth, but I am not ready to say anything. My mouth is dry and several blisters have formed on the edges of my lips from the abuse they have received.

"Oh, my girl," my stomach grows stone cold when I hear his voice. It is Spiro. He had me kidnapped and brought me to him. "I am sorry to see you so ill-treated. If only your Master Nadir would have consented to give you to me to pay his debts, I wouldn't have had to take you by night. Normally, I would never have deigned to take someone of your...appearance, but I couldn't seem to get you out of my mind. Namaah, do take our new servant to her quarters and help her recover from her journey." Couldn't get me out of his mind? Is that the result of my attempts? He sees me forever ugly, but he cannot get me out of his mind. I've created a twisted obsession. Now he wants me here and doesn't know why. At least his appetite for my visage has disappeared.

"I do hope your time here is more comfortable than with Nadir," Spiro calls out. "I do like to keep my servants happy." Happy? How can his servants be happy when they are kidnapped?

There is shuffling next to me as Namaah follows the orders of her master, but she doesn't say a word. Together, we move about the room until we reach a narrow hallway. I feel one side of the wall brushing against my arm as Namaah leads me. When we stop, I hear Namaah open a door to our right. She leads me through it and helps me sit on a bed. Once I am seated, Namaah removes the dark cloth that has been covering my eyes. I pull my face away from the light that is shining into the room. There is a window above the door and the sun is just at the right angle to reach my face. Even if I hadn't been blindfolded for days, the sun would have me squinting.

Namaah is making quick work of removing the ropes from my arms and legs. They are swollen from their imprisonment and the pain of removing the ropes is enough to make me cry. Namaah reaches up and puts her hand on my shoulder. She still says nothing. I look into her face. Her hazel eyes are soft and gentle. Her hair is long and dark and curled like mine, though her skin is more golden. On her cheek is a long scar that cuts nearly four inches across her face. I shudder at what would create something so painful on a person so beautiful. Our eyes meet and she points to her lips, shaking her head.

I don't understand what she is trying to tell me. Am I not supposed to talk? Is she not allowed to talk to me? I blink slowly and she moves her hand to her throat, still shaking her head and I understand. She is mute.

I blink away my tears and nod. Namaah moves to the wall next to the bed and points to clothing hooks. The clothing hanging from the hooks is the clothing of a servant though they are nicer than any servants' clothes I've ever seen. She points to the clothing then points to me. I nod. I know they are for me. Namaah smiles. She walks to a small table near the door where a vase and bowl sit. She pours water into the bowl and dips a rag inside. She gently cleans my face, my hands, my feet. Everything is painful to the touch, but I am grateful it will be cleaned. She rinses the rag then hands it to me, pointing at my body. I take the rag and do my best to wipe the dirt from my stomach and chest. Namaah goes to the clothing pegs and pulls down a nightshirt. She helps me put it on and helps me climb into the bed.

The sheets are softer than I've been used to. They are cool and soothing on my damaged skin. As I lay my head on the pillow, I feel like I am in a real bed, like only the wealthy sleep in. A tiny tear leaves the corner of my eye and creates a tiny circle on the pillow. I mouth the words "Thank you" to Namaah. She smiles and wipes a tear from her own eye and brushes my hair from my face with her fingers. She points to herself, then points to the wall next to me. Her room is next to mine. I give a small smile then close my eyes and sleep.

Chapter 19

I am in my room for several days with no one but Namaah in to see me. She brings me food and fresh water for my wounds and body. She helps me regain my strength and lets me cry when I am too overwhelmed by what is happening. It is a full day before I can use my voice again. It is ragged and scratchy and my throat hurts, but under Namaah's care, it too begins to heal.

The room I am in is brighter than the other rooms I have seen in Greece. Its walls are white, so is the ceiling, so is the floor. The bed is on a raised wooden platform and filled with feathers. The linens are as white as the walls. A white netting hangs from the ceiling and covers the bed, keeping any bugs out. The hydria vase and bowl on the table by the door are covered in a bright mosaic depicting Amphitrite, the water goddess, being captured by the dolphin who returned her to Poseidon. Another table nearer to the bed is empty, waiting for my personal belongings.

I sit up straight in the bed, pain shooting through me with the effort. The little pearl! The little pearl was on the table in my shed at the inn! I don't have her with me! A tear opens in my heart, ripping clear to my stomach. The little pearl is gone. Even if I ever get away from this place, there is no way that I will find her again. Anyone else who finds her will think she is a sentimental trinket left behind by a girl who ran away. She will be sold or made into jewelry. And I will be alone.

I want to scream, but my voice won't let me. I open my mouth and scream silently into this pure white room, angry that I am alone again, angry that I have been stolen, angry that I have lost my pearl.

∞ ∞ ∞

The days and weeks go by and I am able to get up from my bed for longer periods of time. I don't see Spiro. This surprises me since he went to such great lengths to bring me here. When I am ready to work, Namaah takes me to the rest of the household to introduce me. As at the inn, there are manservants and maidservants for cleaning, tending to animals, and working in the kitchen. I am left to work with Abdulla, the head cook of the home. She is old and efficient in her work. She says very little and her hands are gnarled with arthritis. I see that my place in the home will be to learn enough to replace Abdulla as head cook. I am relieved that Spiro is no longer interested in more than that.

The estate is huge. Much larger than any I've seen before. And it is remote. I learn from the servants that supply wagons come by here twice a year and it is a two day wagon ride in any direction to the nearest city. It will take time to learn the lay of the land so I can find a way out. Where will I go once I do escape? I don't know the answer to that question, I don't have strong ties to the inn near Sparta, but I cannot deny the pull to something more.

There is a hierarchy here, even among the servants. A class system that keeps us separated. My place is one of honor, a place where Spiro can keep me isolated and controlled, I am expected only to interact with Abdulla and Namaah. I do help manage the other kitchen help, but I learn that I am not to have close relationships with them. When I officially take over for Abdulla, I will be interacting with the family as well, mostly the mother of the home, Rhea. There are other family members as well. A grown daughter lives here with her husband and children. However, they have a large home of their own on the estate so their servants care for their needs. A son, Gileaus, is traveling with his father as he makes his tour of the provinces. Two younger boys, twins Alcmene and Heracles, are with their nanny and tutors most of the day. They do sometimes sneak into the kitchen. Abdullah can be harsh with them, but I sneak small treats to them when she is not looking. When I am in charge of the kitchen, the boys will have more sweets at the ready.

At first the isolation here is overwhelming. To be surrounded by people but have no close relationships is against human nature and every part of my soul fights against it. I want and need communication. I want and need to get out of my own head.

With time and patience, I develop a relationship with Namaah. She is gentle and kind to me and all of the servants. And because she can neither speak nor write, she is trusted by the family. We develop a kind of sign language with one another. She has many signs she has developed in her life and I add one or two more. Over the course of many months, we draw closer as friends.

On a cold and rainy winter night, the travel caravan returns. Namaah knocks on my door and lets me know that I am to report to the kitchen. I dress quickly and make my way down the hall. As I enter the kitchen I almost bump into a young man whom I have not seen before. He is not one of the servants and is not wearing the servants' dress. On his finger is the signet ring that bears the sign of the house of Spiro. So, this is the son, Gileaus. His fine clothing is wet through and the moment I realize who he is, I offer my help.

"Good evening, sir," I say to him. "I am Athena and new to the house of Spiro. I believe you are Master Gileaus. I will have dry clothing and warm food brought to your room for you. Is there anything more I can do for your comfort?"

Gileaus smiles and looks me in the eyes for a moment. I feel like he is trying to see if I will look away, so I maintain the eye contact, assuring him that I am strong and confident in myself. Deciding that he likes what he sees in me, Gileaus answers, "Thank you, Athena. I am glad to have met you and I appreciate your solicitous concern for my welfare. I am sure that my man will have dry clothing prepared for me when I reach my room, but warm food and drink would be wonderful."

"I'll see that it reaches you, sir."

"Please bring it yourself, Athena. It is not every day that we get a new servant. I like to know who is working for me."

I nod to Gileaus and let him pass to the main part of the house before I move into the kitchen. I let Abdulla know I have been asked to bring food to Gileaus. She clucks her tongue and mumbles something about her youth and instructs me which things to take to Gileaus.

I find one of the best trays and lay out the food on it. Pita bread, goat cheese, and some freshly roasted lamb are piled on the plate with grapes on the side. In a large cup, I pour hot milk with a touch of cinnamon and honey, a little trick I learned from Aphrodite to warm the cold winter nights. I include a small amygdalota almond cookie on the side and head to the young master's room.

When I arrive, I knock on the door and it is opened by Gileaus' manservant who is also new to me. He announces to Gileaus that his food has arrived and I hear Gileaus call out, "Oh, good. Have her bring it in and stay for a while."

His manservant bows to me and extends an arm, inviting me into the room. "You can set the tray here," he says as he motions to a round table. By the table is a terracotta brazier with newly lit fuel inside. The heat from the low pot has not yet warmed the entire room, but the area immediately around the table is quite warm.

A moment after I set the tray on the table, Gileaus comes out from his second room, dried and in warm nightclothes. He is taller than most of the young men I've met here. He is only a year or two older than I am and he is very handsome. His eyes are a light hazel and his skin is darker than mine. His hair looks like jet black waves falling around his face. I am waiting for him to sit at the table, so I have a moment to stare.

"Please sit with me," he says as he comes to the table. It isn't customary for the servants of the house to sit with the masters, but it also isn't customary for a servant to ignore an order. I sit at the table with my hands folded in my lap, waiting on Gileaus for more conversation.

"Archantis," he says to his manservant, "I left my wet clothes in the antechamber. When you have cleared them and taken them, I will not be needing your services anymore for tonight." Archantis bows to his master and heads to the next room for his master's clothing. "And Archantis," Gileaus says again, "thank you for your services. I know these trips are not only hard on me but on my companions as well."

"It is an honor to work for you, sir," Archantis bows. He collects the wet clothing from the other room and heads out the main door into the hall. He leaves the door ajar, so Gileaus and I are not locked alone in the bedroom. I am glad for it.

"Please, Athena," Gileaus says to me, "I do hope to not be eating alone tonight. Will you have some of this food?"

"I have had my evening meal, sir," I reply, "but I am happy to keep you company as long as you desire it." The longer I stay to keep him company, the longer I get to enjoy myself. I haven't had a companion my own age in years.

"I do desire it," Gileaus says to me. "It gets so dull spending so many months traveling with politicians. Though I do find much of the adventure interesting, I am still a younger man by comparison. I cannot add to their conversations without being corrected. I cannot ask for their opinions without being reminded that I am without experience. Sometimes I just want to have a conversation with someone my age about anything other than politics."

Gileaus hands me a small bunch from the grapes on his plate. I take them from him and thank him for the food. I am not very hungry, but I eat the grapes anyway. Slowly, so he doesn't offer me more food.

"Tell me about yourself," Gileaus says to me. "I'd like to know where you came from and how you came to work for our family."

I bristle at his question. Telling him about my entire history is definitely out of the question. But what about the second part of his question - how I got here. Do I tell him that his father had me kidnapped and brought here to serve him? Is that kind of thing common in this family or is mine a unique case? I decide to settle on the safest option. Share as little as possible about everything.

"I don't think the life of a servant could be of much interest to a well-traveled man of wealth," I say.

"Bah!" he replies, "I am your equal, Athena. Yes, I have been born to privilege and yes I am a few years older than you, but somewhere our minds must be able to connect. Have you had any education?"

"I have," I answer.

"Well, good," he says. "That is a beginning. Where did you receive your education and which of your subjects did you find most interesting?"

He cannot know who I really am, what I am capable of. I consider using my mind manipulation to sway the conversation, but his eyes are so beautiful. I don't want to give them the blank expression I see when I affect the minds of others.

"I was educated some by the lady of the house where I was born," I tell him. "She had no children of her own and would often take time to play with the servant children and to teach us."

"And what did you most enjoy learning from her?" Gileaus asks.

"That is easy. I enjoyed learning to read," I tell him. He looks surprised at first, then thoughtful.

"Many women don't learn to read," he comments. "You are fortunate to have had such an educated and wealthy benefactress. Tell me, what do you most enjoy reading?"

It has been so long since I have held a book in my hands. Only the very wealthy have bound books. Everything else is written on papyrus and shared family to family. My education in Argos was mainly focused on the memorization of poetry. Yes, there were some written texts, but nothing I could take home. Memorization was key and any writing or arithmetic was completed on wax boards with a stylus. It's a miracle I know how to read at all.

"What I enjoy reading and what I have access to are two different things," I tell him. "I enjoy the sciences, particularly the natural sciences. But what I have had access to is limited to poetry and prose."

Gileaus, leans back in his chair and regards me for a moment. Our culture teaches that a woman has inferior intellect. To hear a woman enjoys the sciences must be baffling his mind right now.

"You are an interesting creature, Athena," he finally says. "Educated, informed, curious, yet still a servant. How ever did you manage it?"

And now I lie. "I was educated by a good woman, but still had to serve to earn my daily bread. Once the house fell into financial ruin, they let their servants go. I worked where I could until I ended up here, serving your family."

"But what house was it you served?" Gileaus asks. I want to be able to remember my lies. I decide to stay as reserved as possible.

"Their downfall brings me no pleasure, sir. I prefer to keep their identity to myself." I know it is a major offense to ignore the questions of my master. To leave him without the answers he is seeking is dangerous for me. I could be punished for it. But I have a feeling Gileaus isn't interested in causing me harm. I have managed to capture his attention and his imagination. He is intrigued by his paradox of a servant. He wants to know more. But it is late. He has had a long day of travel and I have a long day of work ahead of me.

"If you will excuse me, sir," I say to him, "the hour is late and my day must begin very early. If there is anything more I can do to serve you tonight, I will do it gladly. Otherwise, I must have a little rest."

Gileaus has a twinkle in his eye and a slight pull on the corner of his mouth. He holds the smile back, swallowing the many comments he could make to my request. Instead he is gracious, extends his approval for me to retire to my room, and thanks me for the conversation and food.

"I do hope to have more conversations with you, Athena," he tells me as I leave the room. "You are fascinating and I should very much like to get to know you better."

"As you wish, sir," I say as I bow and leave the room. His hazel eyes are on me as I walk away and I can feel his gaze linger long after I am in my bed. I will have good dreams tonight.

Chapter 20

Happy birthday to Athena.

In the months since Gileaus returned to the estate, there has been so much change. I am 16 now. My life feels like it is rushing away from me. Abdullah is still hanging on and a new sous chef has joined the kitchen. A young, plain girl chosen by Rhea. This one wasn't kidnapped.

Whenever I prepare a meal and take it to the family, Spiro dribbles his drunken approval. "A good investment, a very good investment," he always says. He sometimes tries to talk to me in quiet corners, but the subject is always food. I am relieved that his attentions and desires center on my cooking and not my changing body. Rhea is mortified by her husband's constant state of inebriation, but there is little she can do about it. He demands things on a whim and goes to extremes to get what he wants. He recently sent his men to 'acquire' a rare breed of cat. Money was taken with them on their journey, but the same money was brought back. The offer was refused then and the cat was stolen. I feel a kinship with the little creature who is sleek and black with a perfectly formed strip of silver down his spine. We are neither as common as we seem and we are both here against our wills. Though the cat is also treated with uncommon courtesy - down pillows, a silver bowl and gold dishes - it is still a prisoner. As am I.

In the first month of Gileaus' return to the home, he was often busy counseling with his father and other local politicians, giving them the state of things as they found them on their tour of the local provinces. Though I am often asked to cook for these gatherings, I am never allowed inside to serve. Namaah is the only servant whose presence is admitted.

The many meetings and invitations to dinner keep Gileaus occupied. I sit with him once or twice more in that first month, telling him about my history as a servant. I keep as close to the truth as I can so I can remember the tale I am weaving. But the history I share is not exciting or interesting. Instead it is bland and dull and lifeless. I worry that Gileaus will grow bored of our time together and no longer seek my company. But in the ensuing months, when the dinners and meetings die down,

Trapped

Gileaus has me sit with him at least once a week. The door is always open, but we are otherwise alone.

Now we talk about science and about the things Gileaus has learned in his education and life. He is destined to follow in the footsteps of his father as a politician, but not in his footsteps of drunkenness. Gileaus is embarrassed by his father's behavior. He overhears rumors from other politicians and community leaders that his father will not last long in his place.

"I don't want harm to come to my father, Athena," he tells me as we drink warm milk with our amygdolata, "but I am not oblivious to his behavior. He must change or his life is in danger. Already there are men talking to me secretly about taking over my father's place. They think they can control me and rule over me, using my wealth and influence for their own personal gain."

This has become a common theme in our conversations lately. The pressure for Gileaus to take over for his father is mounting. But the only way that happens is if his father dies.

"What can be done?" I ask, hoping there is a way out of this mess for Spiro. If we cannot find a way to change him, I will use my mind manipulation to help him. But that is a last resort for me. It puts me in too much danger. I am already caught in his mind. "Can you talk to him? Persuade him to control his drinking and behavior?"

Gileaus shakes his head. "I have tried, Athena," he says to me. "He is so set in his ways that he cannot see them for what they are. He believes that his drinking isn't any kind of problem. He thinks these men are his friends. And they all pretend to be, Athena. They all curry his favor while reaching out to me behind his back." Gileaus runs his fingers through his hair and rests his head in his hands. "I don't know what more can be done and I see my father slipping away from me."

I reach forward and put my hand on Gileaus' arm, stroking the skin with my thumb. Little touches like this have become commonplace between us as our friendship and intimacy have grown. He doesn't shrink from my touch and I love to give it. It comforts him to know that someone is listening, really listening to him without an agenda.

"Perhaps I can talk to him," I offer.

Gileaus looks up at me and smiles. "And what will you say to him, Athena? Behave or you'll have no more dessert?"

I roll my eyes and sigh, pulling my hand away from him. He is getting caught in the 'women have lesser intellect' trap.

"No," I say firmly. "But he does like me...*and my cooking*...You never know just how far that kind of thing can take you."

Gileaus reaches across the table and I give him my hand. He smiles and strokes my fingers in his. "Thank you, Athena. I didn't mean to offend you. I just didn't see a way it would help. But I believe you have our family's best interest at heart. I trust you to try. Thank you."

I hold his gaze for a moment until I can feel myself blushing. The heat of his stare is rising into my cheeks. I look away and try to pull my hand away from his, but he doesn't let go. Instead, he pulls my hand closer to him, bringing his other hand to hold it as well. He looks at my hand, running his fingers over mine for several minutes, thinking. My heart is racing in my chest and I can hear it pounding in my ears. It is so loud that I wonder why he hasn't commented on the sound. But he says nothing. He just looks at my hand in his.

After several minutes of this intense silence, Gileaus finally raises his eyes again to mine.

"You are a unique woman, Athena," he says. Then, with his eyes on mine, he raises my hand to his lips and kisses the back of my fingers, closing his eyes when his lips meet my skin. My ears feel like they are going to explode with the pressure that is building inside of me. The sensation of his touch is almost more than I can stand. Almost.

He kisses my fingers again and again, my heart swelling and falling more and more with each touch. Then finally he sets my hand down and looks at me.

"Athena," he says, "may I kiss you?" I am his servant. For him to ask for my kisses is unnecessary. He could take whatever he wanted without punishment. I would not be the first servant girl to be taken by her master. But that is not like Gileaus. He is gentle and he is kind and he is respectful. He cares for me and wants my happiness.

I think of his lips touching mine. But as soon as I imagine them brushing my face, I see bubbles and fish and water and steam. I see the faces of two other boys. One has skin so fair, he must come from the north. The other is dark like a Grecian, but his hair is so light it is confusing. Who are they? Why am I seeing them? There is so much Gileaus does not know about me. I am not who he thinks I am. I am not who I have told him I am. I am sick inside and suddenly light-headed.

"I...I..." I stammer instead of answering him. Gileaus just smiles and touches my cheek with his hand.

"Not tonight, then," he says. "We can give it time." He kisses my fingers again. "You are a very special young woman, Athena. I am more grateful to you than you can possibly know."

I smile at him and nod my respect. I stand and head to my room. My head spinning in circles. My heart unsure of the future.

Chapter 21

I wake in a fog this morning. My dreams were peppered with images of those boys, kissing them both, and of Gileaus. My mind is swirling as I stand and get ready for the day. I have promised Gileaus I will talk to his father. He doesn't believe it will do much, but he is willing to humor me. I know it will change everything.

When the breakfast is ready for the family, I take the separate tray of food to Spiro's room. He is rarely up early enough to eat his first meal with his family. The only time he is in the dining room this early is when he doesn't go to bed. But last night, he capped his drinking off early enough to make it to his room.

I knock on his door and hear him mumble inside. I open the door slowly, peeking around the edge to make sure he is dressed. Spiro is still in his bed with the covers strewn all over the place. His nightdress is a mess, but everything is covered. His manservant has not yet been in to dress him. I will have a few moments alone to work on him then.

I breathe a sigh of relief and step in with the tray of eliopsomo bread and ellinikos coffee. Spiro stirs as I set the aromatic tray on his nightstand. He opens his eyes and struggles to see what is in front of him. Once he registers who is there, he lays back on his pillow and coughs.

"My dear girl," he gets out between fits of coughing, "it is far too early for food. Take it away. I will enjoy it later I am sure."

"But, sir, you must get up now and eat. You have much to do today." I send waves of curiosity into Spiro's mind, urging him to ask questions and have an interest in his life today.

His eyes open a fraction and he peers at me through his lashes. "What do you mean, my girl?" he asks, "What have I to do with the day?"

I smile and keep the curiosity flowing. "You have meetings with your political friends today, sir. They are eager to hear the news of your reformation."

"Reformation?" he asks as he sits himself up. "What reformation? I know of no such thing."

"Oh, but you do, sir," I tell him, sending confidence to his thoughts. "You came up with it yourself last night."

"What did I come up with? I don't remember coming up with anything!" Spiro is growing agitated and confused. I direct a visual along with my words and confidence. The quiet and otherwise empty room help me hold my concentration. So much is riding on my success.

"You told Master Gileaus, sir. Last night after you finished your evening meal. You told him you wanted to reform yourself sir."

"Reform myself?!" he exclaims. Then he settles softly into his pillow. "Yes, I...I do remember something about that," he whispers. I send him images from my mind, conjuring a memory for him that was never there.

"Yes, sir," I continue, "you told Gileaus that you were going to let go of your drinking."

Spiro's face snaps up to mine, his eyes wide and worried. "I *did* say that to him! I *did* promise my boy I would not touch the alcohol anymore." Spiro looks into the space before his face, trying to see something that is not there. "But *how* do I stop?" His voice is a whisper again. "I've heard of men who try to give it up! They go stark raving mad!" He is on the verge of screaming. I send soft clouds of comfort and confidence to him.

"But you are no ordinary man, sir," I say to him. "You can do extraordinary things. And you don't have to do them alone. I can help you."

Spiro moves his eyes slowly to mine. "You?" he asks. "You would help me? But why... and how?"

The 'why' of that question lives in the same house as Spiro and calls him father. The 'why' is Gileaus. I am willing to lay myself open to discovery if it means bringing comfort to him. I am doing this to protect him. To help him. To make him happy.

"I have a certain knowledge of herbs and powders that will help ease you out of the worst of the pain and hallucinations. It will be difficult, sir, but it *is* possible. You *can* overcome this thing."

Spiro looks into my eyes with fear. I send him more comfort and more confidence in me. I am not lying. It will be a difficult road. But with my help, it can be done.

∞ ∞ ∞

"Athena! Athena!" Gileaus is calling to me from across the courtyard. I leave the bread I have just finished baking, wipe my hands, and walk toward him. When I reach Gileaus, his face is bright and his hair is wild. He is in high spirits, excited about something.

"What is it, Master Gileaus?" I ask of him. He shakes his head and furrows his brows.

"I've told you to just call me Gil," he says with a frown.

"How am I to do that, sir?" I ask. "I am your servant. If I am familiar with you in front of the other servants, there is no telling what could happen. Soon, everyone will be calling your mother and father by their given names and demanding greater wages. Your family will go broke and I will be forced to find work somewhere else to support the both of us."

Gileaus smiles and shakes his head at me. He takes me by the shoulders and pulls me to him. My heart is already racing, but Gileaus is quick. He doesn't give me time to think. His lips meet mine in a tender, sweet, smiling kiss. When he pulls away, his eyes are shining and his smile is broad.

"You are a very special human being, Athena," he says while he brushes my hair away from my face. "I don't know what you said to convince father, but he just came to me to talk about his plans for reformation. He is promising to give up drinking." I smile, pleased that my Gileaus is happy. "What did you say to him?" he asks.

"I just told him that it was important to you and that he was strong enough to do it," I answer.

Gileaus shakes his head again. "I'm not sure I believe that is all you said, but you have convinced him that he should and can do this thing." He kisses me again, briefly. "There is so much hope for my future, Athena. Because of you, I finally have hope." He kisses me again, longer this time. It is just the two of us. No images of nameless boys running through my mind. Just me. Just my Gileaus. Out in the sunshine of the courtyard where anyone can see.

Making it through the first week of Spiro's recovery is agonizing and difficult. He asks for me constantly, so I am always with him. Gileaus is often there, but has to take over certain duties on the estate until his father is able to do so again. I have done what I can to coax healing and pain relief from the herbs in the garden and fields, but Dom was so much better with the plants than I am. My heart aches for him and I have to take a moment to calm the tears that run, unbidden, down my cheeks. I breathe in the scent of lavender near me and regain my composure. Though I am not as skilled as my brother, I am able to make enough hot drinks, cold compresses, and aromatic incense to bring Spiro out of the worst of his withdrawals.

Trapped

While I care for her husband, Rhea is seeing to the necessary changes in the household. The many hiding places Spiro has around the house are raided. Rhea knows every single one of them. She finds the bottles and jars and pours them all ceremoniously into the garden. Each vessel is washed and cleansed until it no longer smells of the alcohol. The containers that will not lose their smell are broken and buried or given away. The cooking alcohol is given a new home in a cupboard with a lock and servants and family are told to not offer alcohol to Spiro.

"He is making a reformation," I hear Rhea say to her friend and fellow politician's wife. "He is determined to make a new man of himself."

I am glad to hear that she has also bought fully into the idea of her husband's healing. I haven't had to use any mind manipulation on her. Her faith in the process is enough to keep her strong.

Spiro is another story. Despite my efforts with the herbs and remedies, he still struggles against the pain of withdrawal. He is haunted by hallucinations and I do my best to morph those into something of value. I send him images of what his future could be. I show him his wife, happy to be at his side. I show him his children, proud to call him father. I show him his friends, glad for their friend who has made such a change. I show him images of himself, strong and happy in his decision.

But I cannot be always with him. Nights are the worst. He has nightmares and terrors a few days into his withdrawal. I am awakened multiple times each night to come and tend to him. I see what plagues his mind. He is haunted by his past. Haunted by the people he has wronged. He is haunted by the choices he has made and the infidelity he has lived in. His mind is on fire with regret. Each time I am brought to him this way, I work to ease him back to sleep. I coax him with the beautiful dreams of tomorrow, but I am left seeing the terrors he was dreaming.

But it has been three nights since I have been awakened. Spiro's mind has calmed and his body is free again. He treats me like a goddess and tells anyone who will listen that I saved him. The praise is nice, but after a few days I convince him to calm that portion of his memory. I don't want or need the attention.

Spiro never regains the memory of how I came to be a servant in his house. I tell him that he brought me here for my knowledge and skills. I have been treated well here and am falling for his son. I have no desire to leave. Spiro is willing to believe me, so I leave it at that, wondering how many of the servants here were brought the same way I was. The black and silver cat has taken to sleeping in my room.

Gileaus has me into his room more frequently. We eat, we talk, we kiss. Time passes and we are both growing older. Gileaus wants more from our relationship.

"Marry me," he whispers into my hair one night.

I pull away from his embrace, tears filling my eyes and a knot growing in my stomach.

"I can't," I say.

"Why not?"

"I am your servant. It is impossible for you to marry someone in my station."

"Athena, you saved my father's life. I am the son of a wealthy nobleman who stands to inherit everything his father has. I have enough power and you have enough of my family's affection to make a marriage possible."

I shake my head and my heart pulses wildly within me. Why can't I marry him? I haven't thought of escape since the first time I saw Gileaus. I may be a servant in this house until I die. Why not marry the man I love? But a burning inside tells me that escape is still possible - that I must try to run. I still have a mission to fulfill. Marrying this boy will end that mission for me and lead trouble to his doorstep. I don't know the mission and I don't know my future, but I cannot bring myself to hurt Gileaus.

"Please, Gil," I say, "if I honestly thought it were possible, I would marry you today. But there is too much between us."

"Do you not *want* to marry me?" he asks through tender kisses. "I thought you loved me."

"I do love you," I assure him. "I love you more than I ever thought possible." I kiss his lips, running my fingers through his wavy black hair. He holds me close to him and whispers into my ear again.

"I love you, Athena. I want you to be my wife. I want you by my side to turn the estate around. I want your guidance and your counsel when I work with the elder politicians. I want you to be my partner in life. I want to know you are by my side in everything, every day, and every night."

I cannot stop the tears pouring out of my eyes. I lift my head and hold his face in my hands, forcing his eyes to see into mine. What I would give to show him everything about me, but that puts us both at risk. I have lost so much already because of who I have become. I cannot see that same ruin come to him.

"I don't understand, Athena." His eyes are filled with tears and pleading. "It is time in life for me to marry. I don't want anyone else by my side. You are my equal, Athena. How can I lead without your steadying hand? How can I create a life and a family with anyone else? No one else could be the rock that I need to survive. Please, Athena. Please."

He whispers the last word into a kiss. I stay in his embrace, feeling myself melting into him. I let go of my worries and fears for a moment and let my heart dream of what our life could be: children, a home of our own, making a difference in the world. I see all of it.

He sees it too.

I haven't been careful with my thoughts. I wanted so much to share with him that I have actually done it. Gileaus pulls away from my face slowly and looks into my eyes.

"Who are you?"

His question is a whisper, but it stings like a knife. He has seen what I meant to keep hidden. I have to get away. I cannot stay and endanger him.

I run from his room, determined to find a way out of his life.

Chapter 22

It isn't easy to avoid Gileaus for the next several days. I have started finding jobs to do. I start early each morning, preparing the daily meals well before anyone else is awake. I clean everything I can find long after everyone is sent to bed. Whenever I am told that Master Gileaus wants to see me, I persuade the person to tell him they cannot find me. Whenever I hear him coming, I hide.

I am eating little and listening much. I cannot run if I have nowhere to go. I strain to hear every word the servants say. If there is any news of jobs on other estates or a caravan traveling through, I want to know. When I cannot hear what they are saying, I find my way into their minds to learn what they know. I get a whole lot more than what I bargained for this way. If I were a lesser person, I could easily use what I know against them, against anyone. I could bribe and blackmail my way into any position. Theft, affairs, secret plans to harm each other. I see all of it. I see it and I am glad I haven't developed many lasting relationships with the people here. The people I am closest to are Gileaus and Namaah.

Namaah senses that I am in distress. She tries multiple times to get me to talk to her, to let her know what is happening in my mind and in my heart. But with each attempt, I shake my head, unwilling to break my silence. Maybe that is what happened to Namaah. Maybe she loved and lost, too, and that is why she never speaks. Maybe she is protecting someone.

Days turn into weeks and Gileaus leaves to stay a few days in his sister's house. I am relieved to not have to work so hard to avoid him. I hear of a caravan of performers traveling through the area. Perhaps I can find a way into their group.

Tonight, the servants have a night off. Many are heading out to see the traveling performers camped nearby. Some are pairing off in the wilderness outside the estate. The remaining family is on a trip to the coast. This is my chance to escape.

My bag is packed with the few items I own. I take some of the food I have made for my journey and add it to my bag. I will not steal anything of value from

Trapped

this family, though I could certainly feel justified. All I want is a clean break - a chance to get away with as little harm as possible. I want memories of love with me as I run.

The other servants have already left. Many are paired off in couples. Others are excited to have a night of entertainment in the cool evening air. Some take liberties with the alcohol stores in their master's home. Abdulla lays her head on her pillow for the first early night she has enjoyed in decades. Namaah walks to the brook where she listens to the stories the water tells to her.

I leave my room once the house is silent and tiptoe to the outer door. Once I am outside, I keep my eyes and ears open, ready to hide myself and my traveling bag if anyone sees me. After half an hour of walking, I am finally to the outer gates of the estate. I haven't been this far since I first arrived and I have no idea what is on the other side of that wall.

The tall, dry grass scrapes at my exposed ankles and I open the gate to the outside world. I remember vividly the day I first arrived here and how the dry grass scratched the bottoms of my feet. I let the sensation run through me as I reach up to lift the latch on the gate. A crunching sound echoes in the night behind me. A footstep. I pause and listen and its owner pauses and listens, too. I cannot tell where the sound came from. I look around me but see no one. I have to get out and get out now. I have to run.

I ignore the pounding in my chest and I reach for the latch again, this time determined to lift it no matter what. I grasp the iron handle, lift it with all my strength and the door swings open. The cool breeze of freedom brushes my face and neck and hair. I breathe it in and step toward its promise.

A hand reaches my wrist before my foot steps outside. I pull like mad to get free, but the grasp is iron. I look to my captor and look straight into the face of the man I love.

"Gileaus, what are you doing?"

"I was going to ask you the same thing."

"Your family is traveling. The servants have taken the night off. I was going to explore outside the estate."

"With a full traveling bag?" he asks.

I stand in silence and face him. I don't know how to get out of this.

"Athena," he breaks the silence, "do you really want to leave us? To leave me?"

I nod as a hot tear makes its way down my cheek. I tremble with a feeling I cannot understand. Maybe it is fear. Maybe it is anger. Maybe it is something else.

Gileaus strokes my arm where he has hold of my wrist then steps closer to me. I take a step backward, unwilling to be drawn in. I want to leave. I have to leave. I don't want him to stop me.

"Athena, I won't stop you if this is what you really want."

"This *is* what I really want." My answer is a whisper and I cannot look him in the eye.

"Then let me come with you," Gileaus says as he steps closer again. I am surprised by what he is saying. He would be willing to leave all of this, to leave his life for me? I shake my head.

"You can't come with me," I tell him. "Where I have to go is dangerous and what I have to do could hurt you."

"I don't understand what you mean," he says. He comes closer. I don't understand myself. I just know that every step on my path has led to danger to those around me. I don't know how much more I can take and I don't know how to protect him.

I keep shaking my head, tears rolling down my face, Gileaus steps closer, wraps me in his arms and presses his lips to mine. My tears are in the way and I taste the salt intermingled with the kiss. How can I leave him behind?

"Let me come with you," Gileaus whispers again as I rest my head on his chest.

"I don't know how to do that," I answer honestly.

"Then explain it to me."

My heart is pounding and voices are screaming in my ears, "STOP!" they all say. "STOP! These are dangerous waters! He cannot know! You must not tell him!" but I don't have the power to obey anymore. I have to let someone know my secrets. I have to let someone in. I choose Gileaus.

I turn my face up to meet his gaze. His eyes melt into mine and see into my soul. He loves me completely. I know I can trust him. He will keep me safe.

"You don't know everything about me," I begin.

"Then tell me," he says. "There is nothing about you that I don't want to know."

"I know," I say. I brush his cheek with my hand. "We need to talk privately. I don't want to say what I have to say here."

He turns and looks at the vast estate behind him. From the sad look in his eyes, I feel that he is linked to his home. It is a part of who he is, but he is willing to let it go. He turns his eyes to me again and kisses my lips firmly.

"Then let's go for a walk," he says. He takes me by the hand and together we walk through the gate.

The tall, scratchy grass continues to grow outside of the estate. But a road leads through the center of it. We step on the path and walk it hand in hand.

"There is a little olive tree just beyond that hill," he tells me. "I used to climb it when I was young. It is a way off the road, a bit lonely, but a safe place to talk."

Trapped

"To the tree then," I say, my fingers linked through his. Gileaus takes my traveling bag in his hand and carries it for me down the road and up a small hill. I feel its weight when he lifts it from my shoulder. I am lighter without it.

When we reach the crest of the hill, I see the little olive tree in the distance. The night is dark, but the moon is full. I see the silhouette of the olive tree stretching out over the moonlit grass of the hillside. Its branches are outstretched in an open embrace, ready to take me in. A rough grasp waiting to take hold.

We reach the tree and sit on the soft ground by its roots. A small mound of dirt marks the place of a child's buried treasure. We sit quietly in the darkness and I try to find the best way to explain who I am.

"Gileaus, I am not who you think I am."

"Yes, you've told me that before," he says as he squeezes my hand. "I want to know *you*, Athena. I am ready to listen."

I take a deep breath and weave my tale in a way he will understand. I tell him of Nyobi Kadul and her curse on Mama's womb. I tell him about Dom, the twin I lost. I tell him about Acacia. I tell him about the inn. I tell him about his father.

"Athena," he says, horror written in his tone, "Athena. My father. I didn't know. I didn't know. I knew he was horrible and lived a dark life, but I had no idea he took you." He stands and runs his fingers through his hair, pulling at the roots, pacing back and forth. "Athena, what can I do?" he asks. "How can I make this right? I can take you back to the inn. You don't have to be trapped in our home." He kneels on the ground in front of me, taking both my hands in his, trembling as he speaks. "Forgive me for my father's sin," he whispers.

"You need no forgiveness," I say. "You had no part in the wrong that was done to me. You have treated me as your equal from the beginning, Gil. I have been safe in your home."

Gileaus' hands are still trembling as he kisses my fingers. His face is beaded with sweat and he shudders as he lets go of my hands.

"I don't understand why he would do that, Athena. Your whole life was ruined when he took you."

"It wasn't ruined, Gil," I say. "It was changed. I had no real connections with anyone anymore. He didn't take me from a family I loved. He took me selfishly, yes. He is not in a right mind, Gil. But it could have been much worse. I am not ignorant of that."

"Athena. Athena. Athena." Gileaus whispers my name over and over again.

We sit like that together, me with arms wrapped around my knees, Gileaus kneeling at my feet, for over an hour. When his mind goes back to the darkness, he whispers my name again and again. That is the only sound we make.

After some time of silence, Gileaus meets my eyes. "You didn't tell me why you were chased from your home in Argos."

"It's part of the curse from Nyobi Kadul," I tell him.

"She cursed you so you would never have a home?" he asks. "Is that why you won't marry me?"

"No, Gil," I assure him. "It isn't that kind of curse, really. She cursed the children born from Mama's womb to have powers. Powers that would make them hunted."

"What do you mean, Athena?" Gileaus asks. "What kind of powers?"

My heart speeds up again and my mouth goes dry. I have kept this part of the secret for years. I am opening up my life and fears to another person. Someone I love.

"The kind of powers that could rule a nation," I tell him. "I can control objects. I can control living things. I can control people."

Gileaus sits quietly for a moment. I don't know if he believes me or wonders about my sanity.

"Show me," he says quietly in the darkness. "Show me who you really are, Athena."

I will not deny him. I feel the fire of my power growing in my stomach. I breathe slowly to keep myself calm and focused. I run my fingers over the dirt, speaking to it with my mind. It is warm at its surface, but I feel its cold core beneath me. It is willing to speak to me, maybe even to help me.

What do you want of us? The dirt asks roughly to my mind.

I want to show this man that you are alive. I want to show him your worth, I say, remembering the way to praise anything I speak to.

Hmph, the ground is skeptical. *What do you humans know about our worth? You take us and use us for your own gain.*

I know your worth, I say as I send soothing feelings into the earth, *I know you give of yourself. I am grateful to you for all you do for us.*

I feel the earth swell with pride. *Well, we are willing to show this man our power, but only for a moment. We won't be sustaining him forever.*

That is all I ask of you, I say quietly.

I continue to talk to and coax the earth. I feel on the ground for an olive and find one just beginning to rot. I bury it, pit and all, in the earth. Just as it did for Dom, the earth sends its water and nutrients to the little olive and pit. There is no sun for the little plant to grow, so its life will be short. I continue to talk soothingly to the earth and the olive. I hum a tune as I do. My body tells me this is the way it is done. Gileaus stands quietly by my side as I work.

Within a moment, the little tree is sprouting from the ground. It grows rapidly, reaching the height of my shoulders in just a minute or two. Gileaus is holding his breath as he watches it grow.

Trapped

The little tree grows a few inches more and begins to sprout leaves before the ground has done all it is going to do.

There, it says to me, *we don't care how well you sing us to your will, that is all we have to give today.*

I thank you for your generosity, I say. *I will not ask for more.*

The ground sends one more *Humph* to my mind before letting go of the connection.

I turn to face Gileaus. He is paler than the moon.

Slowly, Gileaus turns to meet my eyes. He is trying to look at me, but keeps looking at the small tree behind me instead.

"Are you okay?" I ask. He opens his mouth to speak, but no words come out. He blinks several times, then raises his arm and points at the tree.

When I turn around, I see that the tree is already dying. Gileaus steps closer behind me and puts his hands on my shoulders. We watch as the tree dries up and falls, its roots not at all strong enough to keep it upright anymore.

"You did this," he says into my ears.

"Yes. I did."

We are quiet for another several moments when Gileaus whispers, "Show me more."

I take him by the hand and lead him to the dead tree. "Help me," I say, and together we break apart the dry limbs and stack them on the dirt. I gather some of the dry grass and fill the cavities made by the branches. I open my traveling bag and pull out the small blanket from inside. I lay it on the ground by the woodpile and Gileaus sits next to me.

I close my eyes and sway from side to side, feeling the melody even before I begin to hum it. *Air that I love,* I say. I feel those Mother eyes turning to me. They have been with me for years since I came to this place. I have reached out rarely, but I have always felt them watching me.

Yes, child, they say to me. *How can we help you?*

Please, I ask, *please help me start this fire. I want to show the man I love what you can do.*

Indeed child, the air says in her many voices, *we will help you.*

A distant breeze makes its way down the hillside, a group of air molecules gathers together, whirling in a tight ball. It superheats and dives into the pile of dead wood and grass. A flame bursts from the center, taking hold of the fuel with hunger. For the first time, I feel the fire speaking to me. It responds to the sound of the melody I am humming.

Creator, it says. *Devourer. Creator.* There are many voices to the fire, but they are all speaking over one another. Male and female, old and young. Some of the voices are angry, others are afraid. All of the voices are hungry.

I stop humming and sit still. The fire ceases to speak to me. I feel fear in the pit of my stomach. Though I can communicate with the fire, I feel a limited sense of control over it. It called me Creator, then Devourer. What did it mean? I am too afraid to ask. I let the fire burn as Gileaus holds me close to his side.

Chapter 23

"This is why I can't marry you," I tell Gileaus as we sit in the dark. The embers from the fire have died away and the morning light is beginning to peek over the horizon. "If anyone else discovers the power I have, they will want to use it for themselves."

"Athena," he says, "there is nothing in this world that we cannot face together. There is no reason for anyone else to know what you can do."

No one else *can* know what I can do. That would be fatal for me and for Gileaus.

"Gil, the plants and earth and air are just a part of my powers," I tell him. "I have that kind of power over people too."

Gileaus thinks for a moment before answering, "Is that how you helped my father?"

"It is."

"Why didn't you use your powers to keep him from taking you in the first place?"

"I have to see those I am reaching to mentally," I tell him. "I was blindfolded, gagged and bound for the journey. By the time I saw him again face to face, I was too exhausted to do anything. I didn't know where I was. I was in pain. It was so hard to even think."

Gileaus is silent again.

"Athena."

"Yes?"

"Have you used your mind skills on me?"

"No, Gil," I assure him as I reach up and touch his cheek. "I made the conscious decision to never touch your mind."

"Why not?"

"From the beginning, I wanted to know you and I wanted you to know me. I wanted our feelings to be real."

Gileaus reaches forward and kisses me. Softly at first then with growing intensity. He tangles his fingers in my hair, pulling me into him tighter and tighter. My hands are resting on his chest and I feel his heartbeat through his robes. My own heartbeat is beating in time with his. For this moment, nothing else matters. Not escape, not power, not Athena. Just him. We are one and in love and it is a beautiful feeling.

"Marry me," he whispers as he pulls away. "Marry me and be my wife, Athena. You know me better than anyone in the world and now I know you, really and truly know you. I still love you and you still love me. Please Athena. Will you be my wife?"

So close to him, feeling his heart beating with mine, the sun's rays barely breaking over the horizon, I can only think of one word.

"Yes."

Chapter 24

Now that we are engaged, I don't want to be apart from Gileaus. I return to the estate and look forward to the future before me. My heart aches for the loss in my life, but this is my life now. The pull to move still surges through my chest, but I want to let it go. I am Athena and I want to be happy.

News of the engagement spreads quickly and I am pleased by everyone's reaction. Namaah smiles as she holds my hands. Her eyes shine with joy for me and she presses her heart over and over again. We embrace and I feel the warmth of friendship between us. Abdullah gives me a nearly-toothless smile and congratulations. Since she has a new apprentice, I will not need to take over as head of the household kitchen, though I will soon need a staff of my own.

Gileaus' family are mostly happy for us. His sister raised an eyebrow and offered a cold congratulations when we told her the news. But Gileaus and I will be creating a home of our own, away from the estate. I won't need her approval to be happy. The twins are excited when we tell them. I promise to give them extra sweets whenever they come to visit. Rhea holds me close and whispers a tearful congratulations into my ear. Spiro is all smiles and congratulates Gileaus on making such a sound investment. My heart pricks at his words.

I am working in the kitchen, making a new market list for the week, when I hear a commotion at the front of the house. At first, I think the twins are rough-housing, but it doesn't take long to realize there is something much worse going on.

"Back with you, vermin!" I hear the sentry shouting. "You will not pass on my watch!" I hear animals in the courtyard clucking and braying and kicking in fear. Footfalls run throughout the house and into the courtyard. I leave my place and go to see what is happening.

When I arrive in the entry room of the home, I see several men fighting in the courtyard. I recognize Spiro's guards. Some of the other men are recognizable as well. I have seen them serving their masters at political gatherings here at the estate.

It doesn't take long for more men to arrive through the entry to the estate with clubs and swords raised above their heads to join the fight. Our guards are greatly outnumbered, but brandish their swords with skill before their assailants.

Spiro runs down the hall with Gileaus at his heels. Rhea is close behind them and lets out a scream.

"Back! All of you!" Spiro shouts to the women. "Stay inside and remain safe!"

Spiro pulls his own dagger from its sheath beneath his robes and runs to the weaponry in the courtyard. Gileaus is with him. The other women have retreated to the kitchen, but I cannot bring myself to leave. I must stay and help Gileaus however I can.

Soon, Gileaus and Spiro have joined the fight. Then I see two, smaller figures fighting with clubs. It is Alcmene and Heracles. Why are they fighting? They are too young and too small! They will be killed! I focus my attention on the boys, urging them with my mind to leave the fight. They stop and turn to one another. I cannot hear them, but I am maneuvering their conversation. I urge them to find a safe place to go until the fighting is done.

All of a sudden, I see a large guard with a club approaching the boys. His face is twisted in a disgusting grimace as he draws closer to them, his club raised. He lifts his arm high above his head and I do the one thing I know will stop him. In one swift movement, I remove the hamsa medallion from my neck.

In an instant, the guard drops his club to the ground. I see him screaming and holding his head. Blood is coming from his nose and ears. The twins are so close they can see the man and they run away screaming. Good. They are safe. No one else sees what is happening to the guard. There is too much other noise and mayhem going on.

I place the hamsa back around my neck and look to wherever else I can help. I see several of the intruding guards pushing into our defense. I send my focus into them. I pour fear into their hearts. A few of them stumble backward when the icy fear fills their hearts. I cannot affect all of them at once, so I turn my attention back to the guards who are doing the best. They are strong, physically and mentally. It will take more than fear to turn their focus.

I reach deep inside and pull out a horrifying dread. I snake the dread on the ground and toward their feet. It laces its way up their legs until it reaches their necks. Then the dread snakes its greedy tendrils down their throats. This time the effect is immediate. One of the guards screams. He drops his sword and runs away as fast as his legs will carry him. The other guard sees him running away and begins to cry. While he is distracted, one of the estate guards pushes forward with his sword into the abdomen of the attacker. Looking up from his wound to our guard, the enemy guard kneels to the ground, tears streaming down his face, and curls into a ball. His suffering tears at my heart. I want to give him peace as he dies slowly in the courtyard, but my focus has to be elsewhere.

Spiro is engaged in mortal combat with an enemy guard. Spiro is old and the guard is young. Spiro has all but ruined his body with drink, the younger guard is virulent and adroit. He moves deftly about Spiro, striking at his aging body over and over again. Spiro is skilled in combat, but he is slow. I turn my thoughts to the enemy guard and urge slowness into his bones. The slowing creeps over him until his movements are almost halted. He looks like a man fighting underwater. His face is confusion and frustration. It looks like he is having a bad dream. A dream where he wants to run but all he can do is crawl. I've had those dreams and recognize the fear as it enters his eyes. Fear that I did not even have to send. He knows he is somehow overcome and he knows he cannot survive. Spiro brings his sword down to bear again on the man. His aim is sure and true and the enemy falls to the ground in an instant. His face is blank. His death was instant.

Spiro sinks to his knees, his robes are covered in blood. I run to him, dodging in and out of guards battling their opponents. When I reach him, his hands are holding his abdomen and they are red as the fire of the setting sun. He looks to my face and I kneel beside him. Spiro grasps for me and holds my hand. His hand slips in his blood so he grabs at my shoulder. He stares into my eyes, fear etched in their surface. I send him comfort. I know his time is near.

"I...I...I am sorry," he says to me.

I cannot speak, I am too focused on helping him. I reach into his mind to see the memory he holds there. It is a memory of a conversation. I see him speaking to Nadir. I cannot hear their words, but Nadir is shaking his head violently no. Spiro reaches up to Nadir's throat, squeezing and crushing. Nadir grasps at Spiro's hands, scratching them in an attempt to get free. But it is no use. Spiro is large and strong. Nadir is small and weak. In a moment, Nadir lays on the ground, motionless.

In his memory, Spiro looks at his hands. They are shaking. He looks around and sees no one. He jumps to his feet and runs to wake his guards and driver. They are groggy, but quickly snap awake as they listen to their master. They ready themselves and their wagon with haste. They follow Spiro around to the back of the inn. He points to my shed. My shed. How did he know where I was? Did he kill Nadir because Nadir refused to sell me to him? The guards run to the shed with a rag and a sackcloth.

The memory ends.

I stare into Spiro's eyes. They are wide and unblinking. The hand that holds my shoulder slips down my arm and falls to his side. His lifeless body hovers for a moment before falling to the ground in a silent heap.

My breath catches in my throat. I want to vomit and cry at the same time. Spiro killed Nadir. He killed the innkeeper because he would not give me to him. Spiro killed Nadir and then he kidnapped me. I could not stop him. Why?! Why?!

"Why?!" I scream at his frozen features. I hit his body with my fists. The anger and fear that made me a prisoner come out through my fists. Yes, he treated me well while I was here. But he had no right to me. No right to take me. No right to kill a man who didn't give him what he wanted.

I punch his body until my arms are tired. When I finally slow down, a pair of hands reaches toward me. I cannot see who it is until they have me by the shoulders and are staring me in the face. It is one of the enemy guards. His face is covered in a beard. Food is caught in the whiskers on his face. He smells of wine and vomit. He snarls and I reach into his mind for an image of a woman, his Mother. He thinks he is attacking his Mother. He sets me down, screams an apology then runs away from me.

I am exhausted from the mental struggle and effort I've used today. But I cannot rest. I must find Gileaus.

"Athena!" I hear him yelling my name. "Athena! Help!"

I scan the courtyard like mad, trying to find his face, but he is not here.

"Athena!" I snap my head in the direction of his voice and see his face for just a moment.

He is in the arms of the enemy guards. Three of them are carrying him at once to a wagon that waits outside. I look for the estate guards to help, but they are all wounded or still fighting. I run to the man I love. I grasp the hamsa medallion around my neck.

In a flash before my eyes, I see myself. I am angry and afraid. The hamsa is off my neck and I am focusing everything on one person. My head screams with pain. The vision turns red then goes dark. I have seen the last memory of the guard I killed. I saw myself killing him and I felt his pain.

I shake the violence of the vision from my mind and keep running. I have to get to Gileaus. I run outside the gate to him. When I reach the guards, I breathlessly sing out the tune I sang to the dead olive tree. I feel the fire burning within me. It works itself free from my body and shoots into the eyes of the guards who are holding my love. At once all three of them scream, dropping Gileaus to the ground as they cover their ears. My singing has turned to screaming and all of my anger and fear find a new focus - saving Gileaus.

All of my muscles tense and I hold my arms near my face, my fingers spread toward the guards. I scream and send my burning hatred into them. They scream and twist on the ground. I feel the energy draining from my body. It is more than I can handle. I am getting lightheaded. As I fall to the ground, I see Gileaus running to me. It is the last thing I see.

Chapter 25

My wrists are burning. My ankles are burning. I am sick to my stomach and I turn my head to the side to let it out, but nothing comes. I am sitting in a chair, bound. My wrists are tied behind me. My ankles are tied to the legs of the chair. My eyes are covered.

"She's awake now," I hear someone mumble nearby. Who is it? Where am I? Why am I tied to a chair?

I hear footsteps coming closer to me. They stop.

"What is your name?" This is a man's voice. Not the same one from a moment ago. This is someone else.

I say nothing.

"You don't seem to understand the question." His voice is laced with sarcasm and bitterness. "I said, what is your name, girl?"

Again, I sit silent. I will not tell them who I am. I hear muffled sounds as the man steps away from me. More footsteps come closer to me. There is a whistling sound in the air and I hear a crack as a searing stinging opens on my cheek. My head whips to the side with the force of the blow. I feel the warmth of my blood dripping down the side of my face. I let out a low, pained moan and I cry.

"Let her be for a moment, Demetrius," I hear the first voice again. "It has to sink in a little."

My entire face is wet with blood, sweat, and tears. I smell the dirt on my clothes from the courtyard, but I smell more than that. This room is bathed in mildew. I feel the damp from the walls seeping through my clothing and chilling me to the bone. Each footstep my captors make echoes around me, the crunch of dirt and straw beneath their shoes letting me know where they are at all times. I calm my crying and focus my ears. I know there are at least two of them with me. Are there more? The stinging in my cheek turns to throbbing as I raise my head and square my shoulders.

"There now," Demetrius says in my ear. "Are you ready to tell me your name?"

I refuse to give them my name, but I also don't want to be hit again. I decide if they are going to inflict evil on me, I will give them evil in return.

"My name is Ceto," I say with my tired voice. The name coming through my lips with no thought at all.

"Ceto?" the other voice asks. "What kind of a name is that?"

"It's a made-up name," Demetrius says, "and the wrong answer."

Again I hear the whistle. Again the cracking sound. Again the stinging.

"Demetrius!" the other man growls. "That's enough! We are to question her, not whip her to death."

Demetrius moves away, "I'm not whipping her to death, just motivating her." I hear the rush of his footsteps toward me again. I duck this time and the strike misses my face. I hear Demetrius stumble as he misses his mark. "Why you little…"

"Demetrius! Out! Now!"

There is silence for a moment then I hear Demetrius mumble something to himself.

"Fine," he finally says out loud, "I'll go. But when you're *really* ready to get answers out of her, you'll know where to find me."

I hear Demetrius stalk away from me and out of the room. From the sound of his footsteps, I know that I am facing the door. If only this blindfold would come off. I could get a real feel for where I am. I hear footsteps coming toward me again. I brace myself. The person pauses, sighs, and gently pulls the blindfold from my bleeding face.

"I'm sorry about Demetrius," he says. "He is the most vicious of our guards. I don't know why he is the one always sent to deal with people. I personally believe we can get much more from treating people well." The man is tall and strong, bearded, and wearing the robes and medallions of a soldier. "I am Captain Juri. I help lead the soldiers here. Demetrius is an under guard who serves under me, though we both answer to a higher master. Unfortunately, that limits the control I have over him."

Captain Juri walks to a table about ten feet from me. Two more guards stand by the door, both with swords by their sides and knives in hand. Captain Juri fills a cup with water and brings it to me. "Here," he says, "I'll help you drink."

The water is clear and cool and refreshing. I am grateful to have it in my parched throat. I finish the drink Juri has given me.

"Thank you," I say.

"You're welcome." Juri walks back to the table, refills the cup, and drinks it himself. The guards by the door stare forward, eyes unblinking. I wonder if they are thirsty.

Captain Juri picks up a chair near the wall and brings it to sit in front of me. The back of the chair is toward me, and Juri sits with a leg on either side, leaning his chest on the back while facing me. He scratches his beard then rests his head on his hands.

"Demetrius gets it all wrong," he says. "He thinks the right answer to every question is brute force. I don't think he'll ever learn the difference between getting answers for answer's sake and getting the truth. I honestly don't think he cares."

Juri sighs then straightens his back. "You may have guessed by now, but we already know your name. What we need to do here is hear it from you. That way we *know* that what you are telling us is the truth." He sighs again and shakes his head. "I'm sorry that Demetrius was the first to interrogate you. Our master insisted on it. If you will be honest with *me*, our master won't require Demetrius to come to you again."

"Who is your master?" I ask through the throbbing pain.

Juri clicks his tongue several times. "I'm afraid that isn't how this will work, Miss. I am under orders to not share the master's name with you. Naturally, *I* would want to tell you. But I have my orders, you know. I will do what I can to keep you unharmed, but there are some orders I cannot disobey. Please. Tell me your name."

I blink several times as I think of what I am being asked. A name cannot be a harmful thing to share. But which name do they have? Here, Gileaus is the only person who knows I am also Pearl.

Gileaus.

"Where is Gileaus?!" I yell as I realize he is not here with me. The throbbing in my face grows worse with the effort. I am dizzy and feel nauseous. How could I have forgotten him for even a moment? He is the reason I removed my hamsa medallion.

My hamsa.

I look down and see it hanging around my neck. Relief floods through me. As long as I am wearing it, I can maintain control over my powers. I close my eyes and whisper, "Thank you."

"Gileaus was brought in with you," Juri says in answer to my question. "The guards in the courtyard came running to where you both were when they heard the screams of the other men."

Silence hangs in the air between us.

"What *did* happen to those other men, Athena?" Juri asks. Good, he knows me as Athena. Without even trying I got him to tell me something he already knew and it is something I needed to hear.

"What happened to Gileaus?" I ask in return. I am carefully sending a willingness to share into Juri's heart. He is smart and I am afraid that if I push too hard, he will feel my interference.

Juri gives me a sideways look, eyebrows furrowed. I've pushed too hard so I pull back on my urging. Juri is quiet for another moment before answering.

"Gileaus is here, Athena," he says. "He is unharmed. He will remain that way as long as you cooperate." A threat. So, Juri is not as peaceful as he lets on. He is willing to push if he thinks it will get him what he wants.

"Can I see him?" I ask.

"Not yet," Juri replies. "But soon. First, I want to know more about *you*."

My stomach turns. What does he want to know? Why does he want to know it?

"When the guards reached Gileaus, it looked like he was trying to put that necklace on you," Juri tells me. "Why would he do that?"

I want to answer Juri's questions. The more I can answer honestly, the more he will believe me.

"We are engaged," I say. "Gileaus knows the necklace is important to me."

"So, he wanted to make sure you were wearing a special necklace while men were dying all around you?" Juri asks. "I find that hard to believe, Athena. Even for star crossed lovers. How about you tell me why he *really* wanted to get that necklace on you?"

"I've told you the truth, Captain. Gileaus loves me. He knew I would want the necklace with me no matter what."

Juri considers this for a moment then asks, "Why *is* the necklace so important to you, Athena? What about it is so important that your fiancé knew you'd rather be caught with it on than to escape without it?"

"My sister gave it to me," I say, thinking of Dom and hiding him in a lie. "I lost her when I was young. I am never without the necklace."

"Hmmm..." Juri says. "Well, I'm sorry to hear that. I lost a brother when I was young." He is silent for another moment. "The piece of rope holding your medallion is worn and fraying. Certainly you would want a strong chain to hold something of such value. I would think you wouldn't ever want to risk losing it."

I don't know what Juri is thinking of. His tone is unnerving. I am silent as he continues.

"Yes, Athena. I think I will do that for you. I will make sure you get a strong chain for your medallion. One that cannot be lost or broken so easily."

"Thank you," I say, unsure of what Juri wants, but not wanting to displease him.

"It is nothing," he responds. "Think of it as payment. I'm sure you will help me. I would like to give you this good faith token on my part."

I don't know what Juri wants from me yet. He still thinks I'm Athena, a servant of the house of Spiro and fiancé to Gileaus. There can be nothing special that he is after. Yet.

Trapped

He is quiet for another moment. Then he stands and puts his chair back against the wall. He walks closer to me, pauses, then says, "I think I will call for some food for you. I want you to be fresh and well." He touches my hair and my spine shivers. "I would have you untied, but you haven't proven yourself that far yet. Guard!" One of the men by the door steps forward, "Have some food brought up for two - some for me and some for our prisoner." The guard bows and leaves the room.

Juri turns to leave. "I'll be gone for only a short while, Athena. When I return, we shall eat together and have a little chat. I want to know more about what happened to the guards at the estate." What do I tell him? I cannot reveal my powers. I am in trouble and I have no idea where Gileaus is being kept.

Chapter 26

I don't have much time to act. I turn my attention to the remaining guard in the room. I search his thoughts and find an image of a young girl, a sister. I cough and he looks up. But he doesn't see me. He sees the girl from his memories. He sees his sister, tied to a chair and bleeding.

He gasps, jumps up and runs to my side.

"Isidira. How did you get here?" he asks. "What happened?!" he is untying my ropes and I send him both confidence and fear. Confidence that he can set me free. Fear that if he doesn't hurry, he'll be caught. He unties my second ankle and I stand.

"You are free now, Isidira. You must go home," he says. If only I could obey that command. "It isn't safe here. You'll be harmed if they find you here."

"What is going on here?" I ask, breathless and eager for information.

"I cannot even say the words, Isi," he says. I send him truth and honesty. A desire to share everything with his sister. "Political intrigue," he says. "Sorcery. They are planning a coup in the government. They are killing their opponents and searching for those with powers to make their enemies crumble."

So, that is why Spiro was killed. He was their enemy. Whoever *they* are. Whoever this master is.

"A man was brought here with me," I tell him. "He is a nobleman's son. His name is Gileaus. Have you seen him? Do you know where they are keeping him?"

I hear a creak and the guard and I both turn to the door. Captain Juri steps inside, Demetrius is right behind him.

"Well," Juri says, "and what have we here? Consorting with the prisoners?"

The guard stands between me and Juri. "She is not a prisoner. She is my sister!"

"Your sister?" Juri asks. "What sister? Isidiri? But isn't she dead?"

The blood drains from my face and the guard spins on his heels to look at me. He still sees his sister. I am about to let him see the truth when he returns to facing Juri.

"Isidiri is not dead," he says in a whisper. "She is here and I will not let you harm her."

Demetrius lets out a low chuckle. "Indeed," he mumbles to himself.

Captain Juri puts up his hand to silence Demetrius.

"I tell you, man," Juri addresses the guard, "Isidiri is dead." The guard plants his feet and reaches for the dagger at his waist.

"I'll not listen to your lies," the guard says as he squats low, ready to strike.

"Athena," Juri says. "Why does this man think you are his sister?"

I cannot let him know what I can do. I can only hope to talk my way out of this one.

"I do not know, Captain," I manage to croak out. "He began calling me by another name and undid my bands. That is all that I know."

Juri clicks his tongue and two guards from the hallway enter the room.

"Take this man to the sick rooms," he tells them. "He has gone mad."

"He must be punished," Demetrius interjects.

"He is not a criminal," Juri argues. "He has suffered a hallucination. Time with the physicians will be enough to work the malady out of him." I worry about what will happen to the guard. There is not much hope for him with doctors. I cringe at the thought.

The young guard looks over his shoulder at me and for the first time, sees *me*. He does a double-take and shakes his head.

"Isidiri," he whispers. "Isidiri. What happened? Where did she go? What have you done with her?!" He drops his dagger and takes me by the shoulders, shaking me. "What have you done with her?!" he shouts into my face.

The other guards are on him in a matter of seconds. They wrestle him out of the room, the entire time he is calling out for his lost sister. As he is taken, screaming, down the hall, Demetrius lets out another low chuckle and follows behind.

The second guard returns, bearing a tray in his hands. Grapes spill over the edge of a bowl. The aroma of fine cheese reaches my nose. Olives and breads are piled high next to a mound of sliced lamb. Two wooden cups rest near the plate. The guard places the plate on the table, then resumes his post by the door. Another guard enters to take the place of the sentry I manipulated. I am beginning to think this place has a limitless supply of guards.

"Poor devil," Juri says as he takes a seat at the table. He motions to the other chair next to him. I move to it slowly and take a seat. Juri watches my every move, tempting me to do something in front of him. "It is surprising," he says. "I haven't had a guard let a prisoner free from their bands before. I wonder what could have made him do it." Juri wraps some olives and lamb in a slice of bread, dips it in a little bowl of oil and vinegar and takes a bite. He motions to me.

"Please, have some."

His manner is unnerving. He is calm and collected in the face of his own guard turning treacherous. He welcomes a prisoner and offers her food. I fear what he is hiding. What is it he is capable of?

I reach for the food, eating from the same piles Juri ate from. If I am poisoned, he dies with me. If I am not poisoned, I will have sustenance to help me through the coming days.

"What do you think of the food?" he asks. "You are a cook, are you not?"

I only told him that I worked on the Spiro estate. I never told him I cooked there. Where is he getting his information?

"The food is good, thank you," I respond. "I did cook for the family of Spiro." I take just a few more bites, then a drink of water. I eat enough to kill the hunger and give me strength, but not enough to stuff myself and grow tired.

"Please," I ask, "when may I see Gileaus?"

"I'm sure you will see the young master soon enough," Juri responds. From somewhere in the building, we hear a scream. It is a man's scream, the guard from my room. "Demetrius," Juri says to himself as he shakes his head. "When will that man leave well enough alone?" He sets his food on the table, wipes his hands on a small towel and stands.

"I'm afraid our time together has come to an end today," he tells me as he walks over to the chair I sat in when I first arrived. "I will be here again tomorrow. For now, you had better rest. I would like you to tell me about yourself and about the guards at the estate. Take all the time you need to consider how you want to tell me."

He said '*how* I want to tell him,' not '*what*.' Does he already know I am the reason those guards suffered? Does he already have an understanding of what I am capable of? Have I given too much away?

"Please, Athena," Juri says. "Come back to your seat. I promise to not make the bands as tight this time, but I assure you the knots will be better."

I leave my chair at the table and return to the seat being offered to me. As I take my seat again, Juri pulls out a rope from his waist. He again ties my hands behind my back and each of my feet to the legs of the chair. But, as he promised, he does not make the bands as tight. My skin is not being rubbed as it was before, though it is still tender where the rope touches. Juri turns and walks to the door.

"If she is hungry," he tells the guards, "feed her. When she needs to relieve herself, turn your heads away. Do not speak *to* her or in front of her." He opens the door. "But be *mindful* of her. She is slippery." He steps out and closes the door behind him.

I think about the interaction I've just had and the man I am being held captive by. Juri is cunning and manipulative with words. He is a good match for my powers, but he is still just a man. He cannot compete with me alone. I sit quietly and consider my next move. I need a plan to get out, find Gileaus, and save our lives.

After some time, I start sending feelings of affection and comradery to my guards who sit silently by my door. I send the emotions in small pieces, enough to tickle their senses, but not enough to be noticeable all at once. Finally, I clear my throat and ask for water. One of the guards stands and brings me a cup from the table. He holds it to my lips and helps me take a drink.

"Thank you," I say.

"You are welcome." Good. He is talking to me. He returns the cup to the table and resumes his seat. I start sending them both tired bodies. Their legs are twitchy and they need to move. Soon, both are up and pacing the room.

"Tell me," I say, "what kind of place are we in? Is it a castle or an estate or a government building?"

The guards pause their pacing and look at each other. They shrug at one another and turn to face me.

"It's an estate," the first guard says.

"Yes," says the second guard, "It sits on a hill in the country. We are far from any major city."

"The master only stays here on occasion. He has homes in several cities where he stays when he has government work to do," the first guard continues.

"Is your master here now?" I ask.

"No," the second guard replies. "But we expect him in a few days."

"Who is your master and what does he want with me?"

The guards look to one another again before answering. I send them another dose of comradery and the first guard speaks again.

"This is Master Abraxas' estate. He is the largest landholder in this region. He is working his way up in politics. He has his eye on Athens."

"Athens?" I ask.

"Yes," the second guard responds. "He wants to rule Greece."

An overenthusiastic politician. Certainly one of Spiro's enemies. Abraxas viewed Spiro as a threat to his political aspirations, so he had him killed? But why capture Gileaus? Gileaus said his father's enemies were trying to gain his favor. And why capture me? I am not of much interest to them.

"Alright," I say. "Then why does your Master Abraxas need me?"

Both guards shake their heads. "We don't know," they say together.

"I think you were just in the wrong place at the wrong time," the first guard offers. "You got caught in the fray." The second guard nods his head.

I just got caught in the fray. The other women and children were hiding in the house during the fighting. Alcmene and Heracles made it to safety before I found

Trapped

Spiro dying and Gileaus captured. Am I the only one of the household who was taken?

"Were there others who were captured, besides me?" I ask.

The second guard shrugs his shoulders. "Don't know. I just know you are here now with us."

That isn't good information to go on, but I would rather find a way out of here than to waste my time finding out all the details of the attack. If others were captured, I'll have to discover that and find a way to free them. Until then, the best thing I can do is get Gileaus and me out of here.

I start sending waves of sleep toward my guards. I want them to fall asleep easily when I am ready to make my move. I just need a little more information.

"Tell me," I say, "what is the layout of the estate? And where am I in relation to the young Master Gileaus?"

The guards both yawn and resume their places by the door.

"It's like we said," the first guard tells me. "This estate is huge. It's shaped like the shoe of a horse, almost wraps back on top of itself. There is a courtyard in the middle with a large olive tree in the center." He yawns and scratches his head.

"It's also a very tall building," the second guard interjects, "It goes far underground with lots of secret rooms."

The first guard stands and smacks the arm of the second guard. "You aren't supposed to tell people that," he says.

"I'm not telling anyone," the second guard defends himself as he rubs his arm. "It's just Athena. We can trust her."

I continue sending friendly feelings to my guards.

"I guess," the first guard says. "Your master Gileaus is only a few doors down," he says to me as he points to my right. He only has one guard outside. I watched over him earlier today."

Excellent.

"And how do you reach the exit from here?" I ask.

Guard one answers again. "There are stairs at the end of the hall, but I don't use those. Those are for servants."

More good news. An exit with fewer eyes on it.

"We use the stairway at the center of this wing. Those take us to the front courtyard."

Thank you, guard. That's all I need.

"I'm getting tired," I yawn out. "Could you untie me so I can sleep?"

The first guard looks at me. "That is definitely against regulations."

"No it isn't," I reply. "Captain Juri said to turn your head if I needed to relieve myself. Well, my body needs relief. I need sleep." The guard looks at his partner who shrugs his shoulders.

"I guess that's okay," he says. He comes over and unties my ropes. The throbbing isn't as bad this time, but my wrists and ankles are still red and sore.

"Thank you," I tell him when he finishes untying me. "I will just lie down on the floor to get some sleep." I send more desires for sleep into the room. Both guards yawn again.

"You don't have to stay up for me," I say. "I'll just be sleeping here on the floor. You can rest if you need to."

Guard two chuckles and yawns. "That's not a bad idea."

"Agreed," guard one adds. Both guards stretch and move around to get comfortable in their chairs. I lie on the floor, watching them as they fall asleep. I add all the rest I can into the room without making myself tired, and I wait.

Once the guards have been asleep for nearly half an hour, I get up off the floor. I keep my movements quiet at first, but nothing I do awakens the guards. I move toward them, stepping carefully. I reach the door and ask its favor to open as quietly as possible.

I wouldn't if I were you, it says to me in response.

I must. I don't have time to lose, I utter quickly.

I open the door slowly. It makes no sound.

Thank you, I tell it. There is no response.

I open the door wide and take my first step to freedom.

But I am greeted by Captain Juri, leaning against a banister, arms folded across his chest, three guards on either side of him.

"I was right," he says to me. "You are a slippery one."

A low chuckle echoes from somewhere down the hall.

Chapter 27

It's been three days since I tried to escape. In my second two attempts, I gave away too much about myself. Now they know that I work with minds. They know I have to see the person I am manipulating. My feet are in irons, my wrists are as well. I am heavily guarded. I still haven't seen Gileaus.

Someone is coming into my room. I don't look up. I don't care to see who it is. I don't care to try.

"Athena," Captain Juri breathes my name into my ear. "I have something for you."

I have grown accustomed to Juri's promises. They are always twisted. Always broken. I know to mistrust anything he says to me. I am a prisoner after all. He is my captor. I keep my eyes on the ground.

"Don't you want to see what it is?" he asks. My gaze remains on the floor. I will not look at him.

"This is very disappointing," he complains. "I have been looking forward to giving this to you. I thought you would like to have it."

Hunger growls within me, a fair warning to the man who is addressing me. I have been moved to a lower room. One of the secret rooms I learned about from my guards days ago. It is deep in the earth. No sound reaches me. My sound reaches no one. I am kept under constant vigil, always with at least five guards. I have done what I can to confuse or destroy all that I can. Any who succumb to my power are punished by Demetrius. The price they pay for their weakness. I am tired of sending men to torture within these walls. I am tired of straining to see into the souls of others. I am tired of fooling them all. I am hungry. I am weak.

"Well," Juri continues, "I suppose that a little quiet reflection on your part is understandable. I'll tell you what, I will give you the gift anyway. Think of it as a sign of friendship, my desire to be held in regard by you."

"Here," Juri reaches toward my neck. His fingers slip beneath the neckline of my robes. I shudder at his touch and brace myself. He finds what he is looking for and pulls slowly. My hamsa medallion pulls out of my robes, dangling from the tired necklace which has held it for years.

"I have a replacement for you, Athena," Juri continues. A replacement for the hamsa? Impossible. It would be death for him.

Death.

My mind takes hold of the thought and I give it all of my energy. If I can focus enough of my anger, Juri will die when he removes the medallion. Many will die, but he is the only one I care about. He is the one who has dealt with me the most treacherously.

I focus my anger as Juri's fingers snap the twine around my neck. The hamsa medallion slips from me, into his hands, and I look up into his face. It is only a split second before Juri realizes he has made a mistake. I see the fear in his eyes as the medallion drops to the ground. He reaches for the medallion, attempting to string it through the heavy chain he has brought, but it is too late.

My anger bores into his skull. I make him feel all of it. In a moment, he is screaming. He isn't the only one. Three more guards - more than I have ever affected before - fall to the ground, hands on heads, blood dripping through their fingers, screams echoing through the chamber. They are an unavoidable loss. Collateral damage for the person I intended most to hurt.

Captain Juri writhes at my feet. Another guard, safe for the moment from my power, leaps toward Juri, taking the necklace and medallion in his hands. From the corner of my eye, I see him lacing the chain through my medallion. He is too late, of course. Juri stops stirring, the other guards in the room also lay still. The remaining guard brings my medallion to me, placing the necklace over my drooping head.

A blinding light flashes through the room. I rise to my knees as the medallion burns against my chest then cools in an instant. I collapse on the ground and look down at my hamsa, my protector. No longer is it the wooden image I have grown accustomed to. Now, it burns gold, glistening in this dismal space. But in the center, where its eye resides, is a shining black pearl. She is my pearl. She has come home to me.

Chapter 28

I smell like smoke now, heat rising from the embers of my medallion. The black pearl burns against me. She protects those around me from the damage I can do. She is with me always. I can feel her presence, but she refuses to communicate with me. Instead, she has made herself a part of the thing that keeps me sane. Or as sane as someone like me could be.

Days go by before anyone speaks to me. The bodies are cleared from the room as I faint in the aftermath of my power. When I awake, there is a tray of food barely within my reach. I lunge for it, eager to fill my stomach with anything other than the gnawing hunger trying to eat its way out of me. I eat the bread, moldy. I eat the meat, rancid. I drink the milk, poisoned. I wretch on the floor and lie down on my side. Why torture me with a poison that won't even kill me? What do these people want from me? As much as I want to know, I also want to run from the answer.

Finally, a tray is sent in with a foaming pudding in a bowl. The pudding is green with bits of fruit and grain mixed inside. It looks like something I've had before. I eat it eagerly, hoping that an end to my suffering is near. The food is sweet, delightful and light. I swallow and have a flash of memory: water, ocean, green, octopus. Why are those memories haunting me here? I finish the pudding, too hungry to care if it kills me or sustains me. I drink the water that came on the tray. It is fresh and cool, unlike the water they have been giving to me. I lick the bowl clean and fall asleep on my filthy floor.

The next time I am given food, it is pudding again, the same as I had before. But this time, bread has been added to my meal. Not the stale, molding bread, but the kind of bread I used to make for the Spiro family. I learned it while I worked at the inn. I eat it eagerly, wishing there were more and that my stomach could handle it. Again, sleep overtakes me and I give in to rest.

This time when I awake, I am still in chains, but I am no longer in the same room. My clothing has been changed, my robes are clean. The smell of smoke has been washed from my body and hair. I am not laying on a stone floor, but on a cushioned bed. A bed nicer than any bed I've slept on in the past 6 years. The room is white. The floors are covered in rugs and animal skins. Pillows support my head. The walls are covered in paintings.

A small settee sits next to a chair in the corner. On the settee is the man I love most in the world. Gileaus. I reach for him, but my chained arms keep me bound to the bed. I say his name and his eyes lift to meet my gaze. His beautiful face is covered in bruises, marred by the butt of a whip, cut by its tip. His lip is split. His eyes are blackened. His hair is a matted mess of tangles and blood. What have they done to my Gileaus?

"What was that you said, Athena? Are you calling for your fiancé?" Every light feeling I felt as I saw my love turns to darkness at the sound of that voice. A low chuckle reverberates throughout the room. My blood runs cold.

"I must thank you, Athena," Demetrius says from the darkened corner behind Gileaus. "I have been wanting to get rid of Juri for years. You came along and took him on in less than a week. Really, how can I repay you?"

"Let Gileaus come to me." My voice is firm. My hands are trembling. My hamsa and pearl scorch my skin.

"Certainly, Athena," Demetrius says in his sneaky tone. He steps into the light of the room, grasps Gileaus by the shoulder, and forces him from the settee. I wince as Gileaus moans. He stumbles forward, falling face first on the bed by my feet. His clothing is torn and he is covered in filth. Bruises and dried blood cover his skin. I reach out and touch his cheek with my fingers. He turns his head to look at me through his swollen eyes.

"What have you done to him?" I ask Demetrius who is still chuckling in the corner.

"What have *I* done to him?" he laughs. "Why do you assume *I* did anything to him? Oh, okay I give up. It *was* me. But Athena, it worked. You're little Gileaus told me everything I needed to know to figure you out."

Gileaus moans, "I'm sorry, Athena. I had to make it stop."

I brush my clean fingers across his filthy, bruised cheek. "There is no need to apologize, my love. I understand." A tear falls from my face onto the white linens beneath me. I raise my eyes to the only other person in the room. Demetrius.

"There's no need to try any of your mind tricks on me, Athena," he says. "I've already alerted the guards that if I behave foolishly they are to kill you. Master Abraxas will know soon enough of your powers."

I look into Gileaus' face. His eyes are heavy. "Sleep, my love," I tell him. "Go ahead and sleep."

"Yes, *do* go ahead and sleep young master Gileaus," Demetrius mocks from the corner. "There is plenty for your fiancé and me to discuss. You don't need to be a part of any of it." He waves his hand in the air as though he is swatting away an annoying fly. My stomach turns at the sound of this evil man's voice. Gileaus surrenders to the heaviness and falls asleep at my feet.

"You mustn't be *too* upset with him, Athena," Demetrius continues. "After all, it *is* because of Gileaus that your quarters have been...upgraded." I look around the room, taking in the fine finishes and rich furnishings. Another tray of food waits next to me on the bed, the green pudding, clear water, bread, and even some meat. The smell hits my nose and all I want to do is feed it all to Gileaus.

"I don't understand," I tell Demetrius.

"Oh, then I shall explain it to you," he answers. He moves from the corner to the chair, placing his feet on the settee. "As you can see, the beatings and such that were carried out on your fiancé here did nothing to make him tell me about you. But once *you* were the one suffering, he changed his tone. He promised to tell me all about you if I promised to take care of you.

"But what kind of promise is that, I ask you? I needed evidence first, you know. I wasn't going to risk myself to *maybe* get information. So, your little Gileaus here told me about your medallion. He said that without it, you tend to kill the people around you. That's when I decided to give Juri the chance to test the theory for me.

"He had been talking about that stupid medallion since you got here. He said that a specimen as fine as you deserved a better looking chain about your neck..." Demetrius chuckles again. "Pardon me. I find chains about necks very entertaining, you know." My stomach turns as I listen to this torturer.

"Anyway, I acted as though a fine necklace was a great way to get you to open up. It took a while for the right necklace to arrive, but when it did, you did *not* disappoint. I cannot begin to tell you how giddy I was when I found out what happened. Poor Juri never saw it coming. Or did he?" Demetrius leans forward and looks me in the eyes. "Did you see fear in his face when you were killing him? It's a very unique expression. I like it."

I remain quiet. My stomach turns again. "You see, once I...*persuaded* your young Master Gileaus to tell us more about this mythical creature he called fiancée, I realized we have a real live sorceress in our midst.

"Of course, your man did hold out for quite a while. We knew some kind of power was used on our guards at the Spiro estate. At first, we thought it was Gileaus here, but efforts to draw the power out of him were futile. Then imagine our surprise when your guard let you go."

My cheeks burn at the memory of that first display of my powers in this fortress. Demetrius continues the monologue of his genius.

"We assumed Gileaus would have more information about you than you were sharing. We...*pushed* him quite a bit, but it wasn't until we pushed *you* that he was willing to give us any more information. Your love did well."

I look down at Gileaus, passed out at the foot of my bed. My heart breaks for him. For what he suffered for me. I touch his face again and let my tears flow freely from my eyes. Demetrius sits silently.

"Fix him," I order.

"Oh, the creature thinks to make a servant of me," Demetrius snarls from his chair. "I'm sorry, Athena. It doesn't work that way.

"Oh, who am I kidding? I'm not sorry. You see, you are going to serve *me* as *I* serve Master Abraxas. He is quite powerful, you know. Together, we will find a way to rule Greece."

"Who is Abraxas?" I ask.

"Didn't your guards already tell you, Athena?" his sneer is infuriating. I want to slap him. I hold back. Not for my sake, but for Gileaus'. "Master Abraxas is a politician of no small note here. Of course, he has bigger plans for himself, for Greece, for the world.

"He is traveling from the coasts of Jaffa just now on business, you know. I expect him soon. I expect you to be more... *pliant* when he arrives."

"I will do nothing for you," I say, a tremor in my voice. I *wouldn't* do anything for this evil being or anyone he works for. But everyone has their breaking point. Demetrius knows mine.

"Oh, I don't expect you to do anything for me, Athena," he says. "But I imagine there is a great deal you would do for our young Master Gileaus here."

My eyes flick down to my Gileaus. He is still unconscious, still numb from the pain that has been inflicted on him. It is true. I will do anything for him.

Demetrius chuckles his low, evil laugh from the chair and my eyes return to his. His eyes are filled with mirth. The man is pure evil, finding entertainment in pain and dominion over others. My eyes are filled with fire. Demetrius' eyes twitch once when he meets my gaze. The only thing sparing his life and mine in this moment is the man between us. Demetrius knows it.

"So long as you do as you are told, Athena, no more harm will come to your fiancé. Though I cannot promise that his accommodations will be as nice as yours, I can promise that the beatings will stop and his wounds will be tended to. You may see him once a week if you are a good servant. Anything further must be discussed with Master Abraxas."

"What does your Master Abraxas want me to do?" I ask him.

"Oh, he is not only *my* master, Athena," he replies. "He is yours now, too. And you are a very lucky girl for it. You and I will be bringing to pass a greater regime than the world has ever known.

"But as for his specific wishes, well, he will let you know that in time." There is quiet for a moment before Demetrius asks, "Do we have an understanding then, Athena?"

"We do," I whisper.

"Oh, excellent! You have 15 minutes to be with your fiancé. Though you may find the exchange a trifle one sided." Demetrius chuckles to himself as he leaves my room, closing the door behind him."

I spend the next 15 minutes trying to wake Gileaus and feed him. He barely moves, but I am able to get some of the water into him. That is a start anyway. If he doesn't return to me in one week's time in better condition, that will be the end for all of us. He will be cared for or I will kill us all.

Finally, several guards enter my room to take Gileaus with them. Fire fills my eyes.

"Treat him well!" I shout at the guards. They do not look at me at all but still lift Gileaus gently from my bed. He is laid on a pallet between them and carried from the room. Tears flow unchecked from my eyes as my love is taken from me.

A low chuckle echoes down the hall.

Chapter 29

In the ensuing days I am given the *opportunity* to show my powers. Demetrius is always in the room when I work. I start by growing small seeds into flowers. I move to levitation as I ask the items in my room to move for me. The objects have been in this place for a very long time. They have seen much. They pity me and are ever willing to do what I ask them. They know my life depends on it.

Paintings move from wall to wall. Animal skins on the floor animate and move about the room. A knife slices through my bed linens.

With each thing I do, I prove myself to Demetrius and to the guards who attend him. At first, the guards are silent. They are under orders to not communicate with me in any way. But eventually, even they cannot keep completely to themselves. The animated animal skins tap their arms and make them jump. Demetrius laughs at their discomfort. When the knife slices my bed curtain, a few let out a gasp. With each sound, movement, or interaction, the offending soldier is taken out and whipped. Demetrius always attends those. He demands perfection from his guards, but he takes pleasure when they must be punished for their imperfections. I would have driven him to slice himself to bits, but I haven't seen Gileaus yet. Everything hinges on Gileaus.

At the end of seven days, my heart beats with the excitement of the promised visit with Gileaus. I must know how he is faring since I have complied. Captain Juri regularly broke his promises to me or hid his intentions behind his requests. Demetrius enjoys letting me know his plans and demands. He horrifies me and he likes it.

"Well, Athena," he says on the seventh day. "You have done very well under these new circumstances. If only I had known, I could have had you in finer accommodations from the start."

"Where is Gileaus?" I ask. "It has been a week. You said I would see him once a week."

"This is correct," Demetrius says as he strokes the Grecian beard on his chin. "And see him you will. But first, I have a little surprise for you. A gift for your good behavior."

I'm not sure I want to know what kind of gift Demetrius has for me.

"Certainly you would like to be bathed before you see Gileaus," I feel my heart sink at the insinuation. Demetrius laughs, lightly. It is an unnerving change for him.

"No, no, Athena. *I* will not be bathing you. I don't run that line, you know. But I do have someone here whom I think you will actually allow to bathe you without burning them alive.

"You may come in now," he says to a person waiting outside the door.

At first, I don't see who he is speaking to. All I can see is the large amphora of water and towels they carry in their arms. Then I see the fingers. Fingers I would know anywhere because that is how we communicated. By sign. He has brought Namaah.

She enters the room and her face lights up in a bright smile when she sees me.

"Oh, bah," Demetrius says. "What is there to be so happy about woman? It is only the bathing of a girl." Then he turns his attention back to me.

"You see, Athena. Namaah here is a very valuable woman to have around. She cannot talk. She cannot tell anyone anything she hears or knows. Unfortunately, that means we didn't get any information from her about you or the Spiro family. But it also means that she will keep our secrets."

Namaah's eyes glisten while Demetrius speaks. He only knows we worked in the same household. He doesn't know how well we know each other. He doesn't know how we communicate.

"Mind you," he continues, "we still *tried* to get her to speak. I can't help myself sometimes. But I figured a little reminder of the home you left might help your spirits be even more willing for the cause.

"I'll leave you to it, then."

Demetrius leaves and closes the door behind him. Namaah rests the vase and towels on the settee and runs to my side. She takes quick stock of my condition. My wrists and ankles are healing from the ropes that held them bound for days, but they are still encased in metal. First, she cleans my wounds, gently. I feel her tenderness in every touch. Tears roll down her cheeks and we are both silent as she does her work.

I remember how well Namaah cared for me when I was first brought to the house of Spiro. Her care was the only connection I had to the outside world for so long. She is still my connection. Once she has finished cleansing my body, Namaah helps me into a fresh set of robes. She brushes my hair into a gleaming set of curls. She places braids at my temples, fixing them together at the back of my head. Once I am cleaned and dressed, Namaah moves to a dresser that sits under the window of the room. She looks carefully through the drawers and finds a case of oils. She opens them, smells them, and chooses several to mix together. She brings the mixture to me in a delicate, ceramic bowl from the dresser and applies the oil to my wounded wrists and ankles. The smell is soothing and the effect is calming.

I feel the strain of my situation melt in the care of my friend. The raw burning that has attended my body is cooled as the oils are applied to my inflamed skin. I am grateful for her knowledge and skill. Namaah has been a faithful servant to many by force. She is a faithful friend to me by choice.

When she finishes, Namaah sits next to me and touches my cheek. I see the pain and concern in her eyes. She wants to know that I am okay. I assure her that I am alright. The damage afflicted on me is limited to starving and beatings. I can bare those. I ask after Gileaus.

She has seen him. She tells me that his room is clean and he is being fed. She has been allowed to serve him and has helped to heal his wounds as well. He is safe for the time being. But she has also overheard Demetrius talking to his closest guards. He has plenty of plans for Gileaus if I don't do what he asks of me.

It was a reminder from a friend instead of a warning from a captor. Namaah has faith in me. But she also wants to be sure I understand the risks. I assure her that I will be careful.

I ask about any others that were captured in the raid. Spiro's footman was taken, but she hasn't heard his screams in days. She assumes he is dead. Rhea, Alcmenes and Heracles were all able to escape. One or two maids were captured, tortured for information, then sold. I am sick inside over the suffering of this household. There is a knock at the door.

Demetrius steps inside.

"Ah, I see Namaah has taken very good care of you, Athena. She will be rewarded." Namaah nods to Demetrius, ever the consummate servant - humble, obedient, respectful of her master's wishes and grateful for his kindnesses, no matter how little they come. I love Namaah. I could never be like her. I obey and behave so I can find a weakness, so I can conquer and escape.

"That will be all, Namaah," Demetrius continues. "Athena has another visitor."

Namaah kisses my forehead and rests her hand on my cheek, communicating so much with her eyes. She leaves the room and my heart quickens. I will see Gileaus. I will know how he is doing. And I will be clean and beautiful when he comes.

But Gileaus will have to wait.

Demetrius gives a low bow to someone outside the door and with a flourish, he motions for them to come in.

Again I do not see the person as they enter the room. Instead, I see fabric. It is a fine wool, the kind that is imported from India. The robe is long and trimmed in gold. But the main body of the garment is purple. I hold my breath as he enters.

His face is strong and broad. His nose is angular. His jawline is chiseled. His hair is in ringlets that settle at the base of his skull. He wears a small gold crown around his forehead and hair. His face, though handsome in the Grecian style, is filled with a contemptuous stare. He raises his chin in the air when he sees me. A large pendant of Jade hangs around his neck.

He may be an impressive man to anyone else in Greece. But to me he is the man in the purple robe. To me he is the man who killed my Dom.

"Master Abraxas," Demetrius says, still in his bow. "This is the young girl I told you about. This is…"

"Pearl," Abraxas finishes the sentence as he looks me in the eye. Demetrius stands and looks confused. He knows me as Athena and doesn't know how to correct his master.

"Her name is Pearl," Abraxas repeats. "Though who knows what name she has told you."

"She has been known as Athena, here," Demetrius says. There is a note of embarrassment and anger in his tone. He is embarrassed in front of his master. He is angry with me.

"Athena, interesting," Abraxas says aloud. "The goddess of wisdom and war. And tell me, Demetrius, has she earned that name?"

Demetrius is silent for a moment. To admit that I have outsmarted him makes him look the fool. To deny our interactions leaves him open to suspicion.

Abraxas laughs to himself and it is strange to hear someone laugh at Demetrius' discomfort.

"Don't worry, Demetrius," he says. "You don't have to answer." He looks about the room for a place to sit. He sees the chair in the corner but the settee by its side is still covered in the towels and vase used to bathe me.

"Hmmm…" he says. "Seating is a bit limited here."

Demetrius trembles and bows. "I will have the servant woman beaten for her carelessness," he says.

"Nonsense," Abraxas replies. "That will only make it harder for her to work tomorrow. Just have another chair brought and make sure the oversight is not repeated."

"Immediately, sir," Demetrius says with a bow so low his robes nearly slip from his shoulder. He leaves the room, running down the hall to find a chair suitable for his master. Abraxas walks to the side of my bed. He pauses there and regards me for a moment.

"I see so much of your brother in you, Pearl."

The fire in my soul burns its way to my heart. I let the flame of my hatred reach my eyes.

"Careful, Pearl," Abraxas says to me. "I understand there is someone who lives or dies by your movements."

I think of Gileaus and it is the only thing that keeps me sane in this moment. Demetrius returns to the room with a red, cushioned chair for his master. A guard following him has a golden footrest in his hands. The chair and footrest are set by my bedside so Abraxas can be close and comfortable as he interrogates me. He sits and leans back in the chair, his hands on the arms, and lifts his feet to the footstool. Demetrius stands quietly beside him, ready for any order.

"Some refreshment, Demetrius," Abraxas says. Demetrius bows and gestures to the guard in the room. The guard bows in return and leaves the room to find a servant to carry out the orders.

"It will be attended to immediately, sir," Demetrius says. Abraxas smiles at the ready faithfulness of his servant.

"Demetrius tells me you can do remarkable things, Pearl." I am silent and only return a stony stare to the murderer at my bedside. Demetrius, however, is anxious to have his master answered at all times.

"Yes, Master Abraxas," he says. "She can manipulate the elements and move them and make them grow just by the sheer force of her will."

"But that is not all you can do, is it Pearl?" Abraxas asks me.

Demetrius looks up at my face. His nervousness soon gives out to contempt for my silence. He raises his chin. His nostrils flare.

"Answer him, girl. Or you will not see Gileaus today," he says.

"Ah, Gileaus," Abraxas oozes. The sound of Gileaus' name on Abraxas' lips makes my blood boil within me. "I have heard his name mentioned. It sounds to me like he is the perfect motivation for our little sorceress. Have him brought immediately."

Demetrius bows low.

"At once, sir," he says. He runs from the room. I keep my lips sealed as Abraxas sits alone with me in the room. In a moment, the refreshment Abraxas asked for comes into the room, carried by Namaah. Our eyes meet and she can read the scream I send. Her breath is shallow and short as she serves the fruit and cheese and bread to Abraxas.

"I understand you are an accomplished cook as well, Pearl," he says to me as he eats the food. Namaah's eyes flick to mine as Abraxas addresses me as Pearl. It is the first time she has heard this name.

"Perhaps we will have you cook for us," Abraxas laughs to himself. "No, no. I only jest. You are too valuable to be sent to the kitchen. No, Pearl. I have much bigger plans for you."

Scuffling from the hall makes its way to our ears and we all look to the door. Demetrius enters, a broad grin on his face. Behind him, three guards bring in a fighting Gileaus. My heart leaps within me and I smile. If he is strong enough to fight, he is being cared for. Demetrius has kept his promise.

"Ah, this must be the young man in question," Abraxas says as he stands and walks to Gileaus. Gileaus kicks and thrashes.

"Gileaus, please!" I call out. "Please calm yourself or they will hurt you."

"No, no my dear," Abraxas assures me. "Gileaus remains unharmed as long as *you* do what is asked of you." Gileaus' eyes grow wide and he turns to me.

"Athena, you can't!" he calls out.

"I said I wouldn't harm him, but that doesn't mean I will tolerate his interference," Abraxas hisses. "Gag him." The guards wrestle a gag over Gileaus' mouth. All he can do now is send messages to me with his eyes. And they are pleading.

"Pearl," Abraxas says, turning to me, "I would like a demonstration of your mental abilities please." I pause only for a moment before answering.

"Who would you have me practice on? I will not enter Gileaus' mind," I assert.

"I assumed as much," Abraxas says. "I already have a substitute.

"You will practice on Demetrius."

Chapter 30

Demetrius is chained in the chair now. Two guards stand on either side of him. The smirk that I have seen so often on his face is hidden now. But it lurks beneath the surface. The guards are unnecessary. Demetrius will stay because he is going to enjoy this.

"Now, Pearl," Abraxas addresses me, "I have seen what can happen when you are set free. Theodis' body was buried on my land after you destroyed him." There is a flicker of fear in Demetrius' eyes. He didn't expect that my power to kill would be used.

"But I don't want to go that far...today," Abraxas continues. "Instead, I'd like to see you sway Demetrius' mind."

I look at Abraxas for an explanation.

"I have written your instructions so Demetrius won't know what is coming." Again, the smirk appears on Demetrius' face. Abraxas turns to his manservant who hands him a piece of parchment. Abraxas opens it, goes over its contents and hands it to me.

> *You will convince Demetrius that he has lost favor with me. You will turn his mind so any secrets he is hiding from me will be shared readily in an attempt to regain my favor and trust. Do well at the task and you will be rewarded.*

I set the paper on the bed next to me without looking at Abraxas once. Instead, my attention is focused on Demetrius. He is leaning forward in his chair, eager for the display coming his way. He hopes for physical pain, but he will receive none from me.

Instead, I reach toward him with my mind. The emotions I want him to feel exit my body in tendrils of green that only I can see. It is fear. Fear of discovery. Fear of death. Fear of loss of station. Fear that he has lost his place in the house of Abraxas. The smoky tendrils snake toward Demetrius, slithering through the air and into his mind and heart. At first, he smirks openly. But as the fear takes hold of him, his expression changes. The smile leaves. He raises an eyebrow, creases his brows, and begins to breathe with short, shallow breaths. Sweat beads on his forehead. He grows pale. He looks about him, darting his gaze from one person to the next. His eyes meet the guard at his side and he shrinks into the chair. All the while, my own eyes never leave his face. I send him every fear I have within me.

Finally, his eyes sweep the floor until they see the feet of Abraxas. Demetrius pauses as he focuses on the leather sandals before him. He takes in the gold border on the purple robe then brings his eyes and head slowly up the body of his master, absorbing the deep purple wool before him. As he reaches Abraxas' face, Abraxas raises his chin, his eyes downcast on Demetrius. Demetrius pulls at his chains, forcing himself to his knees, his guards pulling on his restraints to keep him by their side.

"Master, please," Demetrius says to Abraxas, "Please forgive me," he begs. His hands are in a prayer mode before him, fingers clasped - suiting a prisoner begging for mercy.

"What is it I am to forgive you of?" Abraxas asks. I pour deep blue tendrils of honesty into Demetrius that his only desire is to be completely open with his master.

"My lies, Master," Demetrius pleads openly.

"And what lies are those, Demetrius?"

"I am the reason Juri, Captain of the guard, is dead," he confesses.

"What is this?" Abraxas asks. "Was Juri not killed at the hands of this girl here?" He gestures toward me and Demetrius' eyes follow. His eyes meet mine again and the strength of the emotions I send to him is increased ten-fold. His face turns red and giant tears roll down his cheeks.

"She did kill him, Master," Demetrius sobs, "but it was my design. My device that brought it about. Juri was weak. I knew I could get more information with him out of the way." He turns his face back to Abraxas, relief rushing over him when he is no longer under the power of my stare. "Juri suspected that the medallion she wears has some kind of mythical power. I did not believe him at first, I thought him foolish, led astray by a young and pretty face. But once the guards fell prey to her mind games, I thought there must be truth to it."

"And?" Abraxas asks.

Demetrius darts a brief glance my direction, fear striking his face the moment our eyes meet. Good. Feel that fear, Demetrius. It is well deserved.

"I had to be sure of the truth before I made my plans," Demetrius answers. "I tried putting extra pressure on the boy. He is weak, Master. I knew there must be a way to make him talk."

"Do you mean Master Gileaus?" Abraxas asks.

Again, Demetrius risks a glance my direction. Again, his fear only grows. He turns, pale, back to Abraxas. He nods in the affirmative and Abraxas laughs openly.

"I have never seen you so afraid, Demetrius," he laughs. "Please continue."

Demetrius sinks lower to the ground, letting his hands sink into his lap, drowning them in the folds of his robes. His head bows beneath the weight of his fears. Yes, Demetrius, continue.

"I put extra pressure on the boy, Master, but he refused to speak." Of course he did. Gileaus wouldn't shrink before anyone, especially not if it meant saving me. "In his sleep one night," Demetrius continues, "his guards heard him whisper her name and something about the hamsa. It was enough evidence for me to try.

"Juri was taken by the girl. Her power was alluring to him, but her physical beauty only added to his tenderness toward her. He wanted to give her a gift, something to soften her heart toward him. I knew the fate of the estate guards and I knew the boy worried about the hamsa. So, I encouraged Juri in his desire to impress the girl. I know power is only strengthened in metal, so I told him where he could find a chain of iron and gold. One beautiful and unbreakable.

"I knew the strength of the girl was limited, Master. She hadn't killed any of the guards at Spiro's estate. She can only do so much at once. I instructed the guards who went in with Juri that day that if he should fall, they MUST get the medallion on her neck. I sent enough guards to finish the job."

"Indeed...," Abraxas muses to himself. "I believe it was Juri and three other guards who were killed in the incident, was it not?" Abraxas looks at me. I turn my eyes back to Demetrius.

"Yes, Master," he mumbles from the floor. "Three guards."

"And once you were sure of your plan to get rid of Juri," Abraxas continues, "how were you able to learn more about the girl?"

Demetrius shrinks backward now, shame rendering him mute for a moment. Abraxas nods to one of the guards. The guard shoves Demetrius in the back, forcing him to fall on all fours. He is shaken from his stupor and answers his master, head bowed, voice quivering.

"The boy would not cave to pressure, Master. I tried everything I knew to get him to tell me the strength of the girl's powers, but it was no use. He refused to speak. So, I decided to try a different tactic," Demetrius whispers. "I decided to put pressure on the boy by hurting the girl." Abraxas' face darkens.

"Did you?" he asks, low and rough.

"Yes, Master."

"What did you do to her?"

Demetrius is reluctant to share his part in my suffering, no matter the outcome. I am a valuable prisoner to Abraxas. If I am harmed, his plans are ruined. Not to mention I could easily destroy Demetrius. He looks at the ground as he moves his head in my direction. But he will not look me in the eye. The blue tendrils grow thick as I force the truth out of him.

"I had her food poisoned, Master."

Abraxas takes a threatening step forward, yelling, "You did what?! Don't you know you might have killed her?!"

Demetrius lays himself completely prostrate on the ground, begging for clemency.

"Please, Master. I know it was foolish. I wanted only to get the information you would need about the girl. I knew I wouldn't kill her. But I had to convince the boy."

In one fluid movement, Abraxas runs at the prone Demetrius, his foot making contact with the man's ribs. He then stomps on his back twice. I lose my concentration in the outburst, wincing at the sudden attack. A low chuckle escapes Demetrius' lips.

"Insane fool," Abraxas mumbles as he paces the room. "You could have killed the most valuable asset I have." I regain my composure and send the fear and honesty back into Demetrius. I want to know everything.

"The power to kill wasn't all I learned from the boy," he moans from the ground. Abraxas pauses his pacing.

"Well, what else did he tell you?"

"He was very anxious that I shouldn't hurt the girl. Once he saw that I would follow through with my threats against her, he started giving me information. The more he gave, the better she was treated."

Abraxas bends down, grabbing a handful of hair, lifting Demetrius' head from the ground.

"Out with it, man," he says. "What did he tell you?"

Demetrius rolls to his side, looking up at Abraxas standing over him. I cannot see his face, but I send as much honesty as I can in his direction.

"Well, she can manipulate minds, as you can see. She kills without the hamsa around her neck. She ran from her home in Argos when her twin died." Abraxas huffs at this information. He knows I ran when Dom died. He killed Dom.

"She worked at an inn for several years," he continues. "Until Spiro kidnapped her. She has been working in their home ever since." Demetrius is silent. He lies on the floor, breathing heavily. Everything is out. Everything he learned about me is out. I pull back the tendrils of emotion and fall back on the pillows. They are soft and inviting after all I have expended and all I have taken in.

Abraxas turns to face me.

"Nicely done, Pearl," he says to me. I do believe you really got him to tell the truth. I should beat him for his sneaky behavior, but I honestly think he would enjoy it too much." Demetrius chuckles from the floor.

"Get him out of my sight," Abraxas says to the guards. "Take him to the solitary dungeon room. Give him a bucket of water and leave him for a week." Then turning to me he says, "It won't kill him and he will enjoy the pain of starving, but at least I don't have to listen to him laugh over it."

The guards both bow to their master and bend down to take Demetrius. More guards help them carry his laughing, heavy body out of the room. But Abraxas isn't foolish. He still keeps several guards with him. He walks over to me, leaning over the pillows, and takes the chain of the hamsa into his fingers. He hovers over me so I can feel the heat of his breath on my hair.

"Juri may have been a fool to try to put this chain on you himself, but he certainly had the right idea," he says. His fingers are like ice in this hot room. My energy is depleted. I do nothing to pull away from his touch.

"Hmmm..." he says. "You were just a scrawny thing when I last saw you. I can see why Juri would want to impress you." I turn my head away, disgusted. "Oh, you don't need to worry," he continues. "I won't be using you that way. At least, not as long as you do your part." He drops the chain from his fingers and stands, moving toward the door. He stops near his manservant before leaving the room.

"Be sure to send an excellent meal to her, very hearty," he says. "Bring young Master Gileaus in to dine with her." Abraxas turns to face me.

"You and your fiancé will be fine, untouched, and protected, as long as you do what I ask of you, Pearl. You will rise to power *with* me. I want this for you. But know this, try anything, and I mean *anything*, and both you and Gileaus will pay for it."

I am too tired to respond. But his message comes through perfectly clear.

Chapter 31

Weeks go by and Gileaus is healing. As promised, we are fed and untouched. Abraxas brings in a couple of prisoners, seeking the truth from them. Nothing earth-shattering comes from these interviews. It is all petty grievances, the theft of a small item from Abraxas' estate, stealing from a fellow tenant farmer or servant. All of these infractions against Abraxas carry punishments: repayment for the item, a beating from the guards, whipping. Abraxas is exacting, but not as brutal as Demetrius.

I am becoming more familiar with my abilities. I can see truths before they are spoken, I can really read minds. I keep this new ability to myself. Each time I perform obediently, Gileaus comes to my room for a large meal. We are never alone so we cannot communicate freely. But Gileaus is not the only ally I have in this fortress. I have Namaah.

When Namaah is sent to feed me or bathe me, we exchange information silently. We are careful to hide our discourse from the guards in the room (there are always many guards). She tells me that Gileaus is being treated well, other servants who were captured have willingly entered as servants in the fortress. Those who refused were sold or put to death. Namaah is also allowed into the secret meetings Abraxas holds. As was the case with the Spiro estate, she knows more secrets than anyone else.

Abraxas has been meeting with emissaries from Sparta. The city I lived near when I worked for the inn has been a thorn in Greece's peace for centuries. They are known for desiring independence and power and are often at war with other Grecian cities. Abraxas hopes to sway the Spartans to support him in his bid for power. He is just another in a long line of politicians trying to overtake the history of the world. But Abraxas has been more successful than most. He has found the right combination of allies, sorcerers and secrets. I am not the only person with magic he has in his arsenal. There is someone in Jaffa who Abraxas visits periodically. Someone who advises him on what to do and when. Someone with power. He returns from these visits with potions and powders that he uses to his advantage. Namaah has not yet learned what these potions and powders do, just that they are brought into the fortress. But her eyes and ears are keener than most. They have to be. She will learn what is happening soon enough.

After months of doing everything Abraxas has asked of me, he is ready for me to lengthen my reach. He wants to let me out of my room.

"Understanding, of course, that Gileaus will remain with us while you are out," he says. "Do as you are told and he will continue to remain unharmed. Don't do as you are told and he will be hurt." Abraxas has learned the value of keeping promises, even to prisoners. I know I can trust what he says, no matter how evil, because he always does as he promises to do. I do not like being trapped by him, but I have no other choice. Until I can find a way to free Gileaus, Namaah and me, I cannot deny him.

"I'll be hosting a large party of guests at my home in a week," he continues. "You will be in attendance as my cousin. You will receive instructions as the evening moves on." I listen closely, hoping for some inkling of what he has in mind, what he has planned for his future and mine. "Namaah will help you get ready for the evening. I expect this to be a success, Pearl."

I nod, "Yes, sir." The chains that still bind my wrists make a clinking sound on my bed. Abraxas pauses, considering me. He steps closer to the bed, taking my hand in his, running his finger over the shackle on my wrist.

"I think we can remove these now," he says. "You've proven that as long as I have Gileaus, you are not a risk to me." He addresses a guard before leaving, ordering him to undo the cuffs I have been wearing for months.

When the shackles are removed, my skin is rough and red from the wear of the chains against my skin. It is strange to move about without the extra weight of my restraints inhibiting my movements. I feel weightless, like I am floating.

An image flashes through my body. Almost like a memory. It's more of a feeling than anything else: I am floating, weightless, in a sea of blue. The humid air around me is exchanged for water and my body is no longer mine, but the body of a girl who lives many years in the future. The memory is vague but powerful. My heart yearns for the freedom of that life, moving through water. My heart breaks for the memory and I cry out. The guards in the room shift in their sandals, gripping the clubs, swords, and daggers they carry at their sides. They fear me, but there is nothing to fear from the creature before them. I am not bent on destruction. I am seeing someone else's life and it brings me pain. I lay back on the pillows, turn my face to them, and I cry.

Trapped

As promised, Namaah comes to me at the end of the week, arms laden with fresh robes, perfumes, soaps, and oils. We spend our time quietly, with her bathing and cleaning me as she always does. She takes extra time with my hair, weaving braids and curls like the statues of Greek goddesses I am so familiar with. When I am ready, she places oils behind my ears and on my wrists. Oils that will keep me safe from any who would do harm to me. Perfume is placed on my robes. Braided gold bracelets cover my ankles and wrists, hiding the wounds that are still healing from my months of captivity. At last, I am ready - a powerful tool hidden behind a beautiful façade.

A fortress guard is outside my door, ready to escort me to the dinner. I haven't left my room in months. It is surreal to move about, unshackled. My legs are wobbly and weak. I did have some room to stand on the bed and to move to my chamber pot, but my movements have been so restricted, that using my muscles again will take practice. The guard offers his arm to me as we make our way through the building.

When we reach the entrance to the prison where I have been kept, another guard opens the door wide. He looks at my own guard with pity. He has heard the rumors and knows what I am capable of. He is glad he is not in the post of his fellow officer. My guard stiffens as he passes by his comrade and we head into the courtyard where a small cart waits to take us to the main house. I inhale a deep breath and relish the feeling of cool, fresh air in my lungs. I hum lightly and whisper my greetings to the air around me.

Good child, it says to me, *we have missed you and worried for you. We have been in touch with our sisters from within the fortress. Tell us, are you alright.*

I am, I whisper back. *Though I am not where I would wish to be, I am better than I was.*

If there is any way we can help you, we are ready to do it. We know much about the comings and goings of this place.

I thank you, I tell the good air in response, *For tonight, just being able to be out in the open with you and feel you heal my lungs is enough.*

Pleasure rushes over me as the air sends a breeze through my hair. Air plays a vital role in the lives of humans. It, too, wants to be appreciated and cared for. It is happy when it serves well.

I send my gratitude into the air and allow it to hug me as my guards help me into the cart. Two more guards await us when we sit. I am being tested tonight, but I am not yet trusted. Abraxas will not risk losing me.

The ride to the main house takes some time. My eyes move through the dim light of evening, taking in my surroundings. The hills are rolling and dotted with the wispy trees that make up the Grecian landscape. There are few buildings here besides the fortress. I turn to stare at the great building as I leave it behind for an evening. It is two stories tall from the outside. I cannot tell how many levels lie beneath the surface of the earth that houses it. A spiked fence surrounds the whitewashed structure. The fence is made of tall wooden posts, sharpened on the tops and guarded by a dozen men or more. Torches illuminate just the opening gate to the courtyard. All else is encased in shadow.

The fortress is concealed in a valley, surrounded by a copse of trees. Once we have traveled a mile, I can see no evidence of the compound's existence except for the road we are traveling on now. There are no workers in fields, no farms, no orchards and I wonder how much land Abraxas owns to be able to support his life and still have a hidden fortress.

My guards are quiet as we travel and that is just as well. I want my senses alert to the world around me, not distracted by the conversation of humans. We ride in the quiet, my guards eyeing me, me watching the countryside, until I finally see the signs of outlying buildings and farms. We pass through rich fields laden with fruit and then an orchard filled with the most beautiful olive trees I have ever seen. I wonder if the olive business is what brought Abraxas to the home of Grandfather in the first place. These trees are of the same variety as Grandfather's, but a better quality than what we grew in Argos. Knowing the frequency Abraxas came to visit Grandfather, I know we are within a hundred miles of my childhood home. I feel the tugging of my heart pulling east.

We pass through smaller farms and begin to see the frequency of buildings consistent with a large estate. Homes for servants and tenant farmers dot the land. They are clean and well maintained. Field hands returning home look up as our cart passes. Many begin to raise their hands in greeting, but turn away when their eyes see the guards. They are eager to be warm and welcoming to one another, but they know when to keep to themselves. Some of the younger men, risk a second glance when the cart passes. One sends me a smile. I give him a small smile back. It feels good to have new human interaction.

The cart slows and we enter a wide path lined with olive trees. The fruit is perfect, the best example of what Abraxas' estate creates. The lane opens to a tall, clay, whitewashed wall bathed in light. Torches line the outer wall of Abraxas' home. There is nothing hidden here. Except for me.

The cart passes through the gate and into the courtyard. The soft plodding of the horses' hooves turns to a crunch as we roll into the courtyard. Small pebbles fly outward from the wheels of the cart. We pull up to the house, my guard leaps from the cart and again offers his arm to me. I reach for it and place my hand on him for support as I jump down from the wagon. The remaining guards alight from the cart and follow us through the large doors of the grand estate.

Trapped

I am not the first guest to arrive at the home. I am probably the last. Laughing and talking voices reach the foyer. My guard leads me toward them. We are arriving just as the group is heading into the great dining room.

"Ah, Pearl," Abraxas calls when he sees me entering the room. "I am so glad you finally made it." He moves through his guests like a purple snake sneaking through the dried white and gold grass of the hillside. He reaches me, embraces me, and kisses my cheek. I shiver at his touch. His eyes meet mine and he pulls away. He holds my gaze for a moment and I hold his, a quiet assurance that I will behave. "Ladies and gentlemen," he announces to the room, "this is my dear cousin, Pearl, who will be staying with me for a time. Do show her how lovely you all are, won't you?" Happy mutters echo throughout the dining chamber as his guests greet me. Before he leaves my side, Abraxas, squeezes my hand, depositing a small piece of paper within. I grasp the proffered item and hide it within the bands of gold than encircle my wrists.

Abraxas leads us through his gathered company and takes me to a chair beside a grey-haired man in older robes.

"This is Tassos," Abraxas introduces the old man. "Tassos, my cousin, Pearl." The old man bows to me and extends his hand to the open seat beside him.

"I am glad to meet you, Pearl," he says. "I would be pleased to have you as my company this evening." His voice is ragged and old, quavering with each syllable. He has a gentle shake to his body, one of the many markers of old age. I take the seat next to him and my guard stands behind me. Tassos is occupied in getting his robes arranged in his lap and is searching the table for the food. I take the opportunity to open the note Abraxas gave me.

Tassos is to see snakes on the table

The message is clear and I start my work. I don't know what Tassos has done, who he is, or why Abraxas wants him to see things, but I have a job to do. I have lives to save.

The wine is being poured in goblets all around the table. I look at my plate and send tendrils of black toward Tassos. The tendrils make their way to Tassos' ears and slither into his mind. I send images of snakes to his vision. He sees them slithering down the table toward him.

"Ahhhh!!!!" Tassos screams as he jumps up from the table. "The snakes! Abraxas, the snakes!" He points at the table, screaming as he runs into the servers behind him. General pandemonium breaks out as the women and several men scream and scramble from the imagined snakes. I remain in my seat.

"Tassos!" Abraxas yells as he runs to the side of his guest. "What do you mean? What snakes?"

Tassos is pointing wildly, his hair a disheveled mess around his head. "What do you mean, 'What snakes?!'" he yells at his host. "They are covering the table! Have you lost your sight, man?!" The group grows quiet.

"Tassos," Abraxas places his hand on his guest's shoulder, "Tassos. There are no snakes on the table."

Tassos jerks his head around the room. The men that never left their seats are looking at him with widened eyes, the women whisper to one another.

"The snakes!" he yells again, pointing to the table. "Do none of you see the snakes?!" He is shaking wildly now, from his head to his sandals. His eyes are darting around the room. He grows silent and turns his face to Abraxas.

"Come, friend," Abraxas says. "Let me show you to a room where you may lie down. Your day has been long and your mind fatigued. You must rest."

Tassos is shaking and mumbling to himself, glancing furtively to the snake-covered table as his host leads him from the room. The remaining guests return to their seats, talking in low tones to one another. All around me I hear bits and pieces of their conversation. "He is growing old and senile." "What does this mean for the vote next week?" "He must have been poisoned." "The wine hasn't reached him yet." "He is too old to keep leading." "He cannot continue in this manner."

So, Tassos is a political rival. I see. Abraxas has no mercy for his political opponents. With me here, he doesn't have to do anything as reckless as he did to Spiro. He can control the people quietly and obtain his desires through me. I sit quietly throughout the rest of the meal. I eat the food without noticing its flavor. My mind is running through the events of the evening and what they reveal about my captor. He wants power. He is using me to get it. It is less a loss of life than the attack on Spiro's estate. I may hate the man, but if this kind of subversive behavior will win him his elections with less life lost, I will continue to do it. That is, until I can find a way to freedom from his power.

Chapter 32

Abraxas won the election. It was a local election and Tassos was his greatest opponent. Abraxas played the part of the grateful student until Tassos went mad. I stayed in the home for the week, guards in the halls outside my door. Tassos continued to see snakes.

The election was a success and I performed my part well. Abraxas rewards me with an afternoon lunch, outside, with Gileaus. We are heavily guarded. Gileaus' wounds have healed completely and he is being fed and clothed well. Abraxas has been spending time with him in quiet meetings.

"He is offering me a place at his side, Athena," Gileaus tells me as we finish our meal. "He wants me to join him in the political arena."

"After what he did to your family?" I ask. One of the guards near us shifts his feet and glares at me. I will be punished if I am not careful with my words.

"My father was going to lose his place in the political world anyway, Athena," Gileaus says to me. He is playing with a blade of grass as he stares out over the rolling hills beyond the fortress walls.

"But he was your *father*," I don't know why he needs the reminder. Is he seriously contemplating joining this man? "Are you honestly thinking of joining Abraxas?" This time several guards turn their glares on me. Gileaus doesn't notice them. Or he chooses to ignore them. He is silent for a moment before answering.

"It could be good for us," he finally says. "For you and for me." He turns his face to me. His eyes are tired, defeated. "We could marry and have the life we wanted. We could be free."

I search his eyes, hoping to see something hidden there. But nothing is hidden. His thoughts are clearly written on his face. He is weary. He is overwhelmed. He is hopeless. I reach my hand out and lace my fingers through his.

"But what do you *want*?" I ask him. "We made plans to run away before all of this. To leave the political world your father lived in behind. To be on our own. We can find a way to anything, Gil. This doesn't have to be our path." He pulls his hand away and looks again over the fields.

"I know we had plans, Athena, but our world has changed. *I* have changed." I shake my head, thinking of all my love has been through. He was willing to leave his family for me. He was kidnapped for his father's sake. He has been beaten and tortured to save me. What more can I ask him to do? I reach for his hand again.

"Alright," I say. "If this is what you really want, I will follow you." Gileaus turns his face toward mine, searching for something.

"Do you mean it, Athena? Do you really mean it?"

"Do you doubt it?" I ask. "I love you, Gil. You were willing to give up your world for me. If you need this to bring you peace, how could I say no?" A small smile flickers across Gileaus' face. He seems relieved but haunted at the same time. He has been through so much. I don't know how to free him from these past months or give him back the dreams he used to have. I can only hope that on this road together, he will realize this is a dangerous choice and choose to run. If only we can.

He reaches his face toward mine and brushes a gentle kiss across my lips. It is light and fleeting, the first time our lips have touched since being brought here. We have always been guarded or bruised or bleeding. I have missed the warmth of his kisses.

He turns away again and stares silently across the hills. A short while later, our guards come to break us apart. Our reward time is over. I say a silent prayer that Gileaus will be able to open his eyes soon. How could we possibly live willingly in a world created for us by a monster? Abraxas is manipulating our every move and decision. How do I convince Gileaus that this is what is happening? How do I free us both?

∞ ∞ ∞

With Gileaus' decision to join with Abraxas comes more freedom. He is allowed a room nearer to my own and we are allowed time together daily. We are still never alone, however, so our conversations are limited to what can safely be said in front of a guard. I try to send him notes through Namaah, but they are returned unopened. He tells me he has nothing to hide from anyone. He doesn't want to sneak around if he doesn't have to. It's safer that way.

I continue to create hallucinations for Abraxas' political opponents. It is happening so frequently, however, that some are beginning to suspect him.

"I must have some political success without you," he tells me one evening as I eat. "I must travel again next month. I must go without you." He paces the floor, running his fingers through his hair. I watch him pace, wondering at his distress. He has traveled without me before. I am no longer bound and haven't been for some time. He cannot worry that I will betray him at this point. He stops pacing and turns to face me, his hands clasped behind his back.

"There are still things you can do to serve me while I am away," he says. He still doesn't understand that I don't serve him, I survive him. "You may not like what I ask of you, Pearl, but continue to serve well and you will continue to be rewarded. Fail me and see the results." I shake my head.

"Why do you threaten me?" I ask. "For months I have done all you have asked of me. Why do you worry now? What is it that you ask?" He continues to stare at me and I continue to hold his gaze. His eyes flick toward Namaah who is clearing away the dishes from my table. She knows his plans. She is a quiet observer of everything that happens here. Abraxas raises the corner of his mouth in a crooked smile. He feels confident that his secrets are safe and that he is the master puppeteer.

"You will do as you are instructed," he says again. "I will deliver messages to you through Namaah. She cannot divulge anything in them because she cannot read and she cannot talk."

"And if I have anything to tell you?" I ask.

"When I want information from you, I'll ask for it," he says. He turns on his heel and leaves the room in a flourish of purple cloth. I wait for a moment before turning to Namaah.

"Do you know what is going on?" I ask in our sign language. She averts her eyes and checks the door. A single guard remains posted there.

"He travels to another source of magic," she signs in return, "one even more powerful than you. He fears that you will turn on him despite your love for Gileaus."

I would gladly turn on him, I think to myself. All I need is to find a way to make Gileaus turn with me.

"What does he want me to do?" I ask with my hands. Namaah sighs.

"He wants power in all of Greece. In all the world," she signs to me. "He fulfills favors for others and seeks your help with those favors."

"What favors? Who is he doing business with?" Someone stirs outside my door and Namaah and I both turn our heads. There is a knock.

"Who is it?" I call out.

"The only other man allowed to visit your room," Gileaus calls in return. I smile and sigh. Namaah quickly piles the used dishes on the tray and heads toward the door. She opens it and Gileaus takes a broad step inside. Namaah heads out the door and down the hall. My eyes linger on her disappearing form, wondering what she knows.

"I thought you would be more excited to have me in," Gileaus says as he walks toward me. I stand from my chair and embrace him. Though I am granted more privileges, I am still confined to my room most of the time. When I am at the main house, I stay there unless an event is taking place. Gileaus has earned more freedom. I wonder if that same privilege will ever extend to me.

"I am come to bid you farewell, my love," he whispers into my hair as he brushes soft kisses against my cheek. I pull from him and look up into his eyes.

"What do you mean?" I ask. "Where are you going?"

"Master Abraxas has invited me to join him on his upcoming trip," he tells me. *Master* Abraxas. It is a sound I still don't like to hear from the lips of the man I love. He has been brainwashed and really thinks he is serving that monster, that *we* are serving him together.

"Join him?" I ask. "Why does he want you to join him? We are still his prisoners."

Gileaus stiffens and creases his brows together in disapproval.

"I don't like it when you say things like that," he says.

"What am I supposed to say?" I hiss. "That we are here willingly, joyfully even? Gil, Abraxas has had us here under coercion for almost a year. We do not stay here by choice. We do it by force!"

"Athena," he scolds, "you promised me that if this is what I wanted, you would support me in it."

"Gil, that was a promise to help the man I love find freedom, to help him become who he wanted to be. You haven't become anything you have ever wanted. You have only been forced to believe in something that isn't a part of you. Abraxas is using you, Gil. He has complete control over your life." The guard outside moves closer to the door. Gileaus lets go of my arms and turns from me.

"I am not his prisoner, Athena," he says in a voice so low I almost miss it.

"Gil," I begin, but he cuts me off.

"I am not like you," he says. I stop in my place.

"What do you mean?"

"Master Abraxas can trust me because I have pledged my loyalty to him. I have been able to come and go as I please for many weeks."

"Pledged loyalty to him?" I ask. "Did you have to sign some paper that only seals you to him even more? Gileaus! He is *using* you!"

Gileaus spins toward me.

"*I* am not the one being used, Athena. *You* are the one he must force to do as he wishes. *I* am willing to do what he asks of me. I always have been."

"What do you mean you always have been?" I ask quietly. My guard enters the room.

Trapped

"Master Gileaus," he says. Gileaus shakes his head and turns from me, leaving to follow his new master.

"Gil!" I call after him. My guard stops me, sword drawn across his chest. I look at his weapon, puny in his hands compared to what I can do to him. My eyes flash anger and the guard stands taller. I look out the door and watch my Gileaus disappear down the hall.

Happy birthday to Athena.

Chapter 33

I spend the next week in my room. Gileaus kisses my cheek before he leaves on the journey with Abraxas. I am frozen, thinking about Gileaus. Thinking about Abraxas. Thinking about myself. What is in my future? Where am I headed? What will Abraxas ask me to do? What does Gileaus expect from me? It isn't long before I learn the answer to at least one of those questions.

Late one night, I hear screaming and fighting from down the hall. Someone has been captured. That hasn't happened much since Gileaus and I were taken from Spiro's estate. I get up from my bed and open my door to get a view of what is happening.

The one guard left by my room glances at me as I step through my door. I peer over the balcony and see a dozen guards bringing in a group of people. I see an old man, an old woman, and three younger women. It is a family. Mother is screaming for her daughters, daughters are screaming for their mother, father is shouting epithets at the guards hauling them in. One of the guards, a stronger one I recognize from my own capture and time in interrogation, has grown tired of the man's swearing. The guard spins around, his arm held out, and backhands the old man across the face. The old man's head spins back and his body falls to the floor in a motionless heap. His daughters and wife all scream out to him.

I send tendrils of inquiry to the man's body and mind. He is not dead, he is unconscious. I reach out to the wife and daughters, calming their fears so they can see that their husband and father is breathing. Their screams turn to quiet sobs as they are led down a hall. The guard who dealt the blow is standing over the old man, his arms akimbo at his side.

"Wake up, you old fool!" he shouts. The other guards mumble something I cannot hear. "Oh, he can hear me!" the guard yells back at them. "He is just pretending. Trying to get us to pick him up! I'll get him up!" The guard pulls his leg behind him and swings it at the abdomen of the old man. I scream out at the top of my lungs.

"Stop! The man is unconscious! You will only hurt him!" The guard stops midair with his kick, plants his foot on the ground and turns his angry face on me. His dark eyes are on fire and his face is growing red beneath his full beard.

"What did you say?" he growls at me.

"The man is unconscious. You are only going to hurt him. Abraxas will want him for questioning."

The guard snaps his fingers, points at the old man and jerks his head toward the hall. The remaining guards move to pick up the old man. They carry him down the hall that leads to the dungeons. The angry guard ascends the stairs toward me. My own guard moves to my side, hand on dagger, sword drawn. This is the first time a guard has protected me here.

"What are you doing, you fool?" the angry guard addresses the man at my side.

"My orders are to watch the prisoner," he responds. "That includes protecting her." The bearded guard snarls and flares his nostrils.

"Stand down, man," he barks. "I outrank you and I will not be disobeyed!" My guard shakes his head from side to side, remaining silent. The angry man before us draws his sword. I will not allow my guard to be hurt for protecting me.

I reach out to the man's mind with all the intensity I have. What he sees is a wide open field, green grass, billowing clouds and soft, white sheep grazing all around him. He shakes his head to clear his mind, but he is nowhere near strong enough to combat me. I keep sending out the light green and pink tendrils of peaceful vision. The guard stumbles around, trying to make his way around the sheep. The sheep bump into him and he pushes them away with his legs, kicking harder and harder. My own guard and I have backed away and watch as this man succumbs to my vision. Soon he is swinging his sword, trying to stab the sheep, but every time he strikes one, it pops in a flurry of white and becomes three sheep.

"Woman!" he shouts at me, searching for the person he cannot see. "I'll have you hanged for this!" he swings his sword and rushes forward, but I am not where he thinks I am. He runs straight into the balcony railing, flipping over its edge. His feet fly into the air behind him and he screams as I pull the vision away from his mind. It is a split second, but it is enough for me to see the fear register in his eyes. He lands on the stone floor beneath us, his own sword beneath his neck, cutting a gash that he cannot recover from.

The commotion raises an alarm throughout the fortress. My guard grabs me by the wrist. I turn my face to him. He is so young. I am taken by surprise at the youth in his eyes. I am not paying attention. Before I am aware, I am surrounded by guards, my own guard still holding me by the wrist. All are quiet. There is a protocol for when I misbehave. These men have practiced and they know what to do. I don't know the protocol. This is my first act of misbehavior since my chains were removed.

The guards close in around us. Their daggers are drawn, ready to be used in a moment. I don't need the threat. I need the experience. If I know their protocol, it can help me find a way out of this place. I square my shoulders and raise my chin.

Trapped

We stand still for a few moments until they are sure I will not do anything to harm them. They are prepared to strike me if I do. Not to kill me. I am too valuable.

Hands from multiple guards grab the entire length of my arms and I am led in a group huddle down the stairs. It is a slow process to move so many people at once without falling. As we reach the lower level, I turn my gaze to the dead body beneath the balcony. Only one person is near him. Namaah. She is holding a tray of food for my midday meal. Her eyes meet mine, concern is written all over her face. With my arms bound, I cannot sign to her. She tries to follow the group, but a guard pushes her back.

"No food, woman!" he grumbles. He holds her back while the rest of us head down the hall to the dungeons.

Soon, the crying of the family taken earlier reaches my ears. The daughters have been locked in a cell together. The mother and father are not on this level. We move past the cell and head further into the secret hallways and rooms of the fortress. My eyes and ears and mind are alert. I want to know this place inside and out. We travel further down. A low chuckle reaches my ears as the crying behind me fades. Demetrius. I haven't seen his disgusting face since I played with his mind for Abraxas.

"What have we here?" he asks as he laughs at our group. "Has Mistress Pearl been naughty? Does she need to be punished?" he rubs his hands together, looking into my eyes with delight. I send him a quick image of his pleading on the ground before Abraxas. His smile falters for a moment. He raises an eyebrow, his nostrils flare.

"You can't hurt me here, girl," he snarls. "This is *my* domain. If you are here, you have been very bad and you are in *my* power. No questions are asked of what happens here."

A door behind Demetrius creaks open. Two guards come from the room carrying the captured mother in their arms. She is lifeless. I reach my mind out to hers. Nothing. She is dead. Anger flares within me and I turn my gaze to Demetrius. He chuckles.

"Don't look at me that way, Pearl," he mocks. "It wasn't even my fault. Her guards scared her to death before I could even get down here." He lets out a sigh. "It's a pity really. I was looking forward to a husband and wife set. They are much more fun." He smiles. "But never mind. There are daughters." I yank against my guards as Demetrius disappears up the stairs behind me. I scream and pull. I will NOT let him hurt those women! I send out visions of snakes to the guards, purples tendrils reaching into their minds, but there are too many of them. The guards I reach fall backward. The rest push me into my cell. Several more guards fall as I reach them with my mind. I may not be able to get them all, but I will not be shackled now without a fight. I get half a dozen guards away from my cell. All of the guards are shouting. More guards pour into the cell. Soon, I am bound and chained to an iron plate in the floor. The chains are so short I cannot stand. The guards rush out of the cell, bolt the door and disappear. The only light I am left with is what sneaks in through the door's window. The flicker of torches pushes its way into the darkness.

A chamber pot is close enough for me to reach, but the smell tells me it has not been emptied in some time. I sit in my new prison and wait. I do not know how long I will be here, but I know they will not kill me. I am determined to make their lives miserable.

∞ ∞ ∞

I lose count of the days, but I am sure weeks have passed. I do my best to keep track of time based on the timing of my meals. But when I am particularly egregious with my taunting of their minds, meals are missed. The more I hear screams from down the corridors, the more I mess with their minds.

This is one of those days when I miss a meal. I had four guards dancing in my cell when they were supposed to be changing shifts. It was entertaining for me, but after several hours, their superiors arrived. The guards were beaten, I was slapped, and my meal never came. I am getting used to the hunger pains that toy with my stomach.

My door opens and I look up distractedly. It is Gileaus.

"Gil!" I shout when I recognize him. He is to my side in seconds.

"What happened, Athena?!" he asks as he unlocks my shackles.

"I killed a guard," I tell him. He helps me to my feet, but my legs are weak. Gileaus has to support my weight as he leads me to a chair outside my cell. I am very aware of my appearance and smell.

"What do you mean you killed a guard?" he asks as he sets me down. "What were you thinking?"

"He was beating a man, Gil," I whisper in anger. "It was an old man. He would have killed him. When I shouted at him to stop, he came after *me*. I was just trying to keep him away from me, Gil. He fell over the balcony railing and his sword cut his throat." Gileaus stands erect for a moment, thinking.

"It shouldn't matter then," he says. "I'll talk to Master Abraxas. I'm sure he'll let you out of here." His words are flat, unfeeling. The blood in my veins runs cold.

"What do you mean 'he'll *let* me out?'" I hiss. "Why aren't you screaming right now? I was locked in a cell for weeks, Gil!"

"You killed a man, Athena!" he yells at me. "Did you honestly think you would be allowed freedom after something like that?"

"It was an accident and he was after me!" I yell back. "They have been denying me food. I couldn't even stand up in that cell, Gil! Why are you angry *at* me instead of *for* me?!" Hot tears sting my eyes. My nostrils flare with each breath. "None of this would have happened if you were here, Gil, or if you would have taken me with you. Why did you leave me here? You left me for that monster!"

Gileaus stands straighter and pulls his hand away from the chair. Away from me.

"Master Abraxas isn't a monster, Athena," he says. "He is helping me make my way in the world. I have been creating a future for us. You promised to support me and when I get home I find that you have killed a man and have been torturing the guards. What would you like me to feel? You are the one who has betrayed *me*."

I lower my head, shaking it in disbelief. Gileaus, my Gileaus, feels loyalty to the man who captured us and tortured us.

"Gil," I whisper, "what has he done to you?" Gileaus huffs and shifts his feet.

"Master Abraxas was good to me on this trip, Athena," he tells me, "I'm sorry for my harsh words. I won't lock you back in the chains, but you will have to stay in the cell until I can talk to him."

I am numb inside and out. I don't understand what has happened to my fiancé. He is treating me like an ignorant child, not like a man in love with me. He hasn't embraced me or kissed me once. My joints are stiff as Gileaus leads me back inside of my cell. He brings the chair in so I have a place to sit and he closes the door behind me. The click of the lock rings in my ears, stabbing me through the heart.

Chapter 34

I have slept for days. I have a cot now with fresh linens and a clean chamber pot. Meals are being brought to me at regular intervals. All of this because Gileaus is home and has pull with my captor. But I have gratitude for none of it. I have been betrayed by the man I love. Gileaus hasn't been down to see me since the first day he arrived. Various guards have been sent as emissaries to deliver the new goods and to talk to me. I listen to none of it. I don't care what they are telling me. I don't care what they want.

A gentle hand shakes my shoulder. I open my bleary eyes. The person is blurry for a moment. I blink to see better and Namaah, my Namaah, comes into focus. She smiles at me and I sit up to embrace her. I cry into her shoulder for several minutes while she strokes my hair with her loving hands. She has brought fresh robes and a basin and vase of water for washing. I cry silent tears as she cares for my physical needs like she has done for years. When I am clean and calm, we sign.

"My Athena," she signs to me. "I have been so worried for you since you were brought here. I have kept my ears open for news of you. Why do you eat nothing?"

"I can't," I sign in return. "Gil..." I tear up again.

"Young Master Gileaus has been trying to get Master Abraxas to release you from this cell," Namaah assures me.

"Why does he not come to me?" I ask. "Why does he seek the favor and permission of a monster? A monster who captured the woman he says he loves and is devoted to?! Why does he not speak to me of escape?"

Namaah sits still on the edge of the bed. Her hands are folded in her lap. She doesn't know what change has come over Gileaus any more than I do. She doesn't know what could change the heart of a young man so much.

Namaah places her hand on mine, stroking the back as a mother would. "Let me feed you," she signs. "Let me make you strong and we will work together to free you from this place."

"Free *us*, Namaah," I sign back. "Surely we can both be freed."

Namaah nods as a tear rolls down her cheek. "Yes. Us."

I let Namaah feed me broth and bread. I have taken so little food in the past several days. This meal feels at first like it will make me sick. But as we are slow and careful, I begin to feel better. There is nothing we can say while she feeds me. Her hands are occupied. We will wait.

When the meal is finished, Namaah carefully cleans my face. I drink cool water to rinse my mouth. I am tired from the warm food. Namaah promises to stay with me. She holds my hand and sways to a tune that only she can hear and she can never sing. I close my eyes and imagine my own tune and drift off again.

When I wake up, Namaah is still sitting on the edge of my bed. But her head is drooping and her eyes are closed. Her breathing is slow and even. Her head has only a few gray hairs entangled in the masses of curly black. Her skin has aged. She has lines of worry around her eyes and across her forehead. Her hands are scarred from years of abuse and work. The scar across her cheek has darkened with time. I feel guilt when I think of her past. I have never asked her about it and she has never offered. But what kind of friend knows so little about someone who gives so much for them.

I reach out and squeeze Namaah's hand. Her eyes open and she raises her head. She gives me a small smile which I return.

"And how do you feel after your rest?" she signs.

"I feel better, Namaah," I return. "And you? How do you feel after your rest, my friend?" She smiles when I call her friend and pats my arm gently.

"I am always grateful for extra rest," she tells me. Her smile fades and her eyes grow serious. "Are you ready for a conversation?" she signs to me.

"Is there something you have to tell me?" I sign in return.

"I have had my ears open for news of you, but I have learned many other things that you need to know," she tells me. I sit up in my bed and Namaah adjusts so we can sit face-to-face.

"I am ready to know it, Namaah," I sign. She sighs and nods her approval.

"I have heard some of what Master Abraxas has been doing on his travels and it is frightening," she signs.

"What is it?" I ask. "I thought it was a political tour he was making." Namaah shakes her head.

"His travels will help him in his search for power, but he met with no politicians or leaders," she tells me. "He was searching for magic power. He is impatient and seeks to rise to the top as quickly as he can."

That Abraxas is impatient isn't surprising to me. It is the hallmark of a true politician, but something in Namaah's manner of signing worries me. Abraxas already has me to control. I can use my power to mentally torture and embarrass his enemies. That sounds frightening enough to me. What more could he be in search of and has he found it?

"He took Gileaus on a journey through the Sea of Crete and beyond to the coasts of Jaffa."

Trapped

"Jaffa? Gileaus spent time in Jaffa?" I ask. Namaah nods. She does not know my history as Pearl except for what she has overheard within the walls of the fortress. She does not know that my Dom and I were cursed by a witch off the coast of Jaffa.

"What was he doing there?" I ask.

"There are rumors," Namaah signs. She leans in closer like she is going to whisper a secret, but she whispers it with her hands. "There are rumors of a powerful queen in those coasts. She has power to control humans and make them bend to her will." Namaah pauses. "She is rumored to be even more powerful than you, Athena."

I know how powerful the queen is. She is the reason I have powers in the first place. But I keep this to myself.

"Is it possible that Gileaus is under some sort of spell?" I ask. Namaah nods.

"I think it is," she responds. "Abraxas wears a large jade stone. Green is a color forbidden in Jaffa. The stone may be a symbol of the work he does with the queen."

I have seen the stone Abraxas wears. It is always around his neck and stands boldly against his purple robes. It must have some kind of power imbued within it. Nothing as strong as Queen Nyobi Kadul or even me, but power nonetheless.

"It is possible that Master Abraxas was using the power from the stone even before he took Gileaus to Jaffa," Namaah signs. "It is possible."

It is possible. Possible that my fiancé was and is under the influence of mind control. Possible that the real Gileaus, my Gileaus, is hiding underneath layers of control and magic. I nod in response to Namaah and there is a knock at the door. Namaah moves to open it and a guard steps inside.

"If the prisoner is ready," he says, "she is to accompany me."

"I am ready. As you see," I respond. "Where are we going?"

"I have orders to take you to interrogation."

"To interrogate me for what?" I ask. "I have been open with Gileaus and Abraxas. They know how the guard died. What is there to interrogate me about?"

"My orders are to take you there," the guard snips, "not to answer questions about why you are going. You can ask Master Abraxas that yourself when you get there."

So I am going to interrogation with Abraxas. I don't know what knowledge he hopes to gain from me. I'll find out soon enough. I stand and follow the guard. I squeeze Namaah's hand as I pass by her. The touch does not go unnoticed by the guard. "You. Clean up this room and return to your quarters," he tells Namaah. "You go first," he directs me.

I head out the door and am surrounded by four more guards. Their weapons are at the ready. Abraxas is taking no chances that I will try anything on his guards. That is just as well. I'll save my power for him. I walk down the hall, through the underground levels and upstairs until we reach the interrogation rooms.

Interrogation rooms aren't really the right words for them. Torture rooms would be more accurate. It is in these rooms where Demetrius works. These are the rooms where the screams are heard. I am led into the room I passed weeks ago when the old man's wife was taken to her grave. The feeling of death lingers in the air. I feel her presence, cold and accusing, as I pass the threshold. She has a connection to this place where such injustice was done to her. She is determined to remain here, making life uncomfortable for her murderers.

"Ah, Pearl," Abraxas rises from a decorative table and chair that have been placed in the room. "It has been so long since I have seen you." He walks through my circle of guards, takes me by the shoulders, and kisses my cheek. I stiffen at his touch and turn my face away. "Oh, now Pearl," he whimpers. "Surely you and I can be friends. After all, I have been so good to you and to Gileaus." With a sweeping motion, Abraxas holds an open hand toward the table. Gileaus is sitting there. I didn't see him when I first entered. My guards were in the way.

The guards make a pathway for Abraxas to lead me to the table, his hand in the small of my back. When I get to the chair he has set aside for me, I sit with my face toward Gileaus, searching for signs that he is under some kind of spell, hoping to find something that tells me he is still inside. Wanting him to love me. Gileaus reaches his hand across the table and takes hold of my hand. "I have missed you so much," he says. His words are stilted and his tone is flat, like there is forced feeling behind what he says. I don't know if he is lost to me and is trying to save face in front of Abraxas or if he is honestly under his power.

"Haven't you missed your young master?" Abraxas asks with a tone of mocking sincerity. "He has been away for so long and you have been so...uncomfortable. Surely his being here brings you *some* joy."

"Gileaus came to see me when he first arrived," I answer. "We had time to greet one another then."

"I see," Abraxas says. He eyes the two of us, looking back and forth with eyes that move like a pendulum. "Well, since we are all together again, let us celebrate with a meal."

"I ate with Namaah before I came here," I say. Gileaus sends me a reproving look.

"Did you?" Abraxas asks, "Well, I'm glad to hear it. I hope it was enough to whet your palette then. I've brought some very fine foods back with me. I'd like you to try them."

Trapped

If he is demanding that I eat, I can only imagine that the food is poisoned. I don't think he would kill me, but there could be something else going on. He may want to drug me in order to subdue me. I'll eat as little as I can, hiding it away, if possible. I want as much of my wits about me as I can get.

We eat breads, Abraxas drinks wine. I drink cool water and eat grapes. There are jars of food I've never seen before, most of them pickled sea creatures. Their texture is difficult for me to chew. I've never liked rubbery foods. But their flavor is not unpleasant. I eat small amounts of them, always with bread and water, and wait for the effects of drugs to kick in. We spend an hour eating and listening to Abraxas talk about the exotic sights, sounds, and foods of his journey. Gileaus says very little, only enough to confirm and add praise to Abraxas' descriptions. I cannot tell what he is thinking or feeling. I still refuse to send my mind into his. I want our love to just be the two of us, no power in between.

"Well, I have a visitor I'd like to introduce you to, Pearl," Abraxas says as he wipes the corners of his mouth clean. "Guard, bring in Master Hortencio." A guard bows and leaves the room.

"I'm rather excited for you to meet this fellow," Abraxas tells me. "I am highly interested to see what you can do with him. You see, Pearl, Hortencio has been a family friend for years. His father and my grandfather were officials together in the government, but I've had the most difficult time getting his support for some of my reforms." Abraxas takes another sip of wine. "I do hope you'll be able to convince him to join me. There is a great deal in it for you, if you succeed." Abraxas looks to Gileaus then back to me. "I think we could arrange a wedding for the two of you." Gileaus and I both snap our attention toward Abraxas. He smiles at our reaction. "What is it? Don't tell me the fires of love have cooled between you during our absence. It is a weak heart indeed that cannot handle the strain of separation." Another sip of wine. "Besides Pearl, you'll have to get used to Gileaus' being away once you are married. He is going to be a major contributor to my new government. He will rise to the top right alongside me."

"New government?" I manage to ask. "What do you mean by that?"

Abraxas smiles and opens his mouth to speak when we hear a commotion outside the door.

"Ah, my good friend Hortencio must be here," he says. Several new guards enter the room, restraining their prisoner between them. It is the old man. The old man I saved from a beating. The old man I killed a guard for and ended up living in a dungeon for. This is Hortencio.

Chapter 35

Hortencio is seated in a chair, but not at the table. He looks even older than he did when he was brought here. His gray hair has thinned, his face is gaunt, his eyes are sunken in a starved and haunting look. His body is too small for the robes he wears, the same robes he wore when he came here. Bruises and cuts cover his arms and feet. He wears no shoes. He is a man at death's door. I don't know how he can still be alive. What has happened to his daughters?

"Hortencio, my friend," Abraxas says as he stands and walks to the man he has known his entire life, "it has been far too long since we have met together. I'm very sorry it has to be under such difficult circumstances." Hortencio winces as Abraxas lays a heavy hand on his shoulder.

"Where are my daughters?" the old man asks, his voice cracking with the strain of dehydration.

"Why, Hortencio, my friend," Abraxas laughs, "I thought you were close enough to them to hear them calling to you." The old man lets out a painful groan. It's my turn to wince now. Abraxas is torturing his friend. Why?! Just get to the point!!!!!

"Abraxas," I interrupt, wanting nothing more than to free this man from his suffering. Abraxas turns his face toward me.

"Ah, yes," he says. "Hortencio, old boy, I want to introduce someone to you. This is Pearl. You may remember her grandfather Vasilios from Argos." Hortencio lifts his eyes to meet mine. They are almost empty of life, but a fire remains ignited within them.

"Pearl," he croaks. "You have changed."

"Of course she has changed," Abraxas laughs. "She was just a girl in Argos and now she is here, all grown up! A lovely young woman engaged to my apprentice, Young Master Gileaus." Abraxas points to Gileaus and Hortencio turns his head.

"I know your father," he says. Gileaus shifts in his seat.

"I believe you *knew* his father," Abraxas says coolly, "I'm afraid Master Spiro has been dead for some time now." Hortencio's face goes even more ashen than it was when he came into the room.

"I'm sorry to hear it young man," he addresses Gileaus. "But you do your father's memory no credit by allying yourself and your future bride with this man." Gileaus barely registers anything Hortencio is saying. Even if he is under a spell, how can he not fight to break through it?! I am sick to my stomach. Abraxas is not amused. He moves to stand directly in front of Hortencio, blocking his view of anyone else in the room. He mumbles something I cannot hear to the old man. When he returns to his seat, Hortencio's head is lowered and a tear falls from his cheek.

Taking a final draw from his cup of wine, Abraxas is ready to get to business.

"Hortencio, as you know, I am planning a...restructuring of our government. As you also know, I have invited you to be a part of that restructuring."

"Even if I agreed, what you seek is not possible," Hortencio says. "You need armies and support that you do not have."

"Bah!" Abraxas shouts. "You know full well that with your support and my plans, I can make it happen. You have control of all the armies I need! I just need you to fulfill a few simple tasks and it will work!"

Hortencio shakes his head. "I'll not support your plans, Abraxas. No matter what you do to me, I will not support them."

Abraxas chuckles to himself. "Oh, Hortencio," he says, "do you think I would leave this all to chance? I had you captured and brought here because I have the means to make you change your mind." A heavy silence fills the air between us all as we wait for an explanation. Gileaus shifts in his chair. I had almost forgotten he was in the room.

Hortencio looks at Abraxas directly, raising in his seat and squaring his shoulders. "As long as I live, my mind will not be swayed, Abraxas. You seek murder and power and the overthrow of our government, our way of life. I will do all in my power to preserve it."

"Oh, I believe you," Abraxas says. "I am convinced that your mind will *not* be swayed. But the mind is a fragile thing, Hortencio." Abraxas turns his attentions to me. "Perhaps I was not thorough in my introductions a moment ago. This is Pearl, Hortencio. She is more than an acquaintance of our past. She is capable of things you've only heard of. Certainly you heard the rumors that encircled her family years ago?"

Hortencio shifts in his chair and looks at me. I wish he would look away. I don't want this true and honest man to look at me like I am an evil creation. I don't want him to become my next victim. But I don't see that in his eyes. What I see there is pity. He knows. He knows I am here against my will. He knows I am being forced to live and serve this monster.

"Our Pearl here can do wonderful things with the human mind," Abraxas continues, oblivious to the silent understanding between Hortencio and me. "Pearl," he says to me, "do give our guest a little taste of what you can do. And please remember our discussion earlier. You wouldn't want anything to come between you and your fiancé."

Trapped

I look at Gileaus. I look at the jade medallion around Abraxas' neck. I look into the eyes of Hortencio. I am trapped in this room. I am trapped in this life. If I do what Abraxas wants, a government and an entire people's lives are at stake. If I deny him, I will not be given another chance. What will happen to me? What will happen to Gileaus? Will Abraxas continue to keep him as his puppet, forcing me to watch from my prison window?

I move my mind toward Hortencio. His face echoes courage. He is not afraid of anything I can do. I send soft, white tendrils of inquiry into his mind. I want to see what he has there waiting for me. As my mind reaches his, I am pushed backward into my chair. Hortencio hides nothing from me. He welcomes me into his mind. The intimacy with which he accepts me is overwhelming. I have not experienced this before.

I remain focused and see what this aged man has for me to see. I see his memories, the years of battle for his country. I see his motivation, his children and wife, the country he loves and the values he holds dear. I see his fears, too. I see the oppression he knows will envelop the people if Abraxas forces himself on them as their leader. I see torment among the people he loves. I see depravity of every kind. No one is free from the tyranny of a monster once he has control over them. I feel everything Hortencio feels. I cannot force him to change his mind. I cannot manipulate him. He is true. He is right. He is good. I will not change anything in this man.

"Well," Abraxas says with some irritation, "what are you showing to him?"

"I am showing him nothing," I respond. "This man sees clearly." Abraxas stands from the table.

"What do you mean, Pearl?" he asks. "You have a job here, a responsibility to me. You have the opportunity to save yourself. Convince this man to follow me, Pearl."

I sit still for only a moment. Then I slowly shake my head. "I'll not do it," I say. "I will not manipulate this man. You cannot win without him." I look Abraxas in the eyes. "This is how I defeat you."

A whir in the air and a sharp sting to my cheek. Abraxas wears a ring that cuts my cheek with his slap. My ears ring and my vision blurs. Hot tears rise to my eyes. Abraxas moves to me, grabbing my arm roughly in his large hands, the hands that killed Dom.

"You will see, Pearl," he whispers into my ear. "I have given you your chance. Any more opportunities will come at a much higher price." He pushes me back into the chair and turns to the guards. "Bring Demetrius," he tells them. Gileaus stands. He finally stands.

"Master Abraxas," he yells. Has he reached his breaking point? Is he ready to turn against Abraxas no matter the cost? Is a part of him screaming through the fog? "Allow me a moment to try with the prisoner." He begs. "Let me see if I can persuade her." Me. He is calling me a prisoner. Not his fiancé. Not his Athena. Not even Pearl. *The prisoner.*

"There may be another time for that," Abraxas answers. "But that time has not yet come, my young man. I think you had better return to your room."

"But Master, please," Gileaus begs. It's like watching two completely different people living in the same body. He is fighting within himself. He must be under a spell. The false Gileaus holds a thin power over the real Gileaus, my Gileaus.

"Guard," Abraxas calls out. The closest guard to Gileaus reaches for him and takes him by the arm. He is strong and easily controls my fiancé in his weakened state. He leads him from the room and up the stairs. I hear Gileaus calling to Abraxas the entire way. Abraxas reaches for the jade around his neck and Gileaus quiets. Abraxas returns his attention to me.

"Pearl," he says in a condescending tone, "I'm sure you think you are being very noble. I'm sure you think there is nothing so wonderful as to sacrifice oneself for another. Am I correct?" I do not respond. My silence is my answer.

"This is as I expected," Abraxas continues. "But you see, Pearl, I do not live in that kind of world. I am not at all worried about the self-sacrificing people who throw themselves in harm's way to protect everyone around them. No, I deal in more practical ways." Abraxas clasps his hands behind his back and paces the floor between Hortencio and me. I watch Abraxas. Hortencio keeps his eyes on me.

"You see," Abraxas continues, "I learned a very long time ago that people willing to sacrifice themselves for what they call the greater good are not always willing to make that same decision for other people." A small pit of nerves is opening in my stomach. I am willing to sacrifice myself. I don't care what he can do to me. But he is talking about something else entirely. "Your convictions are strong now," Abraxas tells me, "but I have a feeling they will not be so strong when someone else's safety is on the line."

I hear the low chuckle I have been waiting for. I don't even look up. I know Demetrius is here. I thought he was coming for me, but I was wrong.

"Guards," Abraxas commands, "Secure our prisoners."

At least three guards head toward me, others are already behind Hortencio. He is being tied to his chair. It is a ridiculous precaution. In his weakened state he cannot do anything to fight back. My guards reach me and lift me by the arms. They take me to the far wall where chains are attached to the stone. I am shackled into place. I save my strength.

Hortencio still meets my gaze. He is a brave man and he is trying to send his strength to me. But this is the skill I know best. I send out deep blue tendrils of strength and courage. When they reach Hortencio, I see him glow. It is something only I can see. The qualities have found their way into a home where they are already alive and well. I have given him power that he did not need. But that does not mean he will not be harmed.

Abraxas turns to leave the room, but addresses me one more time. "I will be interested in hearing from you tomorrow, Pearl." And with a flash of dark purple, he is gone.

Demetrius rubs his hands together as he comes up behind Hortencio. He is laughing as usual. It is the disgusting laugh of pleasure he takes in hurting others. With a swift movement, he strikes the back of Hortencio's head with the back of his hand. Hortencio's head jerks forward and his chair rocks. Demetrius walks to the table and lays out a leather satchel he has brought with him. He unrolls his bag to reveal the tools of his trade. I only need a moment to see the instruments he chooses. I cannot let the moment pass and do nothing.

I send thick and strong images into Demetrius' mind. His tools are red-hot. Every time he touches them, he thinks he is being burned. He wouldn't mind, but when he looks down at his pained hands, he sees them melt. Only Demetrius knows what I am sending to his mind. Only he can see the vision I have created for him. Only he responds. He lets out a scream of pain and falls to the ground. He pushes his hands into the floor to stop the pain. But as he pushes, I make him see the melting. I make him see his entire body melting into the floor. He is screaming and begging to be saved.

Something Demetrius would never do.

There is a procedure for this, a procedure to be followed when I toy with Demetrius' mind. The guards in the room know I am responsible for his behavior. They have a job to do. The three around me grab my arms. I give them the same vision I am giving to Demetrius. They are melting. They scream and five more guards rush at me. I am doing all I can and I will take as many as I can with me. Two more guards fall when they reach for me, each screaming about his melting hands that are perfectly sound. Demetrius lies exhausted on the floor. I cannot continue to reach him and fight off the onslaught of guards. I am growing weak.

I am finally overwhelmed by the guards rushing at me. I cannot attack them all. Someone behind me, someone I cannot see, someone I cannot attack, throws a black bag over my head. I cannot see. I can no longer attack. All I can do is listen. And I listen for hours. And when Hortencio finally begins to scream, I am listening.

Chapter 36

For more than a week, I have listened to screams, but I am not swayed. In his screaming, Hortencio begs me not to give in. He is willing to die to preserve the government, to keep Abraxas from a tyrannical rule. The memory of his feelings and character are enough to keep me strong. I withstand the repeated messages I receive from Abraxas:

Are you ready to help yet?

A single line for every message. My answer is always the same. No. No, I will not help my captor anymore. I will fight until I am free from his greedy hands. I am strong. But when Hortencio's daughters are brought in with me, my strength cracks.

The first time the women are brought in, I am not wearing a hood. Abraxas wants me to see their faces. He wants me to see the fear he creates in them. But Hortencio's daughters are products of their upbringing. They have the will to fight, to endure. That's too bad for them. Their beatings and torture will be longer as a result. I do what I can to send them imagery of home, helping them to recall why they are here and what they are being used for. I send them strength, courage, and ability to withstand. I send it all until my face is covered again. Then it is back to listening. Listening to screams. Listening to laughter. It makes me sick.

Another week goes by and I am faltering in my resolve. It must show because today has been quiet. No officers have been sent to take me to the interrogation rooms. No screams are heard down the hall. I wonder, and even hope, that Hortencio and his daughters are dead. Then they would at least be released from their suffering. But the thought is selfish, a desire to keep me from their pain as well as them. I want more for them.

There is a quiet knock at my door and it creaks open. I move my eyes toward the entrance of my cell to see who is coming to get me today. It is Namaah. Her eyes are red and puffy. Her hair is disheveled and loose. Her clothing is wrinkled as though she has been sleeping in them.

"My Athena," she signs to me. "My precious friend. I am come to help you." Namaah turns back to the hall and retrieves a large basket. Inside are the items I have come to expect from her visits: clear and clean water and washing rags, fresh robes, even food. She is here to make me over and freshen me up again. Abraxas must want to see me. He never visits his captors until they are clean.

I allow Namaah to care for me, feed me broth, brush my hair and wash my body, but I sign nothing. I do not communicate anything to her. There is too much sorrow to share. Once I am clean, Namaah tidies up the room and sits beside me.

"There is much disturbance in the fortress," she signs to me. "A close friend of Hortencio's has come to Abraxas. He is searching for Hortencio and believes Abraxas has something to do with his disappearance. He is a man with many resources and influence. Abraxas is fearful of him. Some of the other servants are guessing that Abraxas will kill Hortencio and his daughters to keep them from being discovered."

"What's going on in here?" There is a guard at my door and he is watching Namaah as she signs to me. Our ability to communicate has been our secret for so long. I cannot lose it. I send tendrils of memory loss to the guard, but I am too late.

"What is it?" a second guard asks as he, too, enters my room. I am always heavily guarded. I should have known something like this could happen.

"The servant was moving her hands in a strange way while the prisoner watched," answers the first. "I think it is some sort of code. I..." The tendrils of forgetfulness finally hit their mark, but the damage is done. The first guard falls to the ground, speechless. In my fear and distraction, I pulled too much memory away from him. There is no telling how far gone he may be.

Guards spill into the room and surround my cot. One grabs Namaah by the arm and yanks her to her feet. Her face twists in pain, not a sound escapes.

"Put her down!" I am on my feet in a split second. My arms are spread wide and low as I stare down the guard before me. Several guards fall to the ground as though I pushed them away. My feet rise a few inches above the ground. I have never felt this kind of power rushing through me. I can feel it pulsating through my veins.

"I said put her down!" I yell once more at the guard. Someone in the room cries out and I am rushed. Guards jump on top of me, pulling me to the ground. Before I fall, I see Namaah fighting her guard. Someone pulls out the ever present black sack and I am blinded again.

I kick and scream and thrash and pull. I am hit and pulled and carried. We leave the room, a cacophony of sound echoes down the hallways through which we travel. We enter another room and I am forced into a chair. I still kick and scream and bite - whatever I can do. I know I cannot fight them all off, but I want to hurt anyone I can. I hear the muffled sounds of too many men squeezed into the space. Rough, angry hands tie me to the chair. Chains encircle me until I can move nothing but my head. One by one, the men leave the room. I call out and no one answers. I thrash my head about, trying to dislodge the bag, but it is no use. I relax my body, allowing the air to come in and out of my lungs again. More time passes, my breathing slows, and I fall asleep.

Trapped

When I wake up, it is because someone has yanked the black bag off my head. My head whips back, hair is caught in my eyes and mouth. I try to shake it free, but I cannot get everything out.

"Oh, do help her clear her face. I want her to see me."

Unseen fingers brush my hair free from my face. I breathe and I can see. Abraxas is sitting at a table in front of me.

"I had hoped to be meeting with you in one of the upstairs rooms, Pearl," he says. "But as it is, I understand that you have been in communication with one of my servants. Tell me, what has Namaah told you?"

I shake my head. "Namaah has told me nothing," I say. "She was trying to comfort me. That is all."

"Trying to comfort you?" Abraxas asks. "So, you can communicate with her. Tsk tsk, Pearl. Now I cannot send her to you anymore. It's a pity you should lose this one comfort."

I'm not worried about my own comfort. But now that they know I have been communicating with Namaah, she will be punished, maybe even killed.

"Tell me, Pearl," the monster continues, "how have you spent the last several weeks?"

"You know how I've spent them."

"I?" Abraxas asks in a mocking tone. "How could I have known? I haven't been down here at all during that time. I prefer to leave these rooms to Demetrius, you see." The sickening chuckle comes from the corner of the room.

"And how did Demetrius like his time with me?" I ask. The chuckling stops and Abraxas is the one to laugh this time.

"Yes, I heard about that," he says. "That is why you have to be blindfolded from time to time, my dear. You are the one who has to miss out. Demetrius has done some of his best work these past few weeks."

"What's happened to Hortencio and his daughters?" I ask. I am open with Abraxas. I hide nothing from him. It is the best way to get information from him. Direct questioning.

"As I said, my dear," he answers, "Demetrius has done some of his best work in the past few weeks. Surely you've noticed the quiet in the corridors? You are the only one making noise now."

"Hortencio finally agreed to my terms. His forces will be at my disposal."

"How is that possible?" I ask. Abraxas sighs.

"An old man can only watch his daughters suffer for so long, Pearl," he answers. "Hortencio is a good father. He wants his children to be happy. Of course, one of them, the youngest, will still be staying with me. A little incentive for him to stay on course."

"You've got what you wanted then," I spit, "what more do you want from me?"

Abraxas is quiet for a moment. He shakes his head. "That is a dangerous question, Pearl," he says. "Once I no longer have need of you, I no longer need you here. And I am sure you understand that I cannot just let you go once your work is finished." He is silent for a moment before continuing.

"I have a new problem, Pearl. You see, since you were so unwilling to help me with Hortencio, it has taken too much time to get what I wanted from him and he has been missed. One of our mutual acquaintances, a man I detest but must submit to openly, has come to inquire after his friend. Naturally, I have assured him that all is well and that Hortencio is not with me. But the man will not be swayed. He insists that something is wrong and is threatening inquiry."

"Anyone investigating you would find it very interesting, I am sure," I interject.

"Hmmm, yes," Abraxas nods, "I am sure they would. I am a very interesting man." He stands now and uses a gold-covered walking stick as he paces the room. A limp has developed in his right leg. I hope it is painful for him.

"But you see, Pearl," he continues, "I don't *want* to be investigated. I'm sure you can understand."

I let out one laugh and roll my eyes. Abraxas pauses to assess me.

"You didn't do your job very well the first time, Pearl, but I am willing to give you one more chance."

"You must be desperate then," I accuse. Abraxas nods.

"Indeed, I am," he says. "And you know, my dear, desperate times do call for desperate measures."

"You will have a hard time getting me to help you," I tell him. "I think I have already proven that."

"You have, Pearl. You have. That's something I love about you. You are strong in so many ways, difficult to break. There is something so enjoyable about the chase, you know. You make it that much more enjoyable for Demetrius, too."

"Demetrius doesn't frighten me," I say.

"Oh, I know, my dear. I know." Abraxas stands still, facing me head on. "I need you to erase the memory of the man in my home, Pearl. I need him to forget why he ever came here. I know you can do it. You've done it to my guards. I want you to come to my home - kind, willing, submissive - as my cousin again. Dine with me. Take his memory away."

"You have no power over me, Abraxas," I tell him. "Demetrius cannot use any tactic that would make me fall prey to your will and whim."

Abraxas nods. "I know that's how you feel, Pearl. But I don't think you have taken everything into account. I have more on my side than you are thinking of."

Trapped

I stare at him, mute. I wait for him to tell me what he means. He snaps his fingers. A guard comes to his side. Abraxas whispers in the man's ear. The guard nods, turns, and leaves the room. We wait, but it doesn't take long for his plans to become clear.

Within moments I hear the rustling of guards in the hall. They have someone with them. A prisoner. Maybe more than one. Who else will Abraxas be torturing for my benefit? A path clears in the doorway and the prisoners are brought in. Gileaus and Namaah.

"Athena!" Gileaus calls in a loud voice. "Athena! What has happened?! Do nothing for him! I do not know what he is doing! Abraxas! What is happening?! Why is Athena in chains?" Abraxas reaches for the jade around his neck and squeezes it in his hand. Gileaus goes silent and still. Namaah's eyes are wide and pleading. She has endured so much. She does not fear Abraxas as she should. She wants me to save myself. My love for them both has led to their pain.

Abraxas rests both hands on his walking stick, facing me. "I ask you now, Pearl. Will you do as I ask or do I need to apply pressure?"

"Do nothing, Pearl!" Gileaus yells. He is struck by a guard. Demetrius goes to his side and takes his hand. I hear a sickening snap, Gileaus cries out, then he moans. Demetrius takes a step toward Namaah. Beautiful, wonderful, silent Namaah.

"STOP!" I scream. "Take one more step and you will be begging for Tartarus to take you!" But I know that even the prison for the titans will not strike fear in him.

"Oh, Pearl," Abraxas sighs. "Such a threat. What did you think Demetrius meant to do? I'm sure he was only going to give Namaah a gentle kiss or a pat on the shoulder. Isn't that right, Demetrius?"

"Of course, Master," Demetrius responds. His eyes are on Abraxas, but his hand is moving toward Namaah.

"Why don't you prove it to Pearl, Demetrius?" Abraxas says. "Show her you meant Namaah no harm." Demetrius bows and in a flash, he produces a knife from his robes. He is so fast, I don't have time to prevent him. The knife slices the air then slices Namaah's scar-less cheek. Fire fills me and I send the flames straight to Demetrius. I have the satisfaction of watching him crumble to the ground, hands on his head, before the black bag again covers my face.

Chapter 37

I have no idea how long I have been blindfolded. The minutes turn to hours in this cell. I am given nothing to eat and nothing to drink. I am only given screams to listen to.

Gileaus screams to me through the fog and the pain.

"Athena!" he screams. "Athena! Don't give in! We can find a way out of here!" He is always silenced after these outbursts. Gagged from the sound of it. When it is Namaah's turn, I only hear the strikes, the cuts, the twisting of her body. I am left to imagine the worst and I do imagine it. It makes me sick and I vomit into the sack over my head. No one cleans it up.

At least Demetrius isn't a part of their suffering. They are hurting, yes, but he would have inflicted even more cruel and unimaginable tortures upon them. Now, he has his own tortures. The flame I sent to his mind is everlasting. It will never go out. He will always be in maddening pain and burning. But he will live. It is a small act of revenge for the suffering he has inflicted.

Finally, there is quiet. I hear the pained breathing of my love and my friend. My ears are alert to all the sounds in the room. It is still muffled. There are many bodies in the room, but I do not know what they are doing. Something is laid on a table. I hear leather swishing against leather. Something is unrolling. I hear metal. Tools. They have Demetrius' tools.

"No. No. No. No! Please!" Gileaus screams. "She cannot take it! Leave her alone!"

"I am fine, Gil!" I call out across the room. "I am not afraid."

"It isn't you, Athena," he answers. "They are going to work on Namaah." My ears burn as I hear the sounds of tools being prepared.

"Stop!" Gileaus yells again. "Leave her alone! Pick me instead!" Feet move away from Gileaus' voice. They are going to reach her soon.

"STOP!!!" I shout. The feet silence.

"Do you mean you are ready to do as Master Abraxas wishes?" A gruff voice asks me from the darkness.

"Yes. Yes, I am ready! Just leave her alone." Tears stream down my cheeks. "Leave her alone."

"As you wish," the same voice says. "Alert Master Abraxas. Take these prisoners to their rooms. Orders are to care for them as long as the girl obeys."

Feet shuffle and bodies move. I listen as the two people I care for most are relieved of their suffering. What do I care about Abraxas' plans? Why do I care if he wants to overrun a government? Why do I care when the cost is so high? I will do as he asks. I will save someone.

∞ ∞ ∞

I am kept in the interrogation room. I am kept in chains. A new servant woman cleans the vomit from my face and hair. She is not allowed to clean my body. It must stay trapped in iron. I have grown used to the smell. She has not. She gags multiple times as she tends to my needs. She slops my food on my face and must clean it again. When she leaves the room, she doesn't glance back or offer a friendly sign of affection. Namaah would have made sure my soul was fed.

It isn't long before I hear guards again. This time as they enter the room, their swords and clubs are at the ready. Once they have cleared a path from the door to me, Abraxas comes in.

"Goodness, Pearl!" he exclaims as he holds his robe to his nose. "What a horrid smell. I will make this as brief as possible. You have ruined my best guard. Not that I blame you. He wasn't always my favorite, but he got the job done. Enough about that. You have a job to do and you are woefully unprepared. I will have you taken to your old room and properly cleaned. You will be brought to my home to meet the man in question. At dinner, you will remove his memory of the past month. Do you understand?"

I nod.

"Good," he continues. "One wrong move and your life is over. But only after you watch your friends lose theirs." He turns and runs from the room, his nose still covered. The guards nearest me undo my chains. Daggers and swords are pointed at my head as I am escorted through the dark dungeon hallways and back to my old room. The same servant from before is waiting for me there with all the necessary supplies to make me clean and presentable. She says nothing to me and I say nothing to her. Her hands tremble. Either she is afraid of a threat from Abraxas or she is afraid of me. Both, probably. But there is no need for her to worry. She is safe from me. It is as Abraxas said. I have a job to do.

Trapped

When I am cleaned and ready, gleaming and smelling like the relative of a wealthy nobleman, I am escorted again to the main house. Abraxas meets me in the entryway.

"Pearl, darling," he says as he embraces me. "I'm so glad you could make it to dinner this evening. I hope Gileaus and Namaah are well." He steps aside and leads me to the dining room.

"Everyone," he calls out to the room, "most of you remember my cousin, Pearl, don't you? Well, she is here to visit again and has made it just in time for the second course." A small rumble of applause and greetings reaches me from those in the room. I recognize some of them from the last time I dined with Abraxas in his home.

"Let me introduce you to Master Nicos and his wife Hypatia. I do not think they were here when you last dined with us."

I greet the couple coolly, as I imagine a stuffy noblewoman related to Abraxas would. They are seated next to Abraxas at the head of the table. There is not space for me there. I am led to an empty seat near the bottom of the table. I sit between two young men, faces covered in acne. I have a clear view of Nicos and his wife.

Dinner moves on slowly and there is general conversation all around. Politics, religion, uprisings, taxes. The kinds of things that are always talked about at tables wealthy and poor. I keep my eyes directed at the head of the table. I am aloof enough with my dinner companions that they turn their attention away from me and to the pretty girls surrounding them. Right about the time we are getting ready for the final course, I see a heated discussion beginning between Abraxas and Nicos. It isn't long before Abraxas nods my direction and I know it is time.

I reach out with my mind at lightning speed. No tendrils sneak their way to the head of the table. It is a direct hit. Nicos' hand moves to his forehead as his memory is stripped away. His wife leans in to ask if he is unwell and I hit her with the same strength. Soon, her hand is at her forehead.

Abraxas sighs with satisfaction as he looks my direction. Then he offers his assistance to the ailing couple. They are escorted to their room to sleep off a sudden headache. As they move behind me and out the door, several of the men's eyes meet mine. Do they know? Has Abraxas let some of his inner circle in on his secret?

I look around the table. Only those who were at the first dinner are here tonight. The same politicians I have seen for years are eating with my enemy. They are either his allies or his enemies. He keeps both close to him.

Eventually, the eyes move away from my face and turn to one another. There is much discussion between them and several glances my direction.

When dinner is finished and the guests are leaving, Abraxas calls me to him. I join him in a small room filled with scrolls and a few leather-bound books. There is a chair near a desk and he offers me the seat. I take it. He steps from the room for a moment and returns with a group of men. The same men who had their eyes on me at the table.

"What did I tell you, men?" he says as he closes the door. "My Pearl can do amazing things."

"Wonderful things," one man says.

"Spectacular things," another offers.

"Why do you keep her hidden?" someone asks. "You could use her regularly."

"I don't like to overtax her," Abraxas says as he looks my way. "But I think she is growing in strength. She will be ready for more soon."

"You should travel with her, Abraxas," the first man comments again. "There is so much she could do in the larger cities. Consider Bimini, for example, or even Atlantis."

Atlantis. The name sends sparks of energy into my heart. I know that name. I know that place. It is a central hub of activity in Greece, a place where dreams are realized. I have heard it talked about many times. It is almost the hub of the universe. Servants dream of the luxury that awaits the lowest classes there. Nobles fantasize about the life they can create for themselves there. These have never had a draw for me. But the pulling in my heart is suddenly arrow-sharp. There is nothing I want more in this moment than to travel to this magical city.

"I'd love to go to Atlantis," I say as I stand from the chair. All eyes in the room turn to me. Abraxas wears a threat in his gaze. Don't push too hard, Pearl. "I have always wanted to travel there. Master Abraxas couldn't deny such a request to his prize cousin, could he?" I am bold, but I cannot hold back. My soul will not allow it.

The men turn back to their host and lead conspirator. His eyes are still fixed on me.

"I'm not sure," he says. "Would my little prize cousin do well for herself there? Would she keep herself out of trouble?"

"She would," I tell him. A few of the men glance back at me before returning to address Abraxas.

"You should do it, Ab," they say to him. "A power like that is unparalleled. You could take over even sooner than you hoped. You could have her with you for the next elections. You can really change things."

Abraxas is quiet, thinking. He knows my disobedience to him when he last traveled. Does he risk leaving me again or does he risk taking me with him?

"Pearl," one of the men steps toward me. "Tell me, what all can you do? You have caused hallucinations and taken memories. Can you make a man change his mind? Can you force him to feel something he has never felt before?"

"I don't know," I answer. "I have never tried."

"We must get a practice specimen for her Abraxas," the man says. "We must really test her abilities. We must know what she can really do. Then we can take her to Atlantis with confidence."

There are mumbles of agreement throughout the room as the men discuss and make plans together. Abraxas remains still, his eyes on me.

"What do you say, Ab?" All eyes are on Abraxas now as he stares and thinks. He strokes his fingers along his chin.

"We can practice with her," he finally says. "But if there are any issues, I will not take her. I don't want my plans destroyed."

The men all mutter their encouragement and conviction that this is the best move. They pat Abraxas on his shoulder and congratulate him and each other on their plans. His eyes stay on mine for a moment longer before he turns to see his guests out. I sit back in the chair, unwilling to leave when a new window of opportunity has just opened in front of me.

Abraxas returns after seeing his guests out. "I'm surprised you didn't try to leave," he says as he pulls another chair near me.

"It's as you've said," I respond, "I have motivation to stay."

"Ah, yes," he sighs as he leans back. "Your lover and your spy friend."

"Gileaus is my fiancé, yes, but not my lover. And Namaah is not a spy, she is only a friend."

"Do you expect me to believe that the two of you don't communicate? That she doesn't tell you the things she has heard in this house?"

"I don't expect you to believe anything. Though I could certainly try to *make* you believe. What do you say, Abraxas? Would you like to be the first to be tested? Do you want me to try to change your mind about Namaah?" Abraxas stares at me through narrowed eyes like he is looking at a cat he cannot trust, uncertain if I will scratch if he comes too close. I enjoy letting him squirm for a minute.

"No," he tells me. "I think I'd prefer for you to test your skills when there are others around to watch. But tell me, Pearl. Why are you so eager to go to Atlantis?"

"I have my reasons," I tell him. I don't understand the reasons myself, but the pull will not be ignored.

"Ah hah, yes. I'm sure you do, Pearl. But you see, you are going to have to let me know what those reasons are before I am going to let you accompany me."

Now it is my turn to study Abraxas through narrowed eyes.

"Atlantis is a city filled with mystery for me. I learned about it as a child from my father and I have always wanted to go there. It calls to me, you might say." Abraxas laughs.

"Calls to you how, Pearl? Do you have coconspirators there who would do me harm?" I don't know why he thinks I would tell him the truth about anything. Why he thinks this line of questioning will yield honesty from my lips. Why he bothers asking me questions at all. But I keep talking.

"Abraxas. I have told you my draw to the city. I have grown tired of this place. I want to leave it. I could have killed you already and left on my own by now."

"Except for the guards outside the door," he says.

"I would be willing to try my hand at them," I say. "I am cornered, Abraxas. Give me space or I will attack, regardless of what it means to me."

"What about what it means for Gileaus and Namaah?" he asks. "Are you willing to attack at their expense?"

"Would you like to push me on it and see for yourself?" I feel bold in this room, away from the prison and its torments. "I want to go to Atlantis, Abraxas. Take me and I will do what you ask of me. Don't take me and you lose face in front of your followers. How much will they believe in you when they see you cannot even control the prize you've shown them? Will it leave room for one of them to break away, to take the others with him?"

I am playing on his fears. Abraxas wants nothing but total power. Anything that gets him there is worth the cost. Anything that keeps him from total power must be destroyed. But he cannot destroy me and he knows it. I am too powerful for him. He needs me. He ponders my questions and my demands. He reaches for the jade around his neck.

"I wouldn't if I were you," I say before his hand can reach the stone. He pauses then lowers his hand to his lap.

"What do you know about this stone, Pearl?" he asks me. "Do you know what I am capable of when I use its power? Do you want *me* to show *you* how it works?" He grins and raises an eyebrow. I say nothing.

"I see," he says. "You fear the jade and what it can do, Pearl. We always fear what we do not know. It is just as I fear you in some ways. I do not know what to make of you, Pearl. You were so pliant, so willing to obey. Then I leave and when I return I find that you have fought against my men. I push and you are pliant again. I do not know what to make of you. Can you help me understand where your loyalties lie?"

"My loyalties lie with those whom I love and with myself," I tell him. "I will conform when they are treated well and when I get what I am asking for."

"And if I take you to Atlantis," he says, "what then? Will those same loyalties be in play?"

"They will."

Abraxas sighs and stares at me for several minutes, thinking over my words in his mind. Will he trust me enough to take me with him? I am tempted to send my powers into his mind, but I do not know what the jade would do in response. I also do not know what the guards are prepared to do when their master acts out of character. And so I wait. I watch Abraxas and he watches me, each of us waiting for the other to show their hand, to give in, to make up their mind about what comes next.

"Let's say I do take you with me to Atlantis. What's in it for me?" he asks.

"Your friends want to test my abilities, Abraxas. Why not wait to see what that yields? Then we can discuss your terms."

"And what are *your* terms?" he asks. I take just a moment to answer, letting my gaze rest on various objects around the room.

"Gileaus and Namaah come with us," I tell him. "They are allowed freedom of movement and freedom from the power your jade places on them."

Abraxas shakes his head. "I'm afraid freedom of movement is quite impossible, Pearl. You have created too much discord between us for me to allow for that. I would not be able to trust them and when I cannot trust them..."

"Freedom from the jade, then, Abraxas. Whatever power you are using over them, stops immediately." Abraxas smiles.

"I have actually used very little of the jade's power on them. None on Namaah, actually. I didn't see the need. But with your young Master Gileaus, I merely played with his own inconsistencies. The lure of power is strong within him, Pearl. Whatever he may say to you of love, he would have turned from you eventually."

I will not let this man use his words to play with *my* mind.

"Your power over him stops, Abraxas. He and Namaah will be treated well. They travel with us and I will do as you ask."

"After we test your abilities to see if they are worth the risk, my dear," Abraxas replies and smiles.

"Agreed."

I have just made a deal with a monster. But this deal will bring me closer to Atlantis and whatever calls me there.

Chapter 38

*A*braxas' friends and followers are not the greatest scientific minds, but they come up with a series of tests for me to take, tasks to complete to see exactly what I can do. The test subjects they bring are their enemies, their prisoners, and even their servants who are being punished. I do not love what they ask me to do, but none of it is violent. I justify the tests as a means to an end. The more I prove I can do, the more likely I am to travel to Atlantis and find my way to freedom. I don't know any more who I am or what freedom will look like for me, but I choose faith in this journey as my chance to discover it.

Through their various tests and experiments, Abraxas' cohorts discover that I can indeed make a man change his mind. A servant who refused to worship the gods of his master was brought to me. By the time the experiment was complete, he was a zealot for his master's gods. Then they brought me a prisoner who refused to believe that he had done wrong in stealing bread from a vendor in town. When I was through, he was ready to preach in the streets the duty of every man to work and earn his own way in life. But the crowning achievement, the act that sealed my destiny in their eyes, was performed on another politician. For this feat, we traveled to another one of the men's homes for another dinner. A powerful man in the area who had refused to back Abraxas was in attendance at the feast. Abraxas was not even there. By the time dessert was ended, the man was planning a trip to visit Abraxas to swear allegiance to him and offer any help he could.

Gileaus and Namaah and I have all been moved to the upper rooms of the fortress. Their physical wounds are healing, but their emotional wounds are leaving the bigger scars. As promised, Abraxas has stopped using the power of the jade on Gileaus. But Gileaus has not returned to who he was a year ago. He has seen too much, heard too much, been through too much. A life with me is harder to bear than he thought it would be. He is distant from me when we are together. The only thing he ever says is, "I'm sorry." I don't know how much longer I can listen to him saying that to me.

Namaah returns to serving me as soon as she is able. The cut Demetrius made on her cheek is scarring now, a near-perfect match to the scar on the other side. We have stopped most of our communication for now. Both of us wanting to protect the other. I let her care for me and serve me. I feel overwhelming guilt sometimes and I cry the entire time she tends to my needs. But she is quiet and calm. She wraps her arms around me and pats my hair. Once a tear fell from her face onto my robes. We held each other tighter then.

But I have a deal with Abraxas. Whatever the future holds for those I love most, it is only getting better as I do what he asks of me. So, plans are made, travel arrangements are paid for, and we head east to Atlantis. Gileaus has room on the wagons and ship near me. We try to talk to one another, but too much guilt and fear live between us. I don't know if we will ever be able to love each other as we used to. We have been broken by the evils Abraxas has placed on us. If I ever find a way to exact revenge for our sufferings, I will do it. For now, I just want to keep us alive and safe.

After a week of dusty land travel and another two by sea, I hear the clarion call, "There she is! There she is! Atlantis straight ahead!" There is bustling all around me as the crewmen man their posts and prepare to dock. I am drawn to the bow of the ship, eager to see this city in its glory.

Atlantis is a strange island. Years of building have made it a network of ringed land and moats. If I could see Atlantis from above, it would look like a massive target. The land and moat rings furthest from center are largest, each circle shrinking in width until the center island is reached. A giant canal drives through the rings, allowing boats to move between the layers of the island city.

As we pull close to the first band of the island, my mouth falls open. There is an enormous wall made of fiery red stone surrounding it. The top of the wall is shining brass, bolted securely to the rock beneath. I learn from the ship's sailors that the stone walls of each land ring were quarried from the moats. These strange red walls came from the depths of the island itself. Our ship pulls into the Atlantean canal and we wait before enormous gates. The gates are nearly 50 feet high and made of wood and iron. They are decorated with the same brass that rests on the top of the wall. Sentinels stand guard in towers built above the gates. They saw us coming long before our own ship saw their shores.

I feel a hand brushing mine. I turn to see who is at my side. It is Namaah. Tears stream down her cheeks. The beauty of what stands before us is more than she or I ever imagined possible. I turn my attention back to the gates and the gilded sign that announces the city. The sign is made of a black stone and is covered in precious metals. Etched into the stone is one word.

Atlantis

I shudder from head to toe. I have seen this sign before. Whether in dream or in memory, I do not know, but the feeling is overwhelming. I ache inside. I sink to my knees and let my tears flow. Namaah rests her hand on my shoulder, her eyes still on the gates before us. There is a burning in my chest, a yearning for something beyond those gates. I reach my hand to my chest and grasp my hamsa medallion. It burns in my hand. As my fingers brush the black pearl resting in its palm, I see flashes of memory. Large fish with people on their backs. People who are only half human. An octopus with the face of a woman. They call to me like an ancient world reaching into my soul. Are they here? Are they close? Can I reach them?

There is a loud moaning as the gates open for us to pass through. I cannot keep my eyes open long enough. Blinking is an obstacle I would remove if I could. As we pass through the opposite sides of the gate, I see homes and shops, not unlike those in Argos and Sparta. People here mill about, going about their daily business. Few look up when they see the diplomatic colors raised on our ship. They are unimpressed. Ships like ours pass through daily in Atlantis. I allow my eyes and mind to rest for a moment so I can take in the view of the city around me. I stand and move to the side of the ship, Namaah follows.

As I look upon the life of this first ring of the island, I see a lower class of people. Everyone here is a tradesman, a servant, a merchant, or a soldier. There is no nobility here. Tall buildings that house the families are kept clean, but in some disrepair. A few workmen are arguing over how to properly repair a roof they are standing on. Several groups of children are playing together near the edge of the canal, throwing sticks to see whose will travel fastest. There are women gossiping nearby as they wash the fine clothing of their masters. There are also dilapidated buildings on the far edge of the ring where the very poor have made their home. I recognize the signs of poverty in their dirty clothing and thin, drawn faces. Sticks with fabric draped over them build the homes of the most deprived. Sickness grows among them.

It takes only half an hour to clear the outer layer of the island. Our ship is in a new ring of water, facing a new wall. But this wall is not red, it is white. It is clean and pure before us, unblemished by the poverty growing in its sister. It is taller than the first wall and is topped with tin that has images of Greek gods etched into its glistening surface. We stop once more at another gate guarded by large towers and guards. This gate is made of the same wood as the first but has both brass and tin decorating its surface. There is no sign to introduce us this time, so I keep my eyes and ears open. Some of the crew come to join Namaah and me at the edge of the boat.

As we pass through this second series of gates, we enter into the part of Atlantis where the government is run. The buildings are all clean and large. Columns and marble decorate every edifice. There are signs labeling each of the buildings and their purpose. In the distance, I see the shape of the hospital. A small cry escapes my lips and I cover my mouth. In my memory I see a woman with dark hair and eyes, leaning over me while I am tied to a bed. "If you are going to save this world, my love, we had better cut you loose," she says. Her words and voice echo in my mind. My heart burns and I would give anything to see her again. But a memory is all it is.

The ship moves on and soon we are out of the second band of Atlantis. My knees are weak and my heart is heavy. I lower my eyes to the streets and see men, politicians, walking this way and that. Some are talking to one another, some are whispering. Many more look up when they see our ship's flag. Several wave as Abraxas calls out greetings from the prow of the ship.

The ship slows even more as we approach the third wall. This wall is the most ornate of the three. Gigantic black stones with white grains raise it to a height that exceeds the other two walls. This wall is topped with a copper-gold metal, orichalcum, one of the crewmates tells me. The metal is studded with jewels and stones. Merchant ships line the ring around this section of the city, bringing their goods directly to the privileged. Several small openings in the wall allow for these goods to be carried to their destination. The gates here are decorated by the metals of all the Atlantean walls. They, too, are covered in gems and stones. As these doors swing open, a cool breeze blows through my hair.

You are so near, it says to me. I am startled at first by the communication. I usually initiate conversation with the elements.

Please, I say in a hum, *what is it that I am so near to?*

Could she really not know? Has she forgotten? What does it matter if she has? She is here now. The wind's many voices speak to each other before the mother-voice combines to address me again.

You are here to fulfill your destiny, she tells me.

What is my destiny? I don't remember anymore.

Worry not, my child. We will remember for you for we are always here. When the time arrives, we will help you.

There is a sudden rushing of the wind that swirls around me. The burning that has been growing in my pearl is cooled and calmed and the air grows still. All around me, crewmen are straightening their robes and scarves that were scattered by the wind. A few are chasing supplies that tipped over. None of the crew noticed me speaking to the wind. But Namaah did. She brushes a few loose strands from her face and takes my hand. There is so much she tells me in that touch. She knows I can communicate with the elements. She knows the air around us is our ally. She will be there to help me with anything I need. I squeeze her hand in acknowledgement of all she intends and all she means to me. Together, we turn to the inner ring of Atlantis.

This portion of the island is reserved for the elite. Politicians, wealthy merchants, and heirs to vast estates elsewhere in Greece make their home here in this city. All of the buildings are marble-clad homes. Columns and spires, statues, mosaics and murals cover their walls. Gardens abound here. It feels like the Garden of Eden is trying to grow in every corner it can find. Fruit trees and beautiful flowering bushes line the streets and walkways. Women in fine robes, jewels dripping from their necks, walk idly by, talking to one another or staring serenely into the distance. Servants wearing finer clothing than I am used to seeing on this class, run about managing the affairs of their masters' homes. There are even pets in this area of Atlantis. The few children here are playing with small dogs. I see one woman wearing a snake as though it were a necklace.

Our ship slows and I turn my face from the view. Namaah lets go of my hand when I turn away. Gileaus is behind me and then we are face to face. I pause for a moment, not used to being this close to him. He looks into my eyes for just a moment then reaches up to caress my face. He bends forward, kissing my lips so softly I have to lean in to feel it. When he pulls away, his eyes are glistening. My heart is racing and I have a thousand things to say to him. He brushes my hair from my face, staring deep into my eyes and heart.

"I love you, Athena," he whispers in the space between us. "I always have. I'm sorry our lives have come to this." There is something so final in the way he says it; like he knows something I do not. For him, the end is near. He can feel it. I wish I could push those feelings away for both of us.

"I love you, Gil," I whisper in return.

"Will you forgive me for all the wrongs I have caused you?" he asks. The ship is buzzing with the movement of men carrying things to shore. But in this moment, there is just the two of us: just me and Gileaus.

"Always," I whisper. "Gil, I know Abraxas was controlling you." I reach for his hand. He shudders at my touch.

"I gave him room to enter in, Athena," he whispers. "If I had not been filled with pride, had I not wished that I could have everything - you and power in this world - he could not have worked his magic in my heart. "But I want you to know his power is gone, Athena. I haven't given him any more control over me."

"I know."

"But that isn't all, Athena," he continues. "My desire for power is gone. I have seen too much of the evil it can really do. There is so much evil in the pursuit of power and I have seen the worst of it. I cannot live that way, Athena. I don't want that anymore."

He reaches his hands to my cheeks one more time, taking hold of my face softly. He looks into my eyes, his own eyes a pitiful mess of sorrow and regret, and again lowers his lips to mine. This time the kiss is long and soft. We are lost in each other for several moments before some of the crew call out to taunt and tease us. But we do not part. We let them laugh. We let them call out. We are saying goodbye.

As Gileaus, *my* Gileaus, pulls away and lowers his hands to his side again, I feel like my heart is going to break. I am letting go of the man I love and he is letting go of me. I have a destiny to find. I don't know where it will take me and I don't know who it will hurt. This parting is painful, but it is necessary. Maybe in some way, Gileaus will be able to find a way to escape Abraxas and his cruelty. Maybe he will be able to lead a happy life away from the politics and wealth that bring so much sorrow. Maybe I will be able to find what I have been moving toward my entire life. Maybe I will be able to fulfill the purpose I was sent to fulfill. Maybe we will find meaning in all of this.

Chapter 39

We are staying in the home of a wealthy landowner here in Atlantis. From the information I have gathered, he is funding Abraxas' rise to power. The room I am given overlooks the inner circle of Atlantis: the island of the temple. When I sleep, I dream of that temple. I ride the back of a fish. I head willingly toward something that calls to me. It isn't long before that temple fills me with fear: fear of the unknown, fear of the unexpected, fear of failure. Eventually I embrace it and allow myself the chance to live and serve the people of Atlantis. I awake in a heavy sweat, my heart pounding through my chest. I look at the temple, glistening in the quiet moonlight. It calls to me, begging me to remember. Remember what?

I sit for hours each day, watching the temple gleaming across the water. It is domed and covered in plated gold. Priests of the god Poseidon are constantly working on it, cleaning its surface, and tending to the gardens surrounding it. I wonder what urged men to build it in the first place. I wonder what kind of power it holds that it brings me here. I wonder what weakness it suffers that it must be guarded by three rings of land.

I am lost in these thoughts today when there is a knock at my door. Namaah moves past our guard to answer it. I hear Abraxas before I turn to see him.

"Well, Pearl," he says, "I hope you have been enjoying your stay in the city. Atlantis is the center of all that is good in the world." I seriously doubt that considering my present company. "Have you been out to see the government center yet?" I turn slowly in my chair so I can see his face clearly.

"I haven't been to see it," I tell him. "I haven't left my room since arriving."

"That's too bad," he says with a hint of sarcasm. "You could have had your guards ask me if they could take you on a tour at any time."

"I didn't come here for a tour," I say.

"Then why *did* you come, Pearl," he asks. "You said you had your reasons. You said you had a devotion to the place because your father spoke of it when you were a child. If that is the case, why do you not take a chance to see it?"

I rise from my seat and move to the balcony. Abraxas follows.

"I cannot take my eyes off the temple," I tell him. "Something about it is compelling to me. If I am going to tour any part of Atlantis, I want that to be it."

"Perhaps we could arrange that for you," he says. Sarcasm still laces his tone. "But I do have one treat in store for you tonight. In fact, it's the reason I even brought you to Atlantis in the first place." I almost allowed myself to forget that I have a job to do.

"And what is that?" I ask him. "Are you ready for me to sway your favorite politician?"

"Mmmmm…. Not exactly," he answers. "I have something a little more exciting in store for you."

"And what might that be?"

"Oh, I don't think you need to worry over it right now, Pearl. How about you just wait until this evening? Namaah will be given everything you need to get ready." He turns to my servant and friend. "How does that sound to you, Namaah? Can you make our Pearl into a ravishing beauty tonight?" Namaah bows her head to acknowledge the request. "Excellent," Abraxas says. "I shall be by to gather you in a few hours."

I watch as his purple figure leaves the room and heads toward his host. I can hear his footsteps echo down the hall like a ghost in an empty tomb. I shudder at the thought and turn my attention back to the temple.

Within fifteen minutes, there is a knock at the door. A servant woman is there with arms heavily laden with fine silks and linens. Another servant stands beside her with soaps and spices. Namaah allows the women in and they get to work on lighting the fire under the copper tub in my room. One of the women drops a bucket over the balcony to collect water from below. The water is placed in the tub and she returns for more. After several rounds, the tub is finally filling and warm enough for me to get in. My guard moves from the room to wait outside while Namaah and the other servants tend to my bath.

I am bathed and dried, combed and covered in perfumes. My hair is done in elaborate curls and braids. I am given a gleaming white tunic and am covered in the red silk robes Abraxas brought for me. The edges of the robes are embroidered in gold and gold ropes are wound around my waist. The sandals I wear tonight are gold, white pearls decorating my ankles. Pearls, both black and white, drape around my neck and dangle from my ears. Pink and white pearls are pinned throughout my hair and ruby rings are placed on my fingers. Tonight I look the part of the cousin of an aristocrat.

Trapped

Abraxas arrives to my room just as the sun is lowering over the horizon. I am backlit when he enters my room and I leave my seat at my balcony. The golden temple behind me reflects its brilliance around my silhouette. I can see the fiery light before me, my shadow walking in the midst.

"Pearl, you look perfect," Abraxas says as he comes to greet me. He touches my arm and I restrain myself from shrinking away. I must have his trust.

"Thank you," I reply. "Namaah does all of the magic." Abraxas glances at Namaah, wondering if I mean my words literally. She bows slightly and he returns his attention to me. "When will I receive my instructions?" I ask.

"You must learn to enjoy yourself, Pearl," he says. "You will know in good time what I expect of you. For now, let us enjoy the evening together."

As we leave the room, I cast a single glance back to Namaah. She catches my eye and I motion toward the chair on the balcony. She bows slightly letting me know she understands. Under the embroidered cushion on the wicker seat is a small purse. Inside it is a strand of pearls. I was given so many to wear tonight, I allowed one to slip out of sight. The pearls are for her, for my Namaah. I have included a piece of parchment with the picture of a woman running on it. There is also a well-crafted letter of reference for her. If I cannot do what I am asked to do tonight, if I should fail or refuse, I want Namaah to be free from the punishment that would ensue. I want her to run, to buy herself a way out of this place and into the home of someone respectable. I'll not have her suffer any more for my sake.

I smile at the thought of my guards finding my room empty. The thought of freedom for my friend who has been a slave her entire life. I send a prayer to God, my God, for her safety and happiness.

"What are you smiling about, Pearl?" Abraxas asks. "I thought you were determined to be serious."

"My sandal rope tickles my ankle," I reply, grateful for the quick lie.

"You should be used to ropes by now, Pearl," Abraxas says. I bristle at his words. "Oh, do not mistake me," he continues, "I do not mean it as a threat. I mean to tell you of the rewards of the golden ropes and jewels that await you as you serve me well."

"I have never been one who cherished those things," I tell him.

"That's unfortunate. Nonetheless, they will be yours. Your comfort will be my top priority when I have achieved my design." I sigh and he adds, "Of course, that extends to Gileaus and Namaah. As you rise, they rise, my Pearl."

"And as I fall, they fall," I add sarcastically. Abraxas laughs openly.

"As you say. But I have a good feeling about tonight." He reaches for the jade around his neck. When he touches the green stone, I feel my own golden hamsa pressing into my chest. It knows the jade and fears it. But the hamsa is here to protect others from me - that includes the jade. I do not fear it.

Abraxas and I descend the stairs of the mansion and enter a marble-covered foyer where other guests are already mingling. Abraxas takes time to greet guests, again introducing me as his cousin. Their faces blur before mine. My eyes are on one person only. Gileaus.

This is the first time I have seen him since disembarking more than a week ago. He is standing at the entranceway to the dining room, white linens caressing his frame, gold ropes encircling his waist. A wreath of laurels encircles his temple. A large ruby ring is on the index finger of his right hand. A beautiful woman holds to his arm on the left.

I cannot take my eyes from him and I stumble around the room to reach him. When Abraxas notices my faltering steps, he looks to see where my gaze is directed.

"Ah," he says, "I see that you are eager to meet young Master Gileaus. I shall take you to him myself." We move through the crowding room to the doorway where my love stands. When we reach him, Abraxas introduces us as though we have never met.

"Young Master Gileaus," he greets, "May I introduce you to my cousin, Pearl of Argos. Pearl, this is young Master Gileaus, recent heir to the Spiro estate and this is his fiancée, Zenia, heiress of the Karis estate." I can barely breathe.

Gileaus is stiff as he bows. "A pleasure to make your acquaintance, Pearl," he says through tense lips and gritted teeth. I am speechless, but I move to take his hand automatically. Gileaus takes my fingers in his, brings them to his lips, kissing them softly. His thumb brushes the backs of my fingers in the familiar, loving way. "Any relative of Master Abraxas is most welcome, I am sure," he says as he lowers my hand slowly.

I dip in a small curtsy and bow my head. I turn to look at the woman at his side. Her hair is the color of gold, her eyes the color of the sea. Her skin is lighter than mine. She must be from a northern region. Her nose is pointed and her shoulders are sloped. She is the perfect model of Grecian beauty and elegance.

"A pleasure to meet you, Pearl," she says to me with a voice three octaves higher than mine. "Abraxas tells us you are very special. I should love to get to know you better. I do hope you will sit with me as we dine."

I turn my pained face to Abraxas. He is all smiles. "I'm sure Pearl would love to get acquainted with another lovely young woman," he says. "What do you say Master Gileaus? Are you comfortable with having another beautiful woman near you this evening?"

"I could wish for nothing more," Gileaus says with a bow. His eyes meet mine and I read pain in them.

"Excellent," Abraxas responds. "I shall return her to you in a moment then. I have just a few more guests to introduce her to."

"What have you done to him?" I ask in a hoarse whisper as we walk away. "You promised to let his mind be free."

"I had nothing to do with his choice, Pearl," Abraxas responds. "Master Gileaus came to me just after we landed. He expressed a desire to be released from you, though he wants to continue with me in my new government."

"I don't believe you," I say. Angry tendrils of revenge begin to snake their way toward Abraxas.

"I would be careful what you do," he tells me as he stops in place. "Cause a scene here and I will kill your precious Gileaus without a second thought. I tell you the truth, Pearl. I told you the power I had over him before began with his own natural desires. Those desires remain and I no longer need the jade to control him. His fiancée is from a noble family. It is an excellent choice for one who wants to go far."

My head is spinning as the angry tendrils sneak their way back into my heart. Gileaus told me he loved me. We were to be married. Is this his way of protecting me? Is this the goodbye he was giving me on the ship?

"Breathe deeply, Pearl," Abraxas whispers into my ear. "There are plenty of fish in the sea. You'll recover. You'll see. You never know, maybe *I* could take you as my bride one day."

My head snaps up and I meet his eyes. He is uncomfortably close to my face. My skin is crawling and my heart is beating wildly beneath the surface.

"You needn't be so shocked, Pearl," Abraxas whispers. "I am not *that* repulsive. I am actually quite charming when you really get to know me."

"You have taken everything from me. You killed Dom. You destroyed Gileaus. You have enslaved me. What makes you think I could ever want to marry you?"

"That's the beauty of it, Pearl," he whispers. "You don't have to want to marry me. I own you. You will have no choice in the matter."

"And what makes you think you would be safe with me in your hands?" I hiss. "What would keep me from killing you in your sleep?"

"Oh, Pearl. Don't get so worked up about it. I will give you time to get used to the idea. How does three months sound?" I feel sick to my stomach. Abraxas laughs. "Just get through tonight, Pearl. We can discuss *our* future in the morning."

We continue to weave in and out of the guests, Abraxas introducing me proudly to each one. I am dizzy and weak. I want to run, but I can't make it away from him. There are too many people in our way.

Dinner is announced and the guests make their way to the dining hall. Seats of gold with red cushions line the table. Plates of the freshest fruits and baked goods overflow each setting. Abraxas leads me to the seat next to Zenia. Gileaus is on her other side. When I am seated, I watch Abraxas leave to sit near the head of the table. I turn to my companion, the beautiful blonde who will be marrying my fiancé.

"Do you travel often with your cousin?" she asks. It takes me a moment to find my voice, but it finally makes its way out.

"I do," I say, "Though this is my first journey to Atlantis."

"Ah," she says. "And what do you think of it so far?"

"I haven't seen much," I tell her. "I've spent most of my time here at the mansion, in my room."

"Well, we will have to change that!" she gushes. "I'm sure Gileaus wouldn't mind taking us on a tour!" I glance up at her fiancé. His eyes are on his plate and he turns to engage in conversation with someone else next to him.

"That sounds lovely," I tell Zenia. I work up all the false kindness I can get into my voice to ask her about her own life. "Now it's your turn. How long have you been engaged to the young Master there?"

I've hit the right topic for a young woman recently engaged. I spend the rest of the meal hearing about their courtship and deep love. "It all seems so quick, but once father knew about his vast estates, naturally he gave his permission," she tells me. They met the evening we arrived. It must have been just after Gileaus spoke to Abraxas about releasing himself from our engagement. Abraxas introduced them to each other. He is a friend of her father's. They have been together constantly for the past ten days. Reading together, commenting on art, seeing plays. They fell head over heels for one another and Gileaus asked her father for her hand only two days ago.

"Of course, it takes so much time to plan a real wedding," she tells me over dessert, "but my mother thinks we can make it happen in just a month or two."

"You are very fortunate, Zenia. I wish you all the best." My heart is sinking. I love Gileaus. If I cannot be in his life and he cannot be in mine, I do hope the best for him. I just want to claw her eyes out at the same time.

I look up one last time at the man I love. His eyes are directly on mine. He stares without blinking. He is telling me something. He is telling me to look inside his mind.

So I do. For the first time, I sneak tendrils of inquiry into the mind of Gileaus and I extract the information he has for me. It is beautiful and tender and fragile.

I love you, Athena. I always have and I always will. This is the only way to protect you. I must marry. You are only safe if I cannot be used against you. I must stay close to Abraxas. I must ensure that he does not harm you. This is the only way, Athena. I am sorry it has to end this way. But I do it for you.

Protection. Dom wanted to protect me and he gave his life to do it. Now Gileaus wants to protect me and he will be giving his life in a different way. I smile at him before looking away. I will let him live a happy life. That will be my gift to him.

    I look back at my plate. The strain of the evening is gnawing at my stomach, begging for relief. I finish every bite of the sweet bread rolled in nuts and covered in honey. I let the saccharine goodness bring temporary comfort to my soul. When the servant comes to clear away my clean plate, he leaves a note behind. Abraxas smiles at me from the end of the table.

Chapter 40

I pick up the note and let it slide into my robes. I give a final congratulations to Zenia and make my way to the entrance of the dining room. I do not look at Gileaus again.

When I enter the foyer, I search through the crowds of people for a small corner where I can read in seclusion. I find windows against the back wall, their curtains and shutters are spread wide to allow for a breathtaking view of Poseidon's temple. I move to the windows and tuck my body behind the thick fabric of the curtains where I can read privately. The lit torchlights on the patio provide ample light for reading. I check to make sure no one has seen me hiding away then carefully open the seal on the note. Abraxas' handwriting is waiting for me when the paper is opened.

My Pearl,

By now you are aware that your fiancé has promised his love to another woman. I am sorry you had to face this tragedy. Though I played no part in their betrothal, I did know they were likely to be engaged. I am sure your heart is broken, but I know your strength. Certainly you will be able to overcome this setback in your young life.

Perhaps even now, you will be able to find the strength you need to complete the task you have set out to do. You see, Zenia's father Karis is a sort of rival of mine. I have tried to convince him to side with me, but he refuses. In private, he calls me mad and threatens to ruin my reputation with anyone who really matters. He has avoided open conflict in public thus far. Contrary to what others believe about him, the damage he has done to my cause is too great. No amount of persuasion will change what his lies have done. He must die.

Don't worry, my Pearl. I would never entrust such a violent task to your tender sensibilities. No, I intend to use your power for the manipulation of minds in a different way. I want you to persuade young Master Gileaus that his future father-in-law is out to destroy him. Your task is to convince Gileaus to kill Karis.

I am sure you will fear that Gileaus will be executed for his role in the crime, but I assure you this will not be the case. I have enclosed another letter for you to take to him with explanations of how the deed is to be done. He will be protected, Pearl, you have my word. I wouldn't ask this of you for the world, but Gileaus' new closeness to the Karis family puts him in a perfect position to carry out the task.

Though I trust your ability to complete this task, I will nonetheless keep Namaah as a failsafe for the plan. My men apprehended her as she left your room this evening. The string of pearls meant for you were found in a small satchel she carried. You need not worry, she is safely held for the present. I will not yet press charges against her for the theft since I know how you care for her. Complete this task and she will be set free. I will even give her ten strands of pearls with her freedom.

I have faith in your ability to do this thing, my Pearl.

Ever Your Master,

Abraxas

    I reread the letter. Abraxas wants me to use my power on the man I love. He wants me to trick his mind into killing a man. Gileaus would never kill a person. He would live with guilt for the rest of his life. Abraxas would use the crime to keep Gileaus under his own control. I cannot do that to him. I will not do it.

    But Namaah. Abraxas has her. Where does he have her? I don't know. If I had spent more time learning the layout of the mansion and less time staring at

Poseidon's temple for the past ten days, I might have an idea of where to find her. But as it is, I have nothing to go on.

I rest my head against the shutter and it opens to the patio. A fresh breeze enters through the small opening and I allow the cool air to calm my mind and heart as only it can do.

The breeze.

The air.

Oh, beloved breeze and air that spoke to me only ten days ago, will you now help me to free my friend who has done no wrong? I hum quietly into the night air, praying that it will listen to my plea.

Sweet child, I feel it respond, *we have been waiting for you to come to us. We know where your friend is being kept. She is safe for the time being, but it will not last for long.*

Come with us.

I push the shutter open a little more. It is a tall opening and I step over a small ledge to go outside. I follow where the wind whispers, keeping to the shadows as much as I can. Abraxas knows I have my instructions. He will be looking for a sign that I will follow through.

I rush across the back of the mansion and to the darkest corner that leads into the garden. The wind urges me forward so I enter the stone pathway that leads through the trees and flowers. The heavy scent of blossoms from all around me fills the air. The air is tinged with the excitement of spring. It is reckless as it pushes and pulls me this way and that. Finally I come to a gate that leads down toward the water.

Where are we going? I ask the air. *Where is Namaah?*

We are taking you to her, the mother-voice responds. *Hurry, child. The man is seeking after you.*

I push ahead through the gate and down to the water's edge. A small boat is tied to a post at the edge of the moat.

You must get into the boat, the air urges. I do not hesitate. I climb into the boat, moving my flowing robes out of the way as much as I can. They are already muddied, but I do not care. They are nothing but a trap for me. Once inside the boat, I untie it from the post and sit between the oars. With all of my might I row toward Poseidon's temple, the place the wind is telling me to go. When I reach the opposite shore, I jump ankle-deep into the water and pull the little vessel onto the sand.

Poseidon's temple. This island has no wall. There is free access to it around its entire circumference. Once my boat is pulled up high enough out of the water, I let the wind direct me up the grassy hill and onto the steps of the temple itself. I turn for just a moment to look at the mansion behind me. I see the balcony where I was sitting this afternoon, the view into my room is clear. My guard is leaning on the bedroom door, falling asleep as he waits for me to return. Sleep on, my guard. I will not be returning tonight.

I move to the edge of the marble stairs. Gold leafing covers the riser of each step while unpolished marble provides a firm grip for my feet on the tread. The decorative trees that line the stairway provide added secrecy for my movements. Within a few moments, I have reached the top of the stairs and the columned porch of the temple.

The porch is clad in gold leafing and I stand out against it like a dark stain. I rush to the door of the temple, hiding in the shadows of the columns as much as I can. I listen quietly to the sounds around me, waiting to be sure my entrance to the temple will not be noticed. When the coast is clear, I open the door quietly, listening to the still air inside as it directs me where to go.

The foyer of the temple is gleaming white. Brilliant torches line the walls. As my eyes adjust to the light, I look around the room. Gold and jewel gilt frames surround lavish paintings of the upper class Atlanteans wrapped in their white and gold robes. When I look closer at a painting near me, I recognize the faces. They are people from the dinner I just escaped. They must have posed for the paintings for this temple. I'm sure they thought it was a very fine gift they were giving.

I follow the air through winding pathways and empty rooms until I am as lost as I have ever been. I am led to a room at the end of a long hallway. I am drawn to the door of the room. It is of a fine and hard wood, covered in carvings and designs of a Grecian battle against the rebelling armies of Sparta. I reach for the handle and the door swings open effortlessly. *Here,* the air whispers. *This is where you must be.*

I step into the quiet room and take in my surroundings. This is not a square room. It is round. A pearlescent covering lines the walls. The same gold and jewel encrusted frames surround the art on the walls. There are paintings of nobility laughing and singing, their curls painted in a perfect bounce. Other paintings depict the nobility praising their gods, throwing jewels and fruit at the feet of their idols. Still more art shows noble Grecians mourning the death of a loved one. Scarlet robes are thrown across the dead bodies. Noblemen and women languish across the dead in a fit of passionate grief.

I move around the room and take in each painting, suspended from my fears and intentions for just a moment. I move carefully around incredible ottomans and lounging couches that rest under each painting. Some of the furniture is covered in pure, white fabric. Others are decorated with gold and jewels on their arms and legs. Many have ornate pillows covering their seats. I bend over a side table to see a book that is resting atop a pile. I pick it up and read its title, <u>Timaeus</u> by Plato. Everything in the room is still. I move slowly as I look at the next book in the pile,

Critias also by Plato. When I move this aside, I gasp at what lies beneath: *The Sunken Kingdom: The Atlantis Mystery Solved* by Peter James.

    I drop the books and spin around. I clench my chest as a flood of memories, real memories, rushes into my mind. I have been in this room before. This room called to me more than two thousand years from now. I am not who I think I am. I have been living someone else's life for the past seven years. The realization makes my head spin. I look to the center of the room. The place where the pearl was last floating in the watery grave of Atlantis. Nothing is there. Just a beautiful mosaic sunburst outlined on the floor.

    And me.

Chapter 41

*W*hat is happening?! I ask the air. *Where is Namaah?* A gentle breeze encircles the empty space before me. The air moves gently until it reaches me and speaks.

We are Namaah, it says. *We communicate only with those who are worthy. We speak to you, dear child, so we may help you fulfill the quest you began seven years ago.*

I don't understand, I return. What quest? Are you *my* Namaah? How is this possible?

Yes, they reply in their unified voice, *we are your Namaah. We embrace our physical form but rarely, only when it is most required of us. You were in need of a human being. We gave you our human form so we could better comfort you.*

I blink several times to help process what they are saying to me. *So, when Abraxas' men captured you...*

We disappeared...

Into thin air...

I feel a gentle laugh from the breeze. She has a sense of humor as well as a sense of loyalty and devotion.

Why were you so intent on helping me? I ask.

You are a special being, child. Descended from a line of humans whose hearts are pure and just and kind. Since the first day you breathed air into your lungs, we have been with you, watching what you would do, what you would choose. You gave of yourself willingly to overcome a powerful threat to the world.

Abraxas? I ask.

She doesn't understand

    We must tell her

        Do it gently

The voices speak over one another, having a conference as though I am not able to hear. But I hear everything.

No, child. Before Abraxas ever came into your life, you gave yourself to save the world from Ceto.

Ceto.

What do you mean? I ask. *Who is Ceto?* Vivid memories attack my mind as I say her name.

Trapped

Tell us who you are, child. The wind commands. It grows stronger with each passing minute. The pearls in my hair are beginning to bounce to the ground and across the floor.

I am Pearl, I answer, *twin of Domideus. Daughter of... daughter of...*

Daughter of whom? the wind asks. But I cannot remember. I do not know who I am.

I don't remember my mother's name, tears sting my eyes as frustration grows within me. *If I cannot remember the name of my mother, can I ever know who I am?*

Marisol. The wind whispers to me.

Marisol

    Marisol

        Marisol, the voices whisper on top of one another.

Marisol? I ask. *Then, who am I?*

The wind smiles as she answers me.

Evelyn

    Evelyn

        Evelyn

            Evelyn

You are Evelyn, she whispers. I listen to the name over and over again. Evelyn, Evelyn, Evelyn. As I listen, memories flood my mind. Dreams, people, schools, country, yearning, running, swimming, finding, becoming.

I AM EVELYN!!! I rush to the center of the room, filled with energy. I know who I am! I know why I am here! I am here to save the world from destruction twenty-four hundred years from now.

What do I need to do? I ask the air around me. It swirls swiftly, giddy over my excitement.

You must trust us, Evelyn. You must not be afraid.

The man in purple is coming. He is on the temple steps.

Focus on our voice, Evelyn, she says. *Do exactly as we say and you will fulfill your destiny.*

Hurry sisters! He comes! He is not alone!

Evelyn, allow your mind to focus on your heart. What do you feel? I turn my thoughts inward and focus on the fiery beating in my chest.

It burns.

Yes, Evelyn. It burns, but that burning will only make you free.

Will I be able to stand it? I ask.

We will help you. Remain with us and we will take you where you need to be. I nod this time, unwilling to speak and break my concentration.

Pearl, the wind calls. *Pearl!* I am confused and try to answer the air as she speaks, but she stops me.

Remain focused, Evelyn, she says. *We are not speaking to you.* I turn my mind back to my heart. Back to the burning inside. Somewhere down the long corridor, a pounding of footsteps is rushing toward us.

PEARL!!!! The air screams, filling the room with her voice. The hamsa medallion around my neck lifts from my chest and rises into the air.

Pearl, you must release her. The time has come.

What if it doesn't work? I hear another voice in the room. This time it comes from the small black pearl in the eye of my hamsa. It is Pearl's voice. *What if she is not ready and I am trapped forever? What if I...*

You must quiet your fears, Pearl, the wind speaks to her. *She is here and she is ready. You are the one who prepared her for this moment.*

Yes, Pearl responds, *I did. I will listen. Forgive me.*

You need not apologize, our Pearl. You are safe here. We are here to help you both.

Evelyn, the air addresses me. *You must allow the burning to grow. Allow it to take over everything. We will help it to live. You must burn the tie that keeps you tethered to Pearl.*

I will do it, I say. I allow the burning to grow in my chest. As the pain grows the wind grows with it. Soon, I am inhaling all the air I can and leading it to the fire I feel growing within me.

As the fire grows, the door to the room bursts open. Abraxas is here with his followers and soldiers. He is screaming, but I cannot hear anything he says. He points at me, and several guards rush toward me, but the fire within me has grown too large to be contained within my body. I exhale and flames explode from my entire body. The room fills with fire, consuming everyone it touches. They fall to the ground and I continue to burn.

You are doing well, Evelyn, the wind comforts my mind. *Continue with your strength.*

Pearl, it is time to let go. The golden chain that holds my hamsa medallion to me, breaks and the medallion floats alone in the air. The golden hand turns before me in the flame until the black pearl eye is facing me.

Thank you, Evelyn, she whispers. Her voice is soft, but her words pierce my heart and the burning grows. Together, we grow the flame in the temple. It reaches the outer walls and the ground begins to shake. Still, I burn.

As the ground moves beneath my feet, I receive one more command from the wind.

Hold out your hand, Evelyn. You must take hold and do not let go. I force my hand outward through the wind and flame. I open my fingers and wait. The golden medallion melts in the air above my hand. The melted gold falls onto my fingers and to the ground, but I do not feel the pain of it. The black pearl is all that remains.

Trapped

Slowly she pushes through the wind until she is once again in my palm. I wrap my fingers around her small form and pull her to my chest. Once I have her held tightly to me, I feel her pushing toward my heart. It feels like she is trying to push through me. I have no other choices, no other paths to take. I must remain strong.

The pearl pushes and I burn. The ground shakes and the island moves. I am weightless and the entire island falls into the sea. Ocean water pours into the room. Still, I burn. Pearl pushes and pushes. The island moves across the ocean floor, through space and time. It feels like an eternity of burning and pushing and pulling, but it isn't an eternity, it is only twenty-four hundred years.

We slow and the scenery changes. It is murky, dark and cold. The furnishings are deteriorating. The paintings no longer show their smiles. The fire within me cools. The pulling and pushing stop. I look to my hand held tightly to my chest. My robes are gone. The gold and pearls that were entwined around my waist and neck have disappeared. I am wearing tightly fitting clothes instead. Something I have worn before. But I am no longer in the temple of ancient Atlantis. I am in the modern temple of Atlantis, underwater.

I pull my hand away from my chest and unpeel my fingers from around the pearl. It is lifeless now. A simple, voiceless object. But something ahead of me catches my eye. Not far from where I stand, I see a young boy, about ten or twelve years old. His skin is golden brown and his eyes are darker than chocolate. His hair is thick and full and his face is familiar. It is more than familiar. It is Dom, my Dom. Pearl's Dom. I see my Dom and I see through him. His features move in the water. I am seeing his spirit.

He reaches his hand toward me. Before I can reach back, a spirit girl, the same age as Dom, with long, dark, beautiful curls, deep golden skin, and dark eyes walks toward him. She is leaving the pearl and reaching for her brother. Pearl takes Dom's hand and they both turn to face me. They smile and wave then turn away and fade from view. They are finally together again. heading to the world of spirits. I smile and let a single tear escape into the salty water around me. I have saved her. I have saved the Atlantean pearl. The power source that was a girl, trapped in the bonds of a stone, is now free. She is with her Dom, my Dom. They can be happy. My heart is light. In these brief seconds standing here and watching my Pearl reach for her eternity, I have forgotten everything else.

Until I realize I can no longer breathe.

I turn around and see an empty room. I am drowning and there is no one who can save me. No one who will know what happened or where to find me. As my vision goes blurry I see someone coming through the water. They rush to me and wrap their strong arms around my body. I hold my breath as long as I can until everything goes black.

Chapter 42

When I wake up again I am dry. I hear beeping and whirring. Something cool and fresh is blowing softly into my nose through a tube. I hear voices I recognize, but it takes me several minutes to be able to open my eyes. When I do, the most beautiful woman in the world is standing over me, saying my name.

"Evelyn," she says. "Evelyn, darling. It's mom. Can you hear me, Evelyn?"

I blink to clear the blur and I smile. She reaches to touch my face and cries as she brushes her fingers across my cheek.

"Oh, my Evelyn, my Evelyn," she whispers over and over again. "My beautiful girl. I love you so much. You have done amazing things. You are so wonderful. I love you." I fall asleep to the sound of her voice reassuring me that she is here and will not leave my side.

Several days of scattered consciousness go by before I am awake for long periods of time. I have several visitors. Celia, Uncle Russ, and Jack all come to check on me. Jack stays the longest and listens to every word as I tell him and my mom about the last seven years of my life. My mom cries over and over when I retell the sad things that happened to me. She tells me how proud she is of all the good choices I made. She listens quietly and strokes my hand when I tell her about the bad choices. Jack is fascinated by all of it.

"So you were actually going to marry the guy?" he asks when I get to Gileaus.

"I was," I assure him. My heart breaks as I remember and I start to cry. "Life is so different there, Jack. I didn't know how long I would even live or exist there. Most girls were married and had children by the time they were 17. I was making the best of it. To be honest, I actually forgot who I was. I thought I was Pearl."

It takes an entire day to tell them about the biggest events in the last seven years of my life. By the time I finish, Jack excuses himself.

Trapped

"I need to report to Lady Pescara so she knows how you are and what happened to you." He holds my hands as he says it, rubbing his fingers across mine. Before he leaves, he pauses, then leans down to kiss my hand. The memory of Gileaus is overwhelming. I let go of silent tears as Jack leaves the hospital room. We were beginning to share something before I left. But seven years is a long time to hold onto those kinds of memories. And my life changed in those years. I was reborn and remade.

Except it wasn't seven years for them. It was only a matter of hours. When I touched the pearl, a burst of light shot through the water, forcing everyone back. When both sides of the conflict regained their footing, the pearl and I were gone. The battle began again in that very room. The forces of Atlantis pushed until Ceto and Gwen fled with their armies. Lachlan and his forces remained with Atlantis. They were a large part of how Atlantis was able to win the battle.

Jack remained in the temple room, keeping watch in case the pearl and I returned. When we came back, he saw Pearl and her brother leaving together and rushed in to keep me from drowning. I don't know why I couldn't breathe in that moment. Mom says she thinks I was just out of practice. I hope she is right.

When Jack comes again to visit, he has a message from Lady Pescara.

"Lady Pescara sends her good wishes, Evelyn," he says, "and her gratitude. There's no telling what would have happened if Gwen had gotten hold of that stone before you. There may never have been an Atlantis for us in the first place.

"She also wants me to tell you that Atlantis is still in danger. Ceto and Gwen took their forces with them. That was over a week ago. Ceto's fortress is still secured by our army, the two are not there. Lady Pescara thinks they are seeking refuge with Ceto's mother."

"I didn't know Ceto even knew her mother," I interject.

"She does," Jack continues. "Her mother wasn't a part of her life, it's true, but Lady Pescara thinks she may still be willing to help her daughter. Our armies are preparing to travel once we know for sure where they are. Lady Pescara wants you to join us when and if you are ready."

My mom sighs and takes my hand. "You can tell Lady Pescara to..." but I interrupt her.

"Where does she think Ceto is headed?" I ask.

"To the Mediterranean," Jack replies. "Off the coast of Jaffa. Ceto's mother lives there. She is an incredibly old sea witch named..."

"Named Queen Nyobi Kadul," I say.

"Yes. How did you know?" he replies.

I lay in my bed, staring at the ceiling. My mom holds one hand, Jack's hand is resting on my arm. In my fingers, I still hold the small black pearl.

"I know the queen," I tell Jack. "She stole seven years of my life and Pearl's." I turn my face to his. Every fiber of my being tingles with the anticipation of repairing the wrongs in my life. I know my answer. I will be a part of that army.

"I will come."

End of Book Two

Acknowledgments

Writing isn't easy, my friends. It falls into the category of things that are hard, but fun. Like hiking a mountain. Once you reach the top, the view is worth every step (if you have the right attitude). Also like hiking a mountain, writing is easier when you don't go it alone. I have been SO BLESSED to have the best hiking and writing companions in the world and we are reaching a spectacular view!

I have the world's best muse. If you are a writer, you need a librarian of your own. If you are a librarian, you should be writing books. Sarah Bleyl is my librarian muse and I love her. Sarah knows books inside and out and gave me invaluable advice and suggestions during this process. If I had questions and research that couldn't be solved by Wikipedia, I turned to Sarah. Sarah ALWAYS found the right answer. And she LOVED IT!!!! Thank you, my Sarah. I love you.

Erin Salvesen is one of my fantastic beta readers. And I mean FANTASTIC. Erin sends me live notes as she reads. It cracks me up to see her reacting to my work the same way I did when writing it. Thank you, Erin, for your support, your advice, your questions, and your love. You are fabulous in every way.

Anna Simkins jumped in as a beta-reader-in-a-pinch. Her insights and questions made my story better. I loved being able to text her answers to questions and then go add those answers to the book. I'm pretty sure she got a kick out of the process, too. Thank you, Anna. You are the best!

I have known Marlowe Blodgett my ENTIRE LIFE. We grew up together and she is the closest thing to a sister that I have. She loves and supports me and shares my love of good literature. I called Marlowe in as a draft three beta reader when I needed a new set of eyes on my work. As I knew she would, Marlowe read, questioned, advised, and approved in all the right places. Thank you, Marlowe. I love you.

If you are self-publishing, you MUST have a pro in your corner. Knowledgeable and well-read friends can only take you so far. You need someone who knows the business. For me, that person is still TJ MacKay, owner of InD'tale magazine. TJ gave me the kind of advice that only a professional content editor can. Because of her advice, I was able to take my work to the professional level I am looking for. Thank you, TJ. You are completely wonderful in every way!

Trapped

I again sought out Penny Friday Baker of Baker Blooper Editing for my copy editing work. Not only is Penny professional and experienced, but she is also a caring and supportive individual. She reminded me when I needed to slow down and smell the roses so I could enjoy my writing journey and my life. Thank you, Penny. You are a gem of a woman.

My media guru is one of my favorite people in the world. Mindee Thyrring of Post Modern Laundry handles my cover design and branding across all mediums. I get just as many compliments on her work as I do on my own. Not only is Mindee one of the most talented marketing and media specialists in the business, she is also a fun and amazing friend. Thank you, Mindee, for being so fabulously you. We are going to keep doing amazing things together.

I married my favorite writing support and best friend. Steve has worked as hard as I have to help me finish my second book. He cleaned, cooked, shopped, and budgeted with me so I could have all I needed to make this happen. Thank you, Babe, for being my partner. And thank you, girls, for being excited for your mom.

No thanks would be complete without gratitude for my readers. It is because of you that I get to write. Thank you for taking part in my imagination. Thank you for reading and supporting. Here's to many more!

About the Author

EJ lives with her husband and three daughters on the Central Coast of California. She loves days at the beach and going for hikes and long walks. She loves working with children in her local school district and loves, loves, loves to write. You can find <u>Called</u>, Book 1 of the "Called" trilogy on Amazon. Connect with EJ on Instagram @ej_pay_author, EJ Pay on Facebook, or visit her website, www.ej-pay.com

What's Next?

Keep your eyes open for <u>Released</u>, the third and final book in Evelyn's "Called" journey, coming out in early 2020.

Also in 2020, be on the lookout for the "Nyobi Kadul" prequel trilogy.

Made in the
USA
Middletown, DE